And They'll Come Home

And They'll Come Home

Charlene E. Green

URBAN BOOKS

http://www.urbanbooks.net

This is a work of fiction. Any references or similarities to actual events, real people, living or dead, or to real locales are intended to give the novel a sense of reality. Any similarity in other names, characters, places, and incidents is entirely coincidental.

URBAN SOUL is published by

Urban Books
78 East Industry Court
Deer Park, NY 11729

ISBN-13: 978-1-59983-088-9
ISBN-10: 1-59983-088-4

First Printing: March 2010

10 9 8 7 6 5 4 3 2 1

Printed in the United States of America

For my mother, Juliet Lorraine Simpson—
Naturally, it's all about you.
I love you to pieces.
Without you, I wouldn't be here to do this.

Acknowledgments

Well, I'm back, and I never even expected to be here. When I say "here," I mean doing acknowledgments for a sequel to *One Man's Treasure* (*OMT*), because, to be perfectly honest, there wasn't supposed to be one. I did think about doing one very briefly as I neared the end of writing it, but with all that poor Katrice and Weston had been through, I thought, *No, lemme just leave them alone and let them live their lives.* Until . . .

A funny thing started happening. After *OMT* was released in 2007 when I self-published it, and people were reading and loving it, I kept getting bombarded with this question: "Soooo, when's the sequel comin' out?" Although I was flattered that my readers wanted one, I really had no intention of revisiting their story. I had other stories I was gonna concentrate on. But my readers, thankfully, would not leave me alone! What was even funnier to me was that everyone just assumed there'd be one! It wasn't like, "So, is there a sequel?" It was just straight "When's it comin' out?" Each time my response was the same: "Oh nooooo. I'm not gonna do one. I'm just gonna leave them alone." That is, until . . .

Angela B. Brown entered the picture. You can all pretty much thank her for the birth of this story, because if it weren't for her, I can promise you that you would *not* be about to crack open these pages. Angela and I met at what was supposed to be my first book signing for *OMT* when it came out in 2007. That signing didn't happen because of a major obstacle. But my mother and I still went to the venue to meet and greet any people that might show up that didn't know it had been canceled. Angela walked in, and she, my mother, and I started talking. We hit it off right away. She told me that she would get my book and let me know what she thought of it, since she's an avid reader and would be able to give great critical feedback. When my phone rang about a week or two later, Angela had just finished the book and really enjoyed it. But can you guess what she said? Riiiiight . . . "So let's talk about the sequel. . . ." I laughed and told her the same thing I told everyone else. But she brushed me off and then did what no one else had done thus far: she actually broke down, in detail, *why* there should be a sequel. And that, my friends, is when the two-hour sequel conversation took place. By the time I got off the phone with my new friend, I was so psyched about doing this book that I couldn't wait to see it finished. So thank you, Angela B. Brown, for taking the time to convince me that this was necessary. You were 100 percent right! And let me say that out of all my writing projects, this one was the most fun. I couldn't believe how this story just flowed from within me with the ease that it did. I barely slept or ate during the process, and I probably shouldn't have been sitting for such long hours at a time, because I was re-covering from major back surgery, but, hell, I did it, anyway! I'm extremely happy to bring you this new Weston-Katrice-Royce roller-coaster ride, and dare I say . . . I think there may be one more story to tell after this. But we'll see. Don't quote me on that. For now, just enjoy part two!

All right, let me give my thanks so you can get to readin'! Off the top, of course, I must always thank my mother, Juliet Lorraine Simpson, for her love and sup-port, and for believing in my dream to make all this great stuff happen. Loving you from the depths of my soul, Mommy.

To my entire family, I love you with all my heart. (You

wanna see all their names, look in *One Man's Treasure*'s acknowledgments! LOL!) Kevin Cornell Allen, Rebecca Marie Allen, and Lincoln and Cleo Simpson, RIP. I miss you all and wish you could be part of this phenomenal time in my life.

To my crew, Tamika Byrd, LaMonica Gardner, Leslie Harris, Joan Ferrin-Pann, and Tamara Brown, I love you guys more than you know. Thank you for the laughs, the cries, the fun, the mischief (☺), the road trips (woo-*wee*, those road trips!), the encouragement and the honesty, and for holdin' it down with and for me over these (give or take) thirty years. (Forty for Monica and me.)

Thank you to my helpers, attorney James Dromi for all the legal advice you took the time to give me during your hectic schedule (you were the only one who was really willing to give me what I needed); and Warren Hsiao from Parkhurst Art Galleries for your detailed assistance; I hope I nailed it. And a hearty thanks to the Internet, 'cause without that to turn to when I couldn't get information from people, major chunks of the story would not have gotten written.

To my "chapter-by-chapter" readers, Mommy, Angela B. Brown, and James Moore, thanks for reading, literally, as I typed this story up, and for all the helpful opinions and criticisms along the way. To Gerald Brown (no relation to Angela) for the tips and critical eye you gave me for that pivotal scene and for making sure I kept things "manly," and for being one of my "hot-off-the-press" readers, along with Bridgette Gooden and Vernessie Green-Horn.

To my agent, Maxine Thompson, thank you so much for helping me accomplish this dream. To Rosie Milligan, thank you for getting this thing started back in 2003 when I shoved the raw, unedited copy of the *One Man's Treasure* manuscript in your face, stood proud and tall, looked you in the eye, and said: "It's *good*." (Hey, I had to get you to pay attention to me somehow! I guess it worked!) Maxine and Rosie, thank you for continuing to mentor me. I still have lots to learn and I couldn't do this without you two.

And finally I want to thank all of my readers, fans, and supporters, especially all of you who bought books from me over and over and gave them to friends and family members. You have no idea how much appreciation I have for you.

Well, this is the part of the acknowledgments that scares me. I hope I'm not forgetting to thank anyone. If anyone feels they deserve some credit and I forgot them, feel free to give it to yourself right now, because, I tell you, trying to think of and thank everyone who's been by my side through all this is really hard. But if you helped me, you know I appreciate you, whoever you are! LOL!

Okay, I'm done. And I'm excited for you to turn the page and see what's about to go down. So let me get outta your way. Have fun! (Note to the person with this book in his or her hand: If you're about to read *And They'll Come Home* but have neglected to read *One Man's Treasure,* STOP . . . put the book down, and please go read how this saga got started. If you don't, I promise you'll have a king-sized question mark plastered on your forehead the entire time you're reading! LOL!)

Okay, for real. Go to it! See you all in the next book . . . whatever it's gonna be!

—Charlene Elizabeth Green
June 18, 2009
12:41 P.M.

One Man's Treasure

One man's trash
is another man's treasure
and what jewels that man finds
will be beyond measure.

Be careful the thing
that you throw away,
you may wake from your haste
and want it someday.

By the time that you miss
the rare gem you lost,
it may be too late
to retrieve what you tossed.

Then you will say,
if you could go back in time,
you'd change your decision
at the drop of a dime.

Too little too late
is the phrase for those
who walk away, then come back
to find the door closed.

Don't bother pouting.
No need to get mad.
You should have cherished
what you already had.

Now it belongs
to someone more wise,
who saw that your trash
was truly a prize.

They dusted it off,
gave it love and affection,
while you tried to move on
to a better selection.

But mistaken were you—
then you grasped your err—
to what you treated as rubbish,
you found nothing could compare.

Then, oh, how you scrambled,
almost breaking your back,
moving heaven and earth
to win back your lack.

But the universe laughs
at ingrates like you,
who cry like babies
for chance number two.

"I'm sorry," you say
"I didn't realize. . . .
If I could just have it back . . .
I'll open my eyes."

But all your pitiful begging
is of no avail
'cause the blessing you had
has gone down a new trail.

So let go of the past
and find something new.
Maybe another man's trash
can be a treasure for you.

1

KATRICE

September 16, 2007, 11:39 P.M.

I can't believe my babies turned five years old today. Where the hell did all the time go? I just gave birth to them yesterday, didn't I? First Ellie, then Willie, nineteen minutes later. Damn, it was painful. But it was all worth it. I don't think I've ever loved any two people more than my precious twins. My parents and Weston run a close second, but that's a different kinda love that I have for all of them. This love . . . it can't be explained or measured, ever.

So we gave them their very first birthday party today. We figured five was a good age to start having them. They'd be more likely to remember it better. I'm so damn tired! There were so many screaming, laughing, and sometimes-crying kids in the house that I thought I was in the middle of Romper Room *for a while there. Weston's been asleep for over an hour; I told him he was gonna be worn-out. Willie* and Ellie were spastic with excitement. They crack me the hell up. I can't believe some of the crazy things they say, too! Sometimes Weston and I are just floored by what comes outta their mouths. I'm always wondering if I said stuff like what they say when I was a kid. I'll hafta ask Mama and Daddy about that one day, when I'm thinking about it.

Anyway, the party was so fun. I'm glad we did that for them. They ate so much junk, though. They're gonna have attention deficit disorder for, like, the next week behind all the sugar they ingested today. But oh well. It's not every day your babies turn five. It was definitely a day they'll never forget. Weston told me Ellie asked him if they could have another party next week. Weston told her it's not their birthday again next week, and that's what the party was for today. She said they should be able to have another one so the kids who weren't here today could come. She's so funny. Always trying to work a twist so she can get a little somethin' extra.

Genine did pretty good today. I was worried about her for a while, but after things got rolling, she seemed to be okay. I hope she's able to move on soon. It's been a little over two months, and although I can't pretend to know how she feels, I also don't wanna see her suffering over this for years to come. She's always so sad, and that makes me sad. I just don't know how to help her. I guess I can't, really, and that's what hurts me the most.

So, on another note, Angela called me tonight and said some dude's been by the shop for the last two days looking for me. I asked her who it was, and, of course, she didn't know. Actually, she said he didn't leave his name. But she said he was tall, real dark-skinned, and awfully fine. Whatever. Probably somebody who was referred to me by one of my clients. Sometimes that happens. People come in looking for me so they can find out about my services. Whoever *it is'll hafta wait until Tuesday to talk to me. I'm so glad Weston and I planned to take tomorrow off, 'cause this house is wrecked, and it's gonna take us all damn day to get it back in shape.*

Ellie screamed, *"Willieeeeee!* Gimme back my doll! You messin' up her hair!"

He ran past Weston, laughing, with Ellie's favorite doll in his hand, with its legs flying in the air. He screamed back, "I'm gonna flush it down the toilet!"

"Daddyyyyy!" Ellie shrieked.

Weston turned and grabbed Willie by the arm, which brought his running to an immediate halt. "Ay! Boy, what's wrong wit'choo?! Gimme that doll! You not flushin' nobody's belongin's down the toilet!"

Weston snatched the doll and handed it to Ellie. "Here, Boo Boo."

She grabbed it and said, "Thank you, Daddy," and ran off, out of breath.

Then he told Willie, "And git'cho butt back upstairs and put'cho shirt on! Leave yo' sister's stuff alone and go git dressed! Y'all supposta be havin' a party in an hour and you runnin' 'round here half naked and tearin' stuff up!"

I walked up behind them and said, "Willie, for the last time, *stop foolin' around* and go find your doggone shirt!"

Weston asked me, "What happened to his shirt?"

"I don't know. . . . He shoved it somewhere in a pile of clean clothes a little while ago, talkin' about he didn't wanna wear that one. There's five different loads of clothes in the laundry room. I don't know which one he put it in."

Weston looked at Willie and reprimanded him. "Boy, I don't know where you got that mess from, but you gon' stop all that shovin' clothes away when you don't wanna wear 'em."

"But I don't like that shirt. I wanna wear somethin' else."

Weston said, "Did I ask you all that? Now git in there and find it! You got five minutes!"

Willie got ready to start crying, but Weston put a stop to that. "Don't'choo *dare* start cryin'! You ain't got nothin' to cry about yet! If you don't git'cho behind in there and git dressed, you *will* have somethin' to cry about! Now git outta here!"

Willie ran off toward the laundry room, whimpering.

I said, "*Your* son."

He said, "*You* carried him."

I grabbed Weston's behind, copped a squeeze, and then he pulled me in and kissed me.

I asked him, "Can you believe they're five already?"

"Hell, I still can't believe I got three kids."

"Oh, speakin' of that . . . where's Lydia?"

"Yolanda said she's on her way with her."

"Yolanda's not stayin' for the party?"

"Naw, she gotta go to work. Somebody called in sick again."

"Damn. I was countin' on her help around here."

"Rishidda's not comin' wit' her kids?"

"She's coming, but she's not bringing the kids. You know, they're older. They said they didn't wanna go to a kiddie party. But anyway, she's not coming until five."

"Well, your parents'll be here. And Genine and them, too. And I'm here. What about me?"

"I dunno, Weston. What about you and twenty screaming kids? Can you handle that?"

"Well, hell, I can try. I do a damn good job wit' the three I got, so it can't be much harder than that."

"You say that now, but wait until they're all talking and screaming and yelling at the same time. It's different. I've done it before at a bunch of Rishidda's kids' parties. It's not the picnic you think it's gonna be."

"Well, don't count me out just yet. Gimme a chance to show you what I'm workin' wit' first." Then he popped his collar and did a silly shoulder move.

"I know what'cha workin' wit'—that's how we got twins in the first place."

He pulled at my blouse and started feeling my breasts. "And I know you know how to *work* wit' what I'm workin' wit'. Come on, let's go do a little work right now . . . before people start showin' up."

"No. How 'bout you go in there and see what *your son* is doing and I go get *my daughter*'s hair finished?"

"Oh, now he's mine and she's yours. Okay. But don't be flippin' the script when she starts actin' like you, and then you want me to claim her."

"Screw you, Weston James."

"I'll make sure you do that later on, Katrice Nicole."

We went our separate directions in the house to see about our separate kids.

Around seven o'clock, after all the kids had gone home and Weston had taken the twins upstairs to get them ready for bed, I took a break in the kitchen with Sabrina, Genine, Chantelle, and Rishidda. I needed it. My feet were on fire and my back was aching. And I could have sworn I heard ringing in my ears from all the high-pitched screaming that afternoon.

"Well, ladies," I said, "that was fun, but I'm not tryina do it again no time soon. Rishidda, I don't know how in the hell you managed to get through all the damn parties you've thrown for your kids. It's too much work . . . and money."

"Girl, you just gettin' started. Somethin' tells me I'll be back here for more parties than you think."

"Don't count on it. I'ma hafta find another way for them to celebrate in the future, 'cause all this madness is exhausting."

Genine said, "It was nice seein' all the kids havin' so much fun." She sounded a million miles away when she said it, though.

There was an awkward three-second silence while we all kind of looked at each other in search of how to respond. Genine was looking out the kitchen window, so she didn't see us. But she's not stupid, so she felt the vibe.

She turned from the window and looked at us. "You guys, I'm okay. I was just makin' an observation."

Nobody said anything.

"Seriously. I am. Now stop lookin' at me like that."

I said, "Well, we're just worried. You haven't really talked all that much about it, and to be honest, I was afraid for you to even be here today, with all the kids around. Not that I didn't want you here . . . but you know . . ."

"What do you guys want me to do? Talk about it every time we see each other?"

Sabrina said, "No, but when you *don't* talk about it, it makes us wonder where you are mentally with the whole thing."

"Okay, you wanna know where I am mentally with it? Here it is. I'm pissed, I'm hurt, I'm scared, I'm confused, and I'm tired of people lookin' at me like I'm about to fall apart at any moment. It's done. The baby's gone. I can't change it. So now I hafta deal with it. Is that what you wanted to hear?"

Chantelle said, "Well, at least that's a start. That's the most I've heard you say about it since last month. My aunt had a miscarriage, and she was destroyed. She called my mother every day for, like, two weeks cryin' about it."

Genine told us, "You guys, this is somethin' me and Warren hafta work through together. By ourselves. It's not a regular girl-talk topic. He's upset, I'm upset, and we're just kinda goin' through the motions these days. We don't even talk about wedding plans anymore. It just kinda . . . all went out the window after that day."

Rishidda said, "Well, I know how ya feel. Folks was hard-pressed to get a hello outta me after Cash died, much less a conversation. You gotta handle it your own way. Just know that we gon' be here for you if you do need to let some frustration out at the drop of a hat. Until then, just do you, girl."

"Thanks. I am. Now let's change the subject. Let's talk about why you won't give that guidance counselor at Cassius's high school no play. Wassup wit' that?"

I jumped in. "Oh—for real, 'cause from what Cash—sorry—*Cassius*—gotta remember that—said last week when I was at the house, dude's asked about her a few times, now."

Rishidda said, "He think he cute, all of a sudden wantin' to go by his *real* name. Anyway, I told him not to be tellin' that man nothin' about me, either. I'm not tryina git wit' him."

Chantelle asked her, "Why not? What's wrong wit' him?"

"Nothin'. I'm just not tryina go that route wit' him, that's all. I don't need to be involved wit' nobody at my son's school."

Sabrina said, "You shouldn'ta gone up there that day in ya tight-ass Apple Bottoms jeans and ya cleave-teasin' blouse. That's what did it."

Rishidda said, "Can I help it if I got a lot ta offer? If Cash's ass hadn't been actin' up in the first place, I woulda never been up there that day. I had to leave work early, too."

Chantelle asked, "Well, he's not Cash's counselor, is he?"

"No, but still. What I look like datin' some man my son sees every day at school? If it don't work out, it's gon' look bad."

Chantelle looked at Rishidda and twisted up her face. "Why you assume it's not gon' work out? You better *get'choo* some damn dick, girl. That man got a job, probably a house and a nice car, too. He's obviously educated, and if he's nice lookin', then I say give him a little taste of what'choo got ta offer."

"I'll pass. That's uncharted territory to me."

"Well, speakin' of gettin' dick," Chantelle said while getting up, "I gotta go. I got a date in two hours."

I asked her, "Um . . . since when does 'date' automatically equal dick?"

She said, "Um . . . since we've been out four times, and the last date ended with his lips wrapped around my left nipple, suckin' like he needed milk to do his body good."

Everyone fell out laughing. Then Sabrina said, "Well, on that note, I gotta go, too. All this talk about milk and dick is makin' me thirsty. I told Ty I'd be at his house before ten. I'm hopin' he has some milk for me, too. A milk*shake*, baby. Nice 'n' thick."

Rishidda said, "And creamy smooth."

And I added, "And just a *little* salty."

Chantelle laughed and said, "Oooooo, you freaky hoes."

Then I said, "Dammit, all y'all get out. Now *I'm* thirsty."

We all laughed and then filed out of the kitchen.

After I said my good-byes to the girls and they left, I got ready to go upstairs when my cell rang. It was Angela.

"Hey, Katrice."

"Hi. What's up?"

"There's this dude that's been in the shop lookin' for you for the last two days."

"Who was it?"

"I dunno. He won't leave his name. He just comes in the door, looks around, asks if you're there, and when I tell him no, he says thanks and leaves."

"Well, did you tell him I'd be in on Tuesday? It's probably someone who's been referred to me."

"No, I never got that far. He don't wait for me ta say nothin' else—he just leaves. He fine as hell, though. Real dark, tall, and got that kinda silky voice. You sure you don't know who it is?"

I was irritated; it sounded like she was trying to start a rumor on the sly.

"Angela, I have no idea who it is, and right now, I don't really care. I'm tired. If he comes back tomorrow, just tell him I'll be in on Tuesday. Okay?"

"Okay, honey. I just thought you might know—"

"Angela, I gotta go. I hear the kids callin' me. I'll see you on Tuesday."

"Oh—well, okay, then—"

And I hung up on her. Yeah, yeah, rude, I know. But I was having issues with her, anyway, and that call did nothing but irk me. I wondered if I did the right thing by hiring her to replace Tiki after she and Charles moved to Atlanta at the beginning of the year. Talent for doing hair, I knew she had. But some of the things she did and said made me wanna wring her neck. She had only been working at the shop for about a month and a half, and already we were off to a rocky start.

I shook off the Angela call, looked around the ramshackle house for a minute, then thought about all the cleaning Weston and I were in for the next day. But when I pictured my kids' happy, smile-plastered faces, it made the mess totally worthwhile.

I turned off the living-room light, bolted the front door, and headed upstairs to spend the rest of the evening with my husband.

2

ROYCE

I know what I did that night in May was beyond wrong. I'm not proud of it, either. A lot of people are still pissed at me behind that stunt, too. Charles won't even speak to me because of it. I messed around and lost my good friend. He cussed me up one side of the phone line and down the other when he came back from his honeymoon and found out what happened. Called me up and blew my hair back so hard, I was too ashamed to even respond. Told me I was a low-down, dog-ass ho, and then he said I used his wedding to get to Katrice, and that she was the only reason I showed up. That wasn't true. I would've come even if she hadn't been there. I love Charles. He was the truest dawg a brotha could ever have. Now I'm shut down. Permanently. He told me never to call him again, and to leave Katrice alone. Threatened to kill me if I didn't. So I took my Pacific

Bell beating and agreed to move on without a fight. But I wanted to talk to her. I wanted to keep in touch with her. I wanted to keep our connection going. But, of course, with all the threats and whatnot, I was too scared to do that.

A bunch of times I called her shop, since I didn't have her home or cell number, and when she answered, I would disguise my voice and say, "Sorry, I got the wrong number." I just wanted to hear her sweet voice. But her voice didn't sound so sweet. There was an emptiness in her tone every time I called. It made me sad when I heard it, so after about four months, I stopped calling. Plus, I knew I wasn't taking it any further than the crank calls at the moment, so I gave up altogether.

I could try to come up with a decent excuse for my behavior the night of the wedding, but I won't, 'cause there's no point. I wanted what I wanted, and I got it. After all those years, I got it. But . . . actually, I really didn't. Because when I left Oakland to go back to Maryland, I had to leave without her. That hurt me. When she looked at me right before she walked out the door and said, "Bye, Royce," the look in her eye was different. It wasn't the same as when she first turned around to look at me when I came up from behind her at the reception. This look said, "My work here is done. I'm going home . . . to be with my man." When she left me standing there in the middle of the room, naked and vulnerable—yeah, I said vulnerable, 'cause I was—I knew there was no point in chasing after her at that moment. All she could think about was *him*. Going back to *him*. Being with *him*. Figuring out how she was gonna fix the mess she'd made with *him*.

Her man. Who became her husband. Yeah, I knew she married that Weston dude. Bastard. I didn't even know him and I couldn't stand him. I couldn't stand that he had her, when I wanted to be the one she chose to build a life with. I couldn't stand that he fathered her children. I *hated* him for that. He planted his seed so deep in her that she came up with twins. That hurt. I noticed after we shared that night together, I started fading out of her system. I could see it in her expression when she was fumbling all over the place to put her clothes on. Something had changed. When I went to hug her and she moved, that right there was the clincher. That let me know in no uncertain terms that we were off-kilter.

I know. I said that like we had a good thing going on, huh? If I hadn't been such a scared, insecure egomaniac in high school, I can tell you right now that we would have. I would've never let her go. I would've held on so tight to her that she might have smothered. There would've never been a Troy. Weston's punk ass would've never, ever had a chance. But I blew it all, the day I hurt her so bad that she ended up physically scarred for life. I didn't even know I was the cause of that till she showed it to me that night. When I saw it, when she threw it up in my face and pointed at it, I saw—finally saw—the damage I did to her. Man, she was mad at me in that moment. Looked at me like she wanted to throw dirt in my face. I didn't even blame her. I *was* a cold-hearted son of a bitch back in high school. But the ironic thing is that what I said to her that day, I never said anything like that to any other girl. Their fast asses were on my heels every time I rounded a corner. Even though I loved the attention, I ignored a lot of 'em. They weren't worth my time or energy. Oh, don't get it twisted; I banged a bunch of 'em. But it was just recreation. I didn't even like half of the girls that were after me. They were shallow and weak. They were throwing the pussy at me before I even had a chance to ask for it. Hell, some of 'em didn't even care whether or not I wanted it from *them;* they just wanted it from *me.*

But Katrice, well, she was different. I knew she liked me because she silently gushed over me whenever I'd get close to her. Come on, I wasn't blind or dumb. But the key word there is "*silently.*" She kept herself together. She didn't throw herself at me. She had confidence and self-respect. I loved that. Man, did I love that. Because no other girl was working it like her. Not to mention that she was just as fine as she wanted to be; and she was intelligent, too. She wasn't lacking in the brain like most of those dumb bunnies that wanted to be all up in my world. She had it all. A quality package. That scared the *hell* outta me. Even though I wanted to scoop her ass up and parade around school proudly with her on my arm, letting all the haters know that she was mine, deep down I knew I didn't have the slightest idea what to do with her. Remember, I was the center of attention. I was the man and I wasn't used to dealing with women like Katrice. She was the woman. Dudes chased her just like the girls chased me. In my mind, if she was my girl, and I wasn't on top of my game at all times with her, any one of those dudes could've snatched her from me. I didn't want her to mess around and hurt me. I felt it. I could lose myself in her, and she could really hurt me.

So when she basically asked me to be her man in

that card she left me, that blew my mind. She had gotten bold on me, put everything out there in the forefront. She made her move. That scared me even more, because what she was telling me was that she knew she had "the package," and she knew she was worthy. She wasn't asking me for no frivolous dick; it was like she was saying, "Be my man. Me and you—let's do this. I'm the one you want." Unfortunately, what she had was more than I could handle. So in those thirty seconds, standing outside the gym in my moment of fear, I hurt her. I just didn't know how bad.

Over the past eight years, I was in six different relationships that failed. Not because of the women—because of me. Because deep down, I couldn't get Katrice Vincent outta my head. I was so busy wondering if I should've fought for her after that night that I couldn't concentrate on the women that were in front of me.

So I just decided to make my move. I knew she was married with children. I knew she loved that dude. But all's fair in love and war. 'Cause at one time, before she fell for *him,* she wanted *me.* I figured she just might still have feelings for me, even after all the time that passed. So I decided it was time for me and Weston to go to war. Because if I didn't at least try to get her in my life the way I wanted her, I'd never forgive myself. But most important, I knew if I kept walking away, I would never know if she could've been mine. It was my sole intention to make her mine—even if I had to tear some shit up to get her.

3

KATRICE

September 18, 2007, 9:53 P.M.

There are no words to express how scared I am right now. I'm still speechless about what happened today. I just don't understand why this has followed me into my happy future. I mean, I'm not bothering any-damn-body, am I? I'm not putting any silent vibes out into the universe, calling forth unnecessary trouble, am I? I moved on. I left all that trauma behind me. At least I thought I did. So why is it starting all over again? I just wanna be with my husband and kids and live a jolly life. But no. May 25, 1999, has come back to haunt me eight years later, and now everything's all tense between Weston and me. I don't even know why I told him. Yes, I do. I was scared he'd find out some other kinda way, and then he'd be asking me if I knew, and what would I do? Look in his face and lie? I mean, I could, but given everything that happened back then, lying would only screw things up

*even more. Besides, I don't wanna lie to him. It takes entirely
too much energy. Not the lying part, but the living with the
fact that a lie has been told. It's on your mind every millisec-
ond of the day, and you spend every waking moment looking over your shoulder, wondering when it's gonna come
back and trip you up. I can't live like that. I got way too
much going on to be trying to hide a damn lie. My thing
is this: What the hell does Royce want? Why is he even here?
I guess I got my nerve asking that, seeing as how this is his
hometown and all. But that's not the point. He could still be
here and not bother me. Is "bother" the word I'm looking for?
No. 'Cause he's not actually bothering me. At least he wasn't
today. His presence bothers me, though; and that's where I'm
all messed up. I'm nervous. My gut tells me something bad
is gonna happen . . . something that's gonna really make
things difficult. I'm hardly ever wrong when I get that deep
gut feeling. And right now, my gut is burning with fear.
Royce is back, and that's something I never expected to be
dealing with. Now my husband and the man I let turn my
life upside down are in the same town. God, I beg You, please
keep them away from each other. Please, just don't ever let
them meet. That's all I ask of You.*

When I got to the shop on Tuesday morning, all I
could hear from outside the door was Angela's loud-
ass rap music. I like hip-hop—really, I do; but she was
stuck on the same Jay-Z CD, *Kingdom Come,* and it was
driving me crazy. And what was worse, she kept playing "Show Me What You Got" over and over. So,
anyway, when I opened the door and there it was, blaring through the walls once again, I nearly screamed.

The music was so loud that when I said, "Angela!
Hey! Angela . . . can you turn that down some? It's

way too loud!" she didn't hear a damn syllable that came outta my mouth.

She was busy shaking her ass to the beat of the music while looking in her appointment book.

I was so annoyed that when I walked up behind her, I tapped her on the shoulder extra hard—but still soft enough that she wouldn't feel like I was hitting her, which is what I really wanted to do.

She jumped like a scared bunny, threw her arms in the air all dramatic, and said, "*Ooooo!* Child, you scared the *hell* outta me! I ain't even hear you come in!"

I raised my voice over the music, got real close to her ear and asked sarcastically, "You mean you didn't hear me yelling your name even with the music up to concert-level volume, Angela?"

She got the point, then scurried to turn the music down.

"Sorry, honey. I just *love* that damn Jay-Z! I just can't get enougha this CD."

"Clearly."

"Oh—you don't like it? You don't like Jay-Z?"

"I do. But what I don't like is the fact that it's nine in the morning and you're blasting music like you're at the club or something."

"I'm sorry. I just like ta have a little music on when I'm gettin' ready ta open up. I didn't know it bothered you. I'll make sure I keep it down from now on, then."

"Please. Thank you."

Then she really had me incensed when she said, "Oh, yo' white friend called."

I looked at her, bewildered. "Pardon me? My *white* friend?"

"Yeah"—she pointed to the wall behind my customer chair—"the one in the picture with you over there . . . the white girl . . . she called here earlier, lookin' fuh you."

I looked at the wall and saw the picture she was pointing at. "You mean Joan-Renee?"

"Yeah, yeah . . . her."

"Okay, but why does she hafta be my *white* friend? Why didn't you just say Joan-Renee called?"

"I couldn't remember her name. I mean, it was almost an hour ago. I just knew it was the white girl from the picture."

"What do you mean you couldn't remember her name? Didn't you write it down?"

"Girl, no. I didn't have time for all that. I was busy tryina get my customer's weave hair together before she gets here. I had ran outta hair—I coulda swore I had enough—but, anyway, I had ta lock up and rush over ta Francine's house—you know my friend Francine who do hair—anyway, I had ta borrow some from her since the beauty supply wasn't open yet, and that put me behind schedule."

Goddamn her.

"So . . . what did she say?"

"Child, I don't even remember. Somethin' about movin' or somethin' like that. I wasn't really payin' that much attention. I told you, I was busy."

"Angela. When people call here for me, especially if you don't know them, you need to write the messages down, no matter how busy you are. Not only did you forget her name, but you can't even tell me what she said. That is *totally* unprofessional, and that's *not* the way we do things around here."

"Okay, honey, I'm sorry. I was just a little distracted. It won't happen again."

"Please make sure that it doesn't."

"So . . . y'all is really tight, huh?"

"Meaning?"

"I mean, y'all really been kickin' it since high school?"

"Actually, we've been friends since grade school. Why? What's the big deal?"

"And you really trust her?"

"*What?* What kinda question is that? Of course I trust her. She's one of my best friends in the world. Why would you say somethin' like that?"

She twisted up her face and made a funny throat sound, riddled with suspicion. "Child, I'm just sayin' . . . all the white folks I dun dealt wit' in my life was shady as hell. I couldn't trust none of 'em. Damn sho' ain't neva been friends wit' 'em. You just gotta watch ya back wit' them sometimes, that's all."

"Well, I'm very sorry you've had such bad experiences with white people, but I don't have that problem with Joan-Renee. I don't need to watch my back with her—she *has* my back, always will. And in the future, I would appreciate it if you wouldn't refer to her as my 'white friend' or 'the white girl.' It's very disrespectful."

"Woo, now . . . I ain't mean fuh you ta git all salty on me. I was just sayin', sometimes—"

"Yeah, I know . . . sometimes *you* need to watch *your* back. Well, you go right ahead and do that. This conversation is over. I need to get ready for my client."

And I turned and walked into the back room, leaving her ignorant ass standing there with her mouth half open. God, I missed Tiki.

* * *

Angela left early for the day, somewhere around three-fifteen. I was glad to get some peace in my own shop for a change. My last customer wasn't scheduled until four-thirty, so I had a chance to straighten up, put on my own damn music, and do what I felt like doing without her all up under me. I put on my favorite CD in the world, Chrisette Michele's *I Am*, and mellowed out with her deeply soulful sound. And unlike Angela, I had the volume down to a respectable level; it was down low enough for only me to hear. I had to buy Weston his own CD because we kept fighting over who was gonna listen to it every day. We don't usually have that problem with our music, but with this particular CD, it was an issue.

About fifteen minutes after she left, I was over at my area getting products ready for my client, and I heard the door jingle. I didn't turn around, because, truthfully, I thought it was Angela. She's known for leaving stuff and then doubling back to get it. So I just kept doing what I was doing.

But then it happened. Again. Just like it did back in '99. My back was turned, and after the door stopped jingling, I heard him say in the same tone he did eight years prior, "Hello, Katrice Vincent."

I almost dropped the bottle of shampoo I was holding.

Then I froze right where I was, just like I did at the reception. Only this time, I wasn't holding punch. I had my hand wrapped around the shampoo bottle, gripping it so tight that I started denting it because I was so tense. My breathing quickened, and my heart thumped, off beat. I closed my eyes and hoped I was dreaming, because if I wasn't, that meant for the second time in my life, Royce Phillip Jordan III had snuck up on me from behind and turned me from "calm" and "collected" to "speechless" and "nerve-wracked."

About seven seconds passed before I opened my eyes and said in a shaky, raspy tone, "Hello, Royce." I didn't turn around when I said that, either.

I knew then that he was the mystery man who had been looking for me, and now he was back. And I wished to the highest heavens above he had continued to remain a mystery.

He said in the sweetest, sexiest voice, "You not gon' turn around and look at me?"

I didn't say a thing. Instead, I forced myself to put the bottle down, closed my eyes again real hard, and thought, *Oh, God . . . please don't let him look good.* After I opened them, I glanced at the picture of Weston and me at our wedding, my favorite one, and then discreetly and quietly laid it facedown and quickly put some papers and my appointment book on top of it. Then, finally, even slower than I had turned around at the reception, I turned to look at him.

He looked even better than he did that night in May. No lie. He was so fine it was almost laughable. He was leaning against the door, with his jacket lying over his left arm, wearing brown jeans, a thick black-and-brown turtleneck sweater, and some black Timberlands. I could see his chest muscles through the sweater—and the sweater wasn't that tight.

At that moment, I wished Angela really would double back so she could save me from what was about to happen.

He stared at me with a shocked look on his face

for a second, then moved from the door. He started slowly walking toward me, saying, with astonishment in his eyes, "Goddamn. There is *no* reason for a woman to be as beautiful as you. Just no reason."

He stopped walking after he took about ten small steps.

Then we just stared at each other, me with fear in my eyes and him with a look that said he wanted to revisit the hotel experience we had.

And we stared some more. Neither of us moving. Both of us tweaking mentally in our own way.

After some twenty seconds of intense eye-locking, I finally said a strained "Thank you, Royce . . . for the . . . um . . . compliment."

"I'm just tellin' the truth."

As we breathed heavily and gazed at each other—wouldn't you know it—"If I Have My Way" started playing, and I wanted to dive into the corner where the CD player was and turn the song off. It was *too* apropos at the moment, especially with the way he was gawking at me.

Without blinking or taking his eyes off mine, he asked, "Why you lookin' at me like you scared 'uh me?"

I paused, parted my lips to speak, then fidgeted before I answered, "'Cause maybe I am."

"You think I'm here to hurt you?"

I shook my head. "Not that kinda scared."

We went back to having a nonverbal conversation with our eyes.

The silence between us was deafening, and his fineness wasn't helping matters at all. I finally got half a grip and managed to say, "Um . . . excuse me . . ." and pulled my eyes away from his so I could go turn off the song before I started having thoughts that would surely have Weston serving me divorce papers by week's end.

I felt him taking in my every move with his large, intensely dark brown-eyes.

Once I had taken Chrisette out of our mix, I took full advantage of the fact that Royce no longer had me under his spell. I avoided looking at him again as I headed back to my seating area.

He watched me walk, but he didn't speak.

I caught a glimpse of the small, framed picture of the twins off by the mirror, and seeing their innocent faces smiling at me did something to me. It snapped me back to reality. It was like all of a sudden I remembered the importance of my husband and two children. I was vastly disturbed by the fact that Royce's presence had such a profound effect on me that I had to look at my kids' picture to come back to what was real, what was important. I had a solid relationship with the love of my life, and we had two beautiful, brilliantly smart children whom I would kill or be killed for. That picture saved me from regressing thoughtwise back to the night in the hotel, and brought me from a fifteen on the high-point scale down to a five, where Royce was concerned. I finally took a huge breath in through my nose, let it settle in my lungs before I exhaled it through my lips, and turned back around to look at Royce, this time with composure.

I took on my professional tone and asked him, "So what brings you here today?"

About five different answers Rolodexed through his brain before he finally picked the one he knew would make things awkward for me. "I need a cut. You got time?"

I chuckled. His hair, what little he had, was perfect. Then I said, "What's wrong with your hair right now?"

He smiled at the fact that I knew he was bullshitting me. But he still continued. "I want a razor cut."

"You want me to cut you bald?"

"Yep. All the way."

I looked at the clock. It was three thirty-five, which left me plenty of time to cut him. I just wasn't sure I wanted to actually do it.

"I have a client coming in at four-thirty. How 'bout you come back tomorrow and have my partner, Angela, do it?"

"Nah. I don't know her. I want *you* to do it."

"You've never seen any of my work. How do you know I'm any good?"

"I trust you. Completely."

More silence and hesitation.

I wasn't about to tell him right then that razor cuts are the thing I do best where my male clients are concerned. A good week averages me at least ten or twelve of them.

Since it was obvious he wasn't leaving without getting what he wanted—even though what he wanted was a crock of shit—I reluctantly obliged him. "Fine. I'll do it."

He walked over to the chair and said, "I know you'll take special care of me." Then he winked at me and smiled before he sat his scrumptious, good-smelling ass down.

During the first few minutes while I was prepping him, neither of us said anything. The room was totally quiet, but our thoughts were screaming a thousand different things. I was trying to stay focused on what I was doing so I wouldn't start drifting back to the hotel and imagining him with his face between my legs, gobbling and slurping like he had just ended a ten-day fast.

I started shaving his head, and made sure I took my time. I was nervous as hell, and I kept having visions of him suddenly moving and me slicing through his cranium and blood spurting and spattering everywhere. I've never even nicked a client, so I know the only reason I was tripping like that is because it was *him*.

All of a sudden, he threw me for a loop and broke the silence with a hesitant "So you, uh, talked to Charles lately?"

I wasn't sure what kind of answer he was looking for, but I was fully aware of the fact that Charles had kicked Royce to the curb after he found out what had happened. So I just said, "Yup. All the time."

Instead of asking me what he really wanted to ask, he said, "That's good. He and Tiki still goin' strong?"

I didn't really wanna go with him on this particular fishing trip, so I kept my answer short, and to the point. "Yup."

Again he said, "That's good." But he sounded genuinely sad.

I finally decided to change the subject and ask what *I* wanted to know. "So you just out here for a visit or what?"

"Sorta-kinda."

"Care to elaborate a bit?"

"I just got some . . . personal business to take care of. So I'll be here for a minute."

"And then what?"

"And then what, what?"

"And then after your business is taken care of, you plan on goin' back to Maryland?"

"You tryina get ridda me?"

"I'm just asking."

"It all depends on how my business turns out."

"So your personal business has a direct effect on whether or not you go back to Maryland for good?"

"Basically."

His elusiveness started making me feel really uneasy.

"You still workin' with your dad?"

"That's kinda up in the air right now."

"Meaning?"

Then *he* changed the subject: "So how you like your new partner?"

I assumed he heard that Tiki and Charles had moved away. I knew he still had plenty of connections in Oakland, and there were a bunch of people at the wedding that he knew from when we were in high school. It didn't really surprise me that he didn't ask where Tiki was.

"She's okay some days. Other days I wanna snatch her weave out by the tracks and pimp-slap her in the face with it."

He broke out laughing when I said that, and his head jerked slightly.

My heart stopped for two seconds.

"Royce, please don't move. Please. I don't wanna cut you. This razor is sharp enough to slice the air in half."

"Sorry. I told you, though, I trust you. You not gon' cut me."

"Well, I'm glad you're confident about that fact."

"I'm confident about a lotta things that hafta do with you."

I was way too scared to even dignify that with an answer. Instead, I asked him, "How long you been in town?"

"A coupla weeks."

I was about to ask him where he was staying, but then I changed my mind because I didn't want him to think I was overly interested in him or what he was doing. Even though I was.

We gladly welcomed the next couple of minutes of silence between us. I think we both needed to take a break so we could review our mental notes, so to speak, and get ready for the next round on the "Questions, Answers, and Comments Show."

And his next comment took the show to a whole new level.

"So I heard you got married."

"I did."

"Same dude?"

As if he didn't know who I married. I bet he had the entire scoop the next day.

"Yes, siree."

"These your kids in this picture right here?"

"Yup."

He let out a hard breath before he said, "Cute. They look like you."

"Thanks. I would hope so."

"Twins, right?"

"Uh-huh."

"How old?"

"They just turned five on Sunday, as a matter of fact. We had a big party for them, their first one. They had a blast."

He let all that information marinate for a minute.

I tried to hurry the hell up and finish his shave so I could push him out the door before my client got there.

Since he was all up in mine, I decided to get up in his.

"So you haven't made anybody Mrs. Royce Jordan yet?"

"Not yet—but I'm workin' on it."

"Is that right?"

"Yep."

"Somebody you left back in Maryland?"

"Actually, no. She doesn't live in Maryland."

"Hmm. And no kids for you yet, either?"

He chuckled. "Not that I know of. But you know what they say . . . all men probably have at least one kid they don't know about. Hell, you saw *Dreamgirls*, didn't you?"

"Yeah."

"You see Jamie Foxx didn't find out he had a daughter till the end . . . and he had to figure that out his *damn* self. The girl was almost ten."

I smiled and laughed softly. "True."

"But, hopefully, there's no Mini Me runnin' around that I'm oblivious to. I try to be careful."

"Caution is always best."

Then I marinated on the info that I had extracted from him.

A minute later, I decided to poke a little further.

"So, does your girlfriend know you're workin' on makin' her your wife?"

"She's not my girlfriend."

"Oh? What is she then? Seems to me it'd be kinda

hard to make someone your wife who's not even your woman yet."

"She's somebody I have . . . feelings for. And I'm workin' on gettin' to a point where maybe I *can* make her my wife . . . one day in the future."

"Hmm. You plan on lettin' her in on all this?"

"Eventually. Right now, I'm still mappin' things out."

"Well, I hope she's worth it. Sounds like you got your work cut out for you."

"Oh, she's definitely worth it. And I'm not too worried about the work. It might be a challenge, but I was always told if it ain't hard gettin', it ain't worth havin'. And I believe she's worth gettin' my hands dirty for."

I couldn't believe it, but I was actually starting to get a tad jealous. And that pissed me off. Why I would feel that way, when I already have everything I ever wanted in life, was beyond me. Nevertheless, I decided it was time to get off the subject of Royce's hopeful conquest—quick, fast, and in a hurry.

"Oh. Well, good luck with that."

"Yeah. Thanks."

We both took our individual information soups and let them simmer in our heads.

For about the next ten minutes while I finished shaving and cleaning him up, we talked about simple stuff, like movies, TV shows, cars, the news, current events—you know, subjects that we could discuss without getting into trouble and saying things we might regret.

When I finished—and I have to say, I did a bang-up job, with no nicks or scratches—Royce was looking even more delectable than when he had walked in. He stood up, admired himself in the mirror, smiled at what he saw, then looked at me.

"It's real proper, Katrice. I knew you'd do me right."

"Well, thank you. It's a good look for you."

"Yeah. I think I'll keep it. I wore it like this about four years ago, but the dude who was shavin' me wasn't very good. I had razor bumps for months."

"Well, my clients don't have that problem. I have a special technique that keeps the bumps away."

"Don't tell me it's all in the wrist."

"That, and in the bottle of mink oil."

"Mink oil?"

"Yep. It's good for the scalp. I put some on you."

"Really?" He looked in the mirror again. "I don't see any grease."

"That's 'cause it's not grease . . . or greasy. It's one of the oils closest to that of the human skin. It absorbs immediately. It's good for skin conditions, too. My son has eczema, and ever since I started using it on his patches, he's been fine."

"Can I get it somewhere local?"

"You can, but it's not cheap."

"How 'not cheap' is 'not cheap'?"

"Let's put it this way—a two-ounce bottle could run you close to forty dollars. And I use one of the most expensive brands on the market." I gave him a toothless, schoolgirl smile. "And *that* is why my male clients stay posted up in my shop on the weekly to get their shaves."

"I'm sure that's not the only reason."

"You just had to take it there, didn't you?"

"You know it's true, I don't even know why you frontin'."

"*Anyway.* For now, just get some vitamin E. You

have good skin. It's got just the right amount of palmitoleic acid. You'll be okay with just that."

"Palm-what?"

I chuckled. "Palmitoleic acid. It's a fatty acid that the skin produces to keep itself moisturized. People who have a shortage of it, like my son, end up with dry, itchy, scaly skin, and they need products like mink oil, macadamia nut oil—products that are close to the oil that skin produces—to make up for what they don't have."

He looked impressed. "That is *sexy* how you know your stuff like that."

I laughed. "It's my job to know those things. Hair and skin go together."

His expression said he was ready to knock me to the floor, tear my clothes off, and do *me* right. "Whatever. It's still sexy."

"It's . . . just my job, Royce. It's nothing special. They're just things I need to know, that's all."

"Well, I been gettin' my hair cut by professionals for umpteen years, and no one's ever mentioned the stuff you did today."

"I guess today was your lucky day."

"Uh-huh . . . in more than a *few* ways."

And then we stared again. I'll be damned if I wasn't still attracted to his ass. Not like I was back in the day—this was on a much, much smaller level—but there was a spark still there that made me feel guilty as sin.

A few seconds later, he finally asked, "So how much I got'choo for?"

"Just twenty."

He pulled out a folded bill and handed it to me. It was a fifty.

"Oh—hang on. Lemme go to the register for—"

"I don't need any change."

"But this is a fifty."

He stepped *real* close to me. "I know what it is. And I don't need the change."

"I can't take—"

He stopped me in the middle of my sentence by running the back of his right hand softly down my left cheek; then he said, "Thanks for the cut and all that info. You take care, lovely. I'll see you soon." Then he swung his jacket over his shoulder, winked at me again, and turned and walked out.

I just stood there with my mouth hanging open.

Once again, Royce Phillip Jordan III had managed to captivate me. And I had no idea what the hell I was gonna tell my husband when I got home.

When I walked in the house, Weston was in the kitchen washing the kids' dishes. It was his turn to pick them up from preschool and feed them dinner. I didn't get home until after six, and I was a nervous wreck. I had already made the decision that I was gonna tell Weston about Royce showing up at the shop. I figured I might as well just come clean, because eventually he'd find out somehow, just like he did in '99, and then I'd really be screwed. Besides, Weston knows me. He would've known something was seriously bothering me, and he would've used his finesse to get it out of me before the night was over.

The kids were watching TV in the living room, and they jumped up, ran over, and hugged and kissed me.

After I asked them how their day went and what they did, Ellie said, "Mommy, Daddy made us hambiggers for dinner."

Willie added, "Yeah, but you guys forgot to buy the cheese, so they were naked."

Ellie looked at Willie and frowned. "They weren't naked, Willie. We had ketchup and mustard."

He shot her an aggressive look and spat, "Burgers are naked if they don't have cheese. The cheese goes over the burger, like a shirt. It's like clothes. If there's no cheese, there's no clothes, and it's a naked burger."

I didn't feel like listening to them argue about food the way they always do, so I cut that conversation short.

"Okay, okay . . . we'll make sure there's clothes to go on the burgers next time. Now go sit down, both of you. I'm gonna go see what your daddy is doing."

Willie ran back to the living room, but Ellie asked me, "Mommy, are you mad today?"

"No. Why?"

"'Cause you look like you had a bad day at work."

"No, I'm not mad. I'm just tired. It was a long day, that's all."

"Okay. Well, then, you hafta tell Daddy you're gonna go to bed early tonight so you can get lots of sleep."

I laughed at her; then I said, "I'll make sure I do that, Ellie Kat. And I'll tell him you said so."

"Okay." Then she darted off, calling out to her brother, "Willie, turn the channel back! The show's not over!"

I stepped in the kitchen, stood in the doorway, and looked at Weston in all his sexiness. He had on one of his wife beaters and his favorite black lounge-around-before-bed cotton shorts, with all his beautiful muscles waving at me. I smiled to myself and thought about how lucky I was to have such a gorgeous specimen for a husband. And if I wanted to keep him, I knew I needed to nip the Royce thing in the bud, pronto.

Weston felt me staring at him, and said, with his back turned to me, "My wife gets real jealous when other women ogle me."

I walked up beside him and slipped my arms around his waist. "Then maybe you need to get rid of that possessive wife of yours and come see about *me*."

He turned away from the sink, put the dish towel down, and then ran his hand through my hair. "Nope. Sorry. Not gon' happen. But I'll tell you what . . . you can slip me a little tongue right now and we can just keep that between us."

I said, "That'll work"; then I pulled his face down to mine and gave him a soft, tender, and full-of-tongue kiss.

Once we came up for air, he smiled at me and said, "Hi, wife."

"Hi, husband. How was your day? Did you talk to that guy about opening the gym?"

We untangled ourselves from each other and went to sit down at the kitchen table.

He said, "I'm supposed to meet wit' him on Friday. We got a lot to work out, but if all goes well, we might be able to make a go of a partnership."

"I hope this guy is better than the last one. You been tryina do this for years. I wanna see it happen."

"It will—I just gotta find the right doctor to work with."

"Well, I think opening a physical-therapy gym around here is a great idea. There's lots of money in PT. And if you team up with a really good therapist, you guys shouldn't have any problems pulling in lots of business."

"Yep. I'ma make it happen. Somehow."

I decided to go ahead and dive on in with the news before we got off into a whole other happy conversation.

"Um . . . I don't mean to change the subject all abruptly, but . . . I kinda have something I need to tell you."

"Uh-oh. You not pregnant again, are you?"

"No, but after I tell you what I have to tell you, you'll wish that's what it was."

"Well, damn . . . how bad could it be?"

"Uhhhh . . . well . . . you remember the other night when I told you Angela said some dude was looking for me?"

"Yeah. Why? Who was it?"

I gave him an uneasy look before I rocked his world.

"It, um . . . it was . . . Royce."

His eyes lit on fire; then he leaned his hands on his thighs, pushed his torso forward, and asked— through clenched teeth—a question he already knew the answer to. *"Royce . . . who?"*

My tone was apologetic. "The only Royce there is."

He closed his eyes and started breathing really heavy. Then, a couple of seconds later, he opened them, scooted his chair back, jumped up, and yelled, "Fuck!"

"Shhhhh . . . Weston . . . you're gonna scare the kids. Don't yell, please."

"How the hell am I not supposta yell?"

I got up, too. "Wait . . . seriously . . . please don't get mad."

He kept yelling. "Don't get *mad*! What did he want? Some more *pussy*?"

That got me pissed. "Hey. Wait a minute. That was *totally* uncalled for. And you know what? We need to take this upstairs, 'cause now you dun made me mad. So let's go."

We stormed out of the kitchen. On the way past the living room, I told the kids, "You guys stay down here and watch TV for a while," and kept right on walking.

They just looked at me with question marks in their eyes.

When we got up to our room, Weston walked in first, and I stepped in behind him and slammed the door.

He turned and looked at me. "Oh, now you slammin' doors? What's that all about?"

"What it's about is that *nasty-ass* comment you made in the kitchen! Don't talk to me like that! Don't even go there with me!"

"Well, what'choo expect? You come up in the house talkin' 'bout this mu'fucka been lookin' for you for a goddamn week—"

"Oh, stop exaggerating! It hasn't been a week! It's only been a coupla days!"

"Same difference! The point is his ass is *lookin'* for you!"

"*Was* looking for me!"

"Ohhhhh . . . so I guess he *found* you, huh? What he do, come up in the shop today or somethin'?"

"Yeah, he did."

He stopped and thought about what that meant. He went from enraged to wary in less than two seconds. Then the grilling began.

He walked up on me and gave me the evil eye. "So you saw him."

"Yes."

"What time?"

"Around three-thirty."

"Any clients there wit'choo?"

"No."

"Was Angela there?"

"No, she left early today."

He mumbled to himself under his breath, "Ain't this a *bitch*"; then he asked me, "How long was he there?"

"Less than an hour."

"Less than an hour . . . what's that supposta mean? Y'all was up in there gittin' y'all *visit* on? Tell me what exactly less than an hour means. Five minutes? Ten? Twenty? What?"

"It was like forty-five minutes."

He blew up. "Forty-five minutes? What were y'all doin' all alone up in the shop?"

"I cut his hair! And stop insinuating things! You're actin' like I'm sneakin' around or somethin'!"

The only thing he heard out of that outburst was that I cut Royce's hair.

"You cut his *hair*? Whose bright idea was that?"

"It was *his* idea! And stop doing that!"

"What?"

"Stop saying stuff to make it look like I was encouraging him!"

"Why did you cut his hair, Katrice?"

"Because he asked me to!"

"No . . . I mean, why did *you* do it? You didn't hafta do it!"

"I just told you Angela was gone already! Who else was gonna do it?"

"You missin' my point, and it's pissin' me the *fuck* off!"

"Well, make your point and stop beatin' around the bush!"

"Why didn't you tell him to come back another day and have Angela do it?"

"I *did* suggest that, but he didn't want to!"

"Of course, he didn't! 'Cause he wanted *you* to do it! And my point *is* . . . you didn't demand for him to come back and have her do it! You wanted to do it!"

"Weston, that's stupid! Why would I demand something like that when I could've just as easily done it myself instead of wasting time arguing about it?"

"Wouldn'ta been no argument if you'da just told him you didn't have time for that shit and sent his janky ass packin'! If you'd quit fuckin' around and just admit that you *wanted* to cut his hair and stop tryina pretend like you didn't have no choice, we could move on!"

"Move on to *what?* You're makin' me sorry I even told you about this!"

"Yeah, and you probably thought about *not* tellin' me, too!"

"You damn right! Because I knew we'd end up doin' exactly what we're doin' now!"

"What did y'all talk about? I know y'all didn't sit up there in silence the whole time!"

"We just talked about regular shit! You're makin' this seem like we had a rendezvous or something!"

"Did you charge his ass?"

"Of course, I charged him!"

"Yeah, but how much did he *give* you?"

Okay, now *that* I did lie about. Things were way too heated; and if I had told him Royce gave me a thirty-dollar tip and I accepted it, he might've jumped through a window . . . and tried to take me with him.

"He *gave me* the price of the damn cut!"

"Why don't I believe that, Katrice?"

"'Cause you don't want to!"

He turned away, took a breather, then turned back and looked at me fearfully. "I don't like this. Why is he here? Why is he poppin' up at the shop?"

"I don't know, and I really don't care. He said he's here because of some personal business. I didn't even ask what it was. Baby, I have everyone and everything I need and want right here in this house. There's no way in hell I will *ever* put us in jeopardy again. Ever. So whatever the reason Royce is back, that's his business. *My* business is standing in front of me and sitting in the living room." He looked down at the floor and started wiping his palms on his shorts. "Weston, look at me. I am *not* the person I was back in high school; I'm not fifteen anymore. And I'm no longer obsessed with Royce anymore." His eyes kept shifting away from mine. "Are you . . . Weston . . . look at me. Do you hear me? Don't let Royce's being back in town bother you. There is *nothing* he can do for me now. I told you back in '99 that I was done with him, and I meant that."

He asked me with a scary amount of suspicion, "Have you talked to him since that night?"

"Don't you *dare* ask me a question like that. That's just plain insulting."

"Well? Have you?"

"Of course, I haven't. Why would you ask me that?"

"I mean, would you tell me if you had? Really?"

"I'm not gonna have this discussion with you. You're about to make me madder than I already am, and if that happens, it is *not* gon' be cute around here."

"Katrice . . . it's a simple question. Don't avoid it. Just give it to me straight."

"No, I'll tell you what. I'ma take you back to that day when you told me that I always get all hypothetical, and that you *hate* that about me. So, no, I'm not gonna go there with you on this question, because you know what? It's hypothetical. You're asking me if I had spoken to Royce, would I tell you. The operative word is '*if.*' The reality is no, I haven't. But if I had, guess what? I have no idea if I would tell you or not. Now, I'm going back downstairs to spend time with the kids. If you wanna join me, fine. But be advised—we're not talking about this anymore. I *mean* it."

And I left him standing in the middle of the bedroom, stewing in his own mental juices, and went to attend to my beautiful children.

4

WESTON

I love my wife and children in ways that scare me. I mean that literally. Sometimes I have these thoughts of one of them dying or something terrible happening to one or more of them, and I can feel my soul collapsing, sinking into a deep place that I think only crazy people know about. Then I wonder if I'm crazy, because I take these thoughts all the way to the most deranged points. I see Katrice's funeral. I see myself jumping on top of her casket as they lower it into the ground so they can bury me with her, because without her, I'm dead, too. I see one of the twins lying in the hospital, barely clinging to life. I see myself as a widower. I see the twins being kidnapped. I allow these thoughts to nearly bring me to a cracking point. Then after I've tortured myself enough for the moment, I bring myself back to reality. Come back into the present, where my kids are playing happily with each other, and my gorgeous, sexy wife is curled up in her favorite chair, reading her hair magazines, looking more content than a woman has the right to look. She has no idea where I've just come from mentally. I visit that dark place more often than I'm gonna admit.

But as dark as that place is, there is one darker place I visited so much that it made me feel as unstable as a button hanging off a shirt by a thin piece of thread . . . about to drop off at any moment . . . subject to fall, roll, and end up anywhere . . . without any warning. That place is called "The Return of Royce." I'm a man. Hell, I'm all man. But I'll just go ahead and tell you that when I would think about the possibility of him coming back and trying to take my wife from me, tear us down like he did back in 1999, I turned into a weakling in the brain. I wasn't strong. I was soft as Jell-O. Because there is only one man in this world that I had come to be scared of. That man was Royce Phillip Jordan III.

Don't get me wrong. My wife loves me so much it's sick. Tells me and shows me in ways I won't even get into. Her love for me leaps from her big, beautiful, almond-shaped brown eyes every time she looks at me—even when I've pissed her off. I know her heart. I have total confidence in what we have. She's the mother of all mothers. She's dedicated to our children 500 percent. Lydia included. Katrice treats her like she gave birth to her. To be honest, sometimes I forget that Yolanda is her mother when Katrice is with her. One time, about a year ago, Lydia accidentally slipped up and called Katrice "Mommy," and I had to have a talk with her about that. Had to explain the difference between

Katrice and Yolanda to her, and explain why she couldn't call Katrice "Mommy," but that she was her stepmother. That was a helluva hard conversation to have with a six-year-old. But that's how much Katrice loves my daughter. So much that the child gets confused as to whose womb she came out of. That's a woman right there for you. So when I thought about that bastard Royce trying to move in on my life, my happiness, on everything I cherish, I started seeing red, and I was ready to do things to him that might get me twenty-five to life.

I knew Katrice hadn't spoken to him since that night. I'm mad that I even asked her that question, because it was nothing but an insecure move on my part. But again, he scared me. Even though I know how devoted Katrice is to me, I still couldn't get the thought out of my mind that if he had what it took to break her down back then, after fifteen years, what if his game was stronger, tighter, better, and he broke out the big guns and somehow was able to pull her away from me . . . for good? There was something about him back then that was so undeniable that she couldn't resist him, even as much as she loved me, which always disturbed me at my core. That is *some kinda muthafucka* that can pop up on a woman after a decade and a half and lay down game so smooth that she ends up in bed with him hours later, knowing she has a man she loves and wants to marry.

I never told her this, but I always knew he'd be back. I felt it in my gut. When she told me the story about that night and everything he said to her, I knew it. He had feelings for her. Real, probably-will-never-go-away feelings. Even when I was kickin' the knowledge to her about dogs and getting played, something inside me said, "But he'll be back for her . . . someday."

Then, of course, there's the fact she gave it up. I don't know in what way or for how long, but I know my wife's bedroom techniques, and let's just say . . . I've never been more satisfied sexually with any other woman—and believe me, pre-Katrice, I had more than my share of satisfying encounters. So I know his bitch ass left even more hooked than before. My wife is stunningly beautiful, smart, witty, resourceful, funny, sexy as hell, and strong. There is no man that could not want her. Especially if they had a chance to get close to her intimately. He had. Now he was back, sniffing around the shop, trying to push up on *my* wife. *My* territory. Trust me when I say I was ready to dig . . . his . . . grave.

5

ROYCE

I was right on the money. She still had feelings for me. It was all in her eyes, and in the way she moved, and the way she spoke to me. I still did something to her, and it took everything she had to fight it. It was perfect. She was perfect. Man, motherhood sure did her justice. Her body was amazing. Her breasts were twice as big as when I last saw her, and her hips had taken on an even more voluptuous shape. Her face had that special glow and fullness that motherhood gives women. Her hair was caressing her face just right, in that cute little neck-length bob she wore, and her lips were succulent with that ruby-red lipstick she had on. When she looked at me with those huge, hypnotizing brown eyes, it took everything I had not to pin her up against a wall and lay one of my slow, sensuous, I'm-'bout-to-fuck-the-shit-outta-you French kisses on her that I've given so many

women over the years—including her that night in
May—that makes them all melt into the floor and
causes their panties to drop in three seconds flat.

What I really couldn't believe was how perfect it
was that she was alone when I got there. I didn't
even *try* to do that. I was fully expecting to see her
partner and a bunch of customers in there. All I
was gonna do was go in, make my presence known,
say hi, try to have a short conversation with her,
shake her up a little bit mentally, and be out. But
something so much better was in the cards. What
were the odds that I would be able to get her alone
in the middle of the day like that? Next to none,
that's what. I couldn't have planned that if I tried.

I knew she hadn't forgotten one single detail of
what we shared. Probably had flashbacks that made
her nervous, just like I was having. Except I wasn't
nervous. I knew exactly what I was doing, why I was
there, and what I wanted to find out *while* I was
there. I found out all but one thing, which was a
gamble, anyway, because it wasn't necessarily a
given. I saw the picture of the kids, which distressed
me a little bit, but I had to move past that pretty
fast and keep it pushing so I could get to the other
items on my list. I was really looking for a picture
of Weston. I wanted to see what I was up against,
but I didn't see one hanging or propped up anywhere. I was looking hard, too. When I saw the
kids, I tried to get an idea of what he might look
like, but they looked so much like her beautiful ass
that I couldn't see past that. I did notice their eyes
were really light. Not quite hazel, but definitely not
all the way brown, either. I figured he must have
some kinda funny-ass-colored eyes. They had caramel-

colored skin, so that told me he wasn't one of the special-dark crew, like me. I guess light-skinned brothers really did come back in season. Anyway, I purposely didn't ask what their names were. That would've made them even more real. There's something about putting a name to a face that brings that person—or in their case, persons—that much more into existence. It's like, if you don't know someone's name, you can't totally identify that person. That's the way I wanted to deal with them for the moment. Just knowing they were part of the scenario was difficult enough. I could've really done without having seen their picture at all, because after that, their faces were plastered all over my brain. But that didn't dissuade me from my main focus. It was just a small thorn in my side that I had to adjust to.

So once I peeped game on the fact that she still had a thing for me, no matter how small it might have been, I felt like I could still be in the running. If I had walked up in there and gotten no more than a cordial "hello" and "how are you," with total disinterest in her eyes, then I would've had a problem. You know how it is when someone finally gets over you—their whole demeanor changes when they see you. It's like you don't even faze them anymore. Like what they felt for you never even existed. They look at you like you're just another insignificant Joe or Bob that they knew way back when. But that's not the way Katrice looked at me at any point while I was in her presence. That was as good as I wanted it.

She almost messed up my game when she started asking all those questions about my love life. I wasn't really expecting all that from her, and it kinda caught me off-guard. Not like I wasn't tempted to tell her she was the one I was after, but that wasn't on the "to do" list just yet. It was way too early in the game. And I didn't know *what* I was gonna say if she had asked me where exactly "the woman" lived. I was relieved she left that subject alone after I told her she didn't live in Maryland. I was glad to know that she was interested, though. That told me that it mattered to her, even a little. You know if they don't at least *try* to find out who you're laying the pipe to—which is really what that line of questioning is all about—you can be pretty sure they honestly don't give a damn.

Now, we all know I didn't need a cut. As a matter of fact, I know how to do my own razor shaves. After that one dude messed me up back in the day, I learned how to take care of my own head, and started doing it myself. Of course, hers was better; and I really didn't know all the extra information she gave me about the mink oil and stuff; but I didn't need her to do it. I just wanted to feel her touch again, and I knew that was probably the only way I was gonna get her to touch me. I started to try to hug her after she turned around, but when she looked at me all scary, I decided that might not be such a good idea. I couldn't quite tell where her head was at, and I didn't wanna take any unnecessary chances with the situation, so I just kept my distance. Her asking me what brought me there was the perfect segue into that cut, because right before she asked me that, I was trying to figure out what my next move was gonna be. It was also the perfect test, because once I decided to ask her to cut me, I wanted to see if she would say no. She tried, but the bigger test was when I told her I wanted *her* to do it. That was her chance to say no for real, if she really didn't wanna have anything to do with me or wanna be near me. When a woman *truly* doesn't want you around or in her space, she makes that fact perfectly clear. But she took the bait like a hungry fish, didn't even put up a fight. She fell right into my trap.

The last test was right before I left. Actually, there were two, back to back. First was the fifty dollars I gave her. I wanted to see if she'd accept the extra money. Yeah, I know, she tried not to, but again, she didn't *really* reject it. If she really didn't want it, she would've made sure she gave it back to me. But let me make something clear: it wasn't that she wanted the money, like she needed it or something; it was about that hold I had on her—that thing she couldn't deny. When someone is in your heart, even a little bit, you let that person do things like give you a thirty-dollar tip. You're not offended, un-comfortable with it, or put off by it. Because you feel something for that person. It's just human nature. If she had rejected the tip, that would've meant she really didn't want me in her life, and that she wanted to cut the ties, so to speak. That's what you do when you want someone to be gone for good. You cut all ties, no matter how small.

The second part of the test was when I touched her face. That was actually a last-minute decision, but it worked out well. When she was trying to resist the money, my instinct was to attempt to stop her— and the first thing that came to mind was touching her. That always gets 'em. Especially if you touch their face in that special kinda way, which I did. It all tied in, because again, if she let me touch her, I knew I was still in there. Women most *definitely* don't let you touch them if you're assed out—and if she still took the money after that, well, that was all I needed.

In the end, she confirmed everything I hoped for. After eight years, she still felt enough for me to not kick me to the curb. That's all I needed to know on that first visit. The foundation of phase one of my project was laid, which made preparing for phase two that much easier.

6

KATRICE

September 21, 2007, 11:57 P.M.

I tell you, if I didn't have my girls in my life, I'd never get through a single crisis, I swear it. They just make things so doable, even when I still don't know what to do in the end. I feel sorry for anyone who doesn't have at least one great friend they can talk to about anything, with no inhibitions—without being judged or criticized. I mean someone who'll tell them the honest, down-and-dirty truth, even if it hurts a little—or even a lot; someone who won't let them get away with lying to them, or themselves; someone who can help lead them down the right path, because that's how much they're loved by that friend . . . or those friends. Which is how it is in my case. My girls never give me a break in the truth department. And I need that, because, otherwise, I'd lie to myself at least five times a day.

I still don't have the slightest idea how I'm gonna get

through this whole Royce situation. I am sure of one thing, though, which is that I'm not in love with him, and I don't wanna be with him. But that doesn't matter, anyway, because he's not trying to be with me, either. He's making plans to lasso some other woman. Which is actually a relief. But even with all of that, there's still this "thing" between us that we can't seem to get past or get rid of. It's very disturbing and horrifying. If Weston ever found out that I'm even remotely attracted to Royce, even though I have no intention of acting on it—because that part of my life is over—he'd lose his mind, for sure. He's already halfway there just knowing Royce is in town. I hope he wraps up whatever business he has and makes his way back to Maryland, because I can't stand the thought of him being here for too much longer.

I waited until Friday night to get together with the girls so I could fill them in on the happenings at the shop on Tuesday and my fight with Weston. It was too much to try to have four separate conversations about it; plus, I wanted all of their input at the same time. We planned a girls' night in—at Rishidda's, over Zachary's pizza and beer—to have the sacred discussion.

After I had pored over every detail of the time Royce was in the shop, everyone had something different to add or ask. After several small, easy-to-answer questions, things got a little deeper. No, a *lot* deeper.

Genine asked me, "So why did you cut his hair, Trice? I mean, why didn't you tell him you couldn't do it? You know having him around is dangerous. Why'd you put yourself in that position?"

"You sound like Weston. He asked me the exact same thing. If I didn't know better, I'd swear you were a fly on the wall during our fight."

She asked, "Well, what was your answer?"

"Actually . . . the question never got totally answered, because the fight took a different turn right after that."

"So, again," she started, "what's the answer?"

"I guess . . . because I wanted to talk to him. I wanted to find out what the hell was going on . . . what he was doing. Not just in the shop, but here in Oakland, in general. I knew if I sent him away, I wouldn't be able to find out much."

Chantelle asked, "You think that's really it?"

I asked her, "You think that's *not* it?"

Then Rishidda said, "You know what I think? I think you want him to be hooked on you, but you don't necessarily wanna be hooked on him, even though you kinda still are."

I looked at her, confused. "That doesn't make any sense."

She broke it all the way down. "Yes, it does. See, part of you is still operating from the mind-set of the jilted high-school Katrice—the girl who wanted Royce's attention but couldn't have it the way she wanted it. That was a really big issue for you back then. So now that you *have* the attention you always wanted from him, you wanna hold on to it—even though you have no real intentions of takin' things any further. It's like—havin' his attention *now* makes up for all the years you longed for it. Even though, technically, you got him out yo' system back in '99, meanin' you probably don't need to do him again or get all physical. You like the fact that he wants you—and you don't wanna let it go. It's kinda like now the tables are turned, and you wanna make *him* suffer like you did."

We all looked at her in amazement, and then Chantelle said, "*Dayum!* How the hell did you come up wit' that? I mean, that's some deep, psychological Dr. Phil talk that actually *does* make sense, girl." She looked at me. "I think she's right, Trice. You still got a few issues to work through about him."

Rishidda said, "Girl, my therapist, Dianne Bye, man, she was the bomb. I learned so much from her, I could be a psychiatrist myself and not even need a degree."

I said, "Well, hang on—I need to marinate on all that for a minute—but back up, first. What does everything you just said hafta do with the reason I cut his hair?"

Everyone looked at Rishidda like she was E. F. Hutton.

"Because you're great at what'choo do. It was yo' chance to show out a little, let him see how you work yo' professional thang. He dun already seen yo' freaky, sexual side—"

I laughed, then said, "Shut the hell up."

She chuckled, then went on. "No, seriously—he has. So it was time for you to show him yo' other skills. You know ain't nothin' sexier than someone who's good at they profession. And men like that, girl. They like to see a woman be good at more than just ridin' the 'd' all day and night. But anyway, cut-tin' his hair was the perfect chance for you to step up yo' game and get him even more hooked."

I was totally astounded. I looked at all the girls in disbelief, then said, "You know what? She has the nerve to be *right*, y'all. I mean about the men liking that kinda stuff. Because we got into a discussion about the product I used on his head and the condition of his skin, and I said a few knowledgeable things about it, and he sure did say it was sexy that I knew my stuff like that."

"See, I know what I'm talkin' about, girl. If you give it enough thought, you'll see I'm right about everything I said."

Sabrina said, "Well, goddamn, Sheed! When can I sign up for *my* counselin' session? I got a few thangs *I* need to discuss!"

Everyone cracked up.

She said, "Ay, I'm just kickin' knowledge based on all them years I spent sittin' up in Dianne's office tryina work through my own trauma over Cash. But on the serious tip, Katrice, maybe you should go see her. She could really help you work past this. 'Cause sorry to say, but you still got feelin's for the dude. They might be different than before, and, like I said, you might not be tryina git wit' him again, but this fire and desire ain't over between y'all."

Genine jumped in. "Tell the truth, girl—are you still attracted to him?"

Then Sabrina asked, "Yeah, does he still make ya pussy throb?"

We roared at that one.

Chantelle said, "Leave it to this freak to say somethin' like that!"

Sabrina said, "I'm serious! Y'all know how it is when a man got'choo all jacked up in the head. If he looks good, ya pussy throbs. If he smells good, ya pussy throbs. If he stands too close to you, ya pussy throbs—and if his ass *touch* you, ya pussy starts beatin' like a

kick drum! Now you tell me that didn't happen at
least *once* while he was up in the shop, girl!"

Everyone was practically on the floor laughing.

Once we all got ourselves together, I finally said,
"You know what? And I can only tell *you* guys this,
but my pussy throbbed *the whole time* he was there.
And when he touched my face, it was beatin' *harder*
than a kick drum."

Sabrina said, "See! I told yo' ass!"

Then I got real serious. "But you know what,
y'all? This really isn't funny. This is actually past bad
and on its way to detrimental. I have a husband that
I have no intention of *ever, ever* walking away from
or cheating on again, and kids that I would throw
myself into an inferno for at the drop of a dime.
And then there's Royce . . ."

"Who still makes your pussy throb," Genine said
solemnly.

I looked at all of them in despair. "Yeah. He does.
And I don't know what to do to make it stop."

That rendered everyone in the room speechless
and put an end to the entire conversation altogether.

7

WESTON

After Katrice told me Royce's grimy ass was all up in the shop grinning and skinning with her—and probably trying to figure out fifty-eight different ways to hit it again—I pretty much lost my mode, and things ended up being strained and tense between us all week. We tried to put on a good front for the twins, but they're smart as hell, so it didn't work. Ellie kept asking Katrice if she was mad at her; and about eight different times, Willie told her she looked sick. She's never been good at keeping her feelings off her face; so whenever she's upset, the kids know.

Me, on the other hand, I try to keep things cool; but for a couple of days, I was pretty transparent myself. Willie asked me three times if he was about to get a spanking. I told him no and asked him what made him think that, and he said I looked like I was about to bring out the belt. I had to laugh, because he's so much like me; and Mama said he acts just like I did when I was his age. She told me I used to ask Pop that same type of question all the time. That was because I was always into something I wasn't supposed to be into, and I knew it.

I went to pick Lydia up on Wednesday evening to take her to buy some new shoes and then to dinner at Round Table Pizza, her favorite place, and she asked me why I wasn't talking to her like I usually do. I told her I was tired, and you know what she said? My baby girl told me I was telling her a fib, and I needed to check myself—then she rolled her little neck and pointed her finger at me like a sassy black woman. I busted up laughing. I asked her where she got that phrase from, and she said she heard Thomas telling some dude on the phone one day that if he didn't check himself, there was gonna be a big problem. I told her to stop repeating things she hears grown folks say, because she doesn't know the meaning of what she's saying. She told me she knew what "check yourself" meant. When I asked her what, she said, "It means you better get it together. So get it together, Daddy, and stop tellin' me fibs." I cracked the hell up. She's so damn funny. All three of my kids are. Man, I never thought I would see the day that I had three smart, gorgeous kids who take my breath away every time I look at them. I know that sounded corny, but I don't give a damn; it's true.

Anyway, me and Katrice's vibe was all out of whack, so when she told me she was gonna go hang out with the girls, I said fine. Friday night is usually our night to chill, but since neither one of us was in the mood to chill with each other, we broke that little tradition.

I put the kids to bed early and went to work on my business proposal so I could be ready for my next meeting with Dr. Owen the following Tuesday. I had been trying to open a physical-therapy gym for a minute and was having a hard time finding the right therapist to work with. We met that day, but he had to leave early and said he wanted to reschedule. That was best, because I still didn't feel totally ready. So while Katrice was out gabbing with the posse, I took care of business.

When she got home, she did her usual routine and wrote in her journal before bed; then when she got in, she was acting like she wanted some, but I just wasn't in the mood. I turned over and pretended like I was too tired for any kind of action. She huffed and puffed about it for a minute, then finally scooted over on her side of the bed and pouted till she fell asleep. I know she was pouting, because she fidgets and breathes heavy, and then she starts tossing and turning to try to get my attention. She ain't slick. I ignored her. I was still pissed about the haircutting incident. I was on *fire* behind that. Why she would stand up in my face and try to play me for stupid about something like that, I'll never know. I couldn't believe she tried to get around the fact that it was obvious she wanted him there, and that she wanted to cut his hair. Do I think she was thinking about cheating on me again? *Hell* no. If she didn't know anything else, she knew better than to pull that shit again. Besides, I knew she was past that. But do I think she still had a minor thing for him? Yeah. That's what pissed me off. I think what made it worse was the fact that she didn't feel like she could just admit that she was still

slightly attracted to him. I mean, I know the difference between cheating feelings and human nature
feelings. Okay, yeah, I would have obviously felt
better if she despised the man, and all attraction
had melted away. But, hey, there's several exes of
mine that if I saw them today, my dick would probably get hard. Some people you just always have
an attraction to, even if you don't necessarily want
the person anymore.

But my point is, me and Katrice talk about everything. I mean everything. It bothered me that he
still had some kind of effect on her, and she didn't
have enough respect for me to just admit that; *and*
that she didn't trust that I would trust that was all
she felt. If she had just gone on and said, "Yeah, I
cut his hair, 'cause I wanted to talk to him for a
while and find out how he was doing and what was
going on in his life," I know I wouldn't have liked
it—hell, I'da been furious—but I would've at least
respected her honesty and I wouldn't have felt like
she was trying to keep her feelings from me. I don't
know. Maybe something like that is easier said than
done. Yeah, I flew off the handle about him being
at the shop, which is probably why she held back,
but that was more about my fear of him—not about
a fear that she wanted to run off with him.

I did know one thing, though: I didn't want him
staying around town too damn long, because the
thought of him popping in and out of the shop
trying to be near her seethed me. If ever there was
a dirty dog, it was Royce; and if he had the chance
to get close to my wife again, he would take it—and
her—and do a hundred-yard dash.

8

ROYCE

I knew I had to be careful. The last thing I wanted to do was make Katrice feel uncomfortable or piss her off. It was a delicate situation, because I knew I was dealing with a married woman with two small children; and while I was definitely trying to win her over, I wasn't trying to make things any more difficult for her than necessary. Every move I made had to be calculated down to the last detail.

So what I planned on doing was using that cut she gave me as the perfect excuse/opportunity to spend time talking to her at the shop. I purposely stayed away for a couple of weeks, even though not seeing her was killing me. I did that partly because I wanted to give her some space so she wouldn't be freaked out or feel like I was stalking her, and also to give her some time to think about me and wonder where I was. But I also did it so I could let my hair grow in a little so that I could go back and have her cut it again.

I nixed the idea of popping up and asking her to go to lunch with me, because I could just see her reaction to that. She probably would've felt apprehensive about that kind of move for a couple of reasons. One, she definitely wouldn't wanna be seen with me out in public; hell, her husband might see us or something, not to mention any friends or acquaintances that might be floating around. Two, she might have felt like I was pushing up on her, which would've been true, but that's not the impression I wanted her to have . . . just yet.

The hardest part about it all was figuring out what kind of conversations to get into without her bringing up her husband. But it's hard to talk to a married woman without her bringing her spouse up in some kind of way. It's almost unavoidable. So that was what had me stumped for a minute. I had to think of a way around all that married-life talk and try to get to some other issues with her that didn't include him. I would've even settled for talking about the kids a little bit, because even after I stole her heart from him, I'd still have to deal with the kids because they were never going away—so that was a doable option. Plus, if we talked about them, I'd have an idea of what kind of mother she was. That would've been valuable info just in case I wanted her to give me a little Royce Phillip Jordan IV someday in the future. In the end, I settled on topics like her parents, which actually was a good one because I really didn't know anything about them, her girlfriends, her career, and any hobbies she might've had. And, of course, the kids.

The whole point was to get her talking to me like a friend, get her to open up and feel real comfortable with me on a mental level. We already had the physical connection down pat. That fire was burning out of control, to be honest, so I wasn't worried about that. The biggest job a man has when trying to conquer a woman is getting deep in her head, which will then take you straight into her heart. If a man can get a woman to talk freely and feel like she can be herself around him—which is what she does with her girlfriends—and why she spends so much damn time with them—he's on his way to paradise. And if he can make her laugh, all the better. Women love men that make them laugh. The ugliest dude can snag the finest woman in the world if he's got the personality she's looking for, and a sense of humor. For some reason, women can't seem to resist a man that can pull out that deep-bellied laugh from them. I definitely had that area covered as well, so my mission was to reel her in through her psyche.

I wanted to get her alone again so bad, but I knew the chances of that happening a second time were pretty much nil. So I was prepared to have to talk to her in the presence of a bunch of other people at the shop. I even planned on making some of my visits close enough to closing time so that I might have a chance at being the "last of the Mohicans" sitting in there waiting for an appointment, instead of one of ten or fifteen. The only thing was, I forgot to ask her what her hours were, when I was in there the first time, so I'd have to take my chances on the next visit and then see what I could find out. But don't get it twisted—I wasn't gonna make it a habit of popping up at the end of her day, because then I would've started looking obvious. The idea was to make her feel like I was coming at her as a trustworthy friend, not as a potential threat to her husband. It would be harder for her to accuse me of pushing up if I were in there among half the city of Oakland than if I crept in during all her quiet times.

I hoped she would let me get in her business and not ask too many questions about mine, because that would make things tricky. But that was something I couldn't really prepare for, because I wouldn't be able to be sure what kind of responses she'd have during our conversations. I realized I would have to just try to stay a few steps ahead and keep on my toes where my answers were concerned, because one thing Katrice is, is sharp. That's most women, though, when it comes to picking men's brains. They know how to slip those slick questions in that make you have to think twice before you answer, so you can make sure you say the right thing. Because for every single question they ask a man they're interested in, they're looking for a specific kind of answer. And they always ask those questions that require some kind of five-paragraph-long explanation. They're not big on one-word answers to their inquiries. Hell no. They need details. But that was fine. I had a good sense of her vibe, and I felt like I could withstand any line of questioning, as long as she didn't start asking me things that had to do with how I might feel about her.

One thing I made damn sure of was that I was looking and smelling my best. I had come to realize that when I sported the fragrance Unforgivable by Sean John, the women damn near tried to pull my dick out and start sucking right where they stood. No joke. I had similar reactions when I wore Euphoria by Calvin Klein, but Unforgivable stole the show. At any rate, I had both fragrances close at hand. I brought all my best gear with me so I would always be looking like I was about to do a *GQ* cover shoot when I was in her presence.

Yeah, I was on point. I was working my way up to going in for the kill. As soon as I eased my way into her soul and started gently drawing her away from that lightweight of a husband of hers, I could finally be with the woman I passed up—all because I wasn't ready.

9

KATRICE

September 23, 2007, 10:16 P.M.

   Well, apparently I have some work to do on myself, because Mama broke me off something surprising today. I was kinda hurt that she put it all out there like that, but maybe I needed to hear it. I don't like knowing that I have these faults that are a serious potential turnoff. I mean, I know everyone has faults; but I just never thought of myself in the way Mama made me out to be today. Well, I'll have to look deeper into what she was saying, because if I need to make some changes, I'll do it. And I'll definitely have to get a second opinion from Daddy.

   It's been almost a week since Royce showed up at the shop, and part of me is glad he hasn't been back; the other part of me, much as I hate to admit it, wants to know where he's been. I'm curious about this personal business he's got. I know I shouldn't be, but I am. If he comes back, I'm gonna make sure I try to find out what's up on the sly. But maybe he won't come back. If he takes care of whatever he's supposed to be doing, he's going back to Maryland . . . at least I hope that's the case. He did say his going back depended on how his business turned out. I wonder if he's trying to get a job out here or something. That's the only thing I can think of in the moment that would be a factor in whether or not he went back. Dammit! Why do I even care? I'm pissed that I'm interested in him like this! Maybe Rishidda's right; I do need some help. This is really disturbing.

Things between Weston and me are finally getting back on track. We spent some quality time together over the weekend, made some seriously passionate love*—he did things to me Saturday night that he hasn't done in months on end—and we started talking like normal again. I was afraid after Friday night, when he didn't wanna have anything to do with when I got in bed, that the rest of this month was gonna be bad for us. But, oh, I do know how to bring my husband around when I need him. I got that secret skill that he loves and needs, and when times get desperate, I pull out the biggest guns I got and take care of Dangerous in very special ways. Yep. That always does the trick. After he rejected me Friday night, I wasn't dealing with that again Saturday, so I had to do what I do best. Once I worked that magic, he fell right into place, and the rest was gravy.*

Yeah, Royce may still make Girlfriend throb, but Weston sets her ablaze. There's no describing the satisfaction I get from my golden-eyed Adonis. Straight up.

Angela was getting on my *last* nerve. For real. She was so damn presumptuous, always doing things without asking and acting like she could do no wrong. If she hadn't been such a *master* at the art of doing hair, brought in so much business, and boosted the reputation of the shop the way she did, I would've put her ass out after the first two weeks of her being there.

The kids and I were on our way to my parents' house so I could drop them off there for the day, and we stopped by the shop so I could pick up the bottle of conditioner I had told Mama I'd let her sample. I never leave my babies in the car, not even for a few minutes, so I took them in with me, even though I knew it would be an in-and-out move. We rushed in, and I bustled by Angela and her customer.

"Hey, Angela." I turned to the twins. "Kids, say hi to Angela. And stay right here for a minute."

"Hi, Miss Angela," they said together.

"Hey there, sweet babies. How y'all doin'?"

"Fiiiiiine." They sounded like a mini opera.

"Katrice, I didn't think you was comin' in till eleven."

I was halfway to the back room when I called out, "I'm not. I just came to get the conditioner for my mama. I'm droppin' the kids off there for the day, and I'm comin' back here."

She didn't respond.

I went to the shelf to get the conditioner, but it wasn't there. I was confused, because I remembered putting it in that exact spot the day before. It was a sampler that I got from the beauty supply store when the regular items that I ordered came in. I had told my supplier that Mama wanted to try it, and he hooked me up with a free sample bottle.

I came out from the back room and looked around aimlessly for a minute.

Willie was sitting in a dryer-head chair, kicking his legs up and down, and asked, with his mouth full, "What'cha lookin' for, Mommy?"

Ellie was standing next to the chair Willie was in, and her mouth was moving as well.

I was disturbed by the loss of the bottle, but noticed my babies were eating something I didn't give them, and that clearly no one asked me if they could have, and that deterred me from the conditioner for a spell.

I walked over to them and asked, "What are you two eating?"

Willie smiled like all was right with the world and spoke for both of them. "Some candy Miss Angela gived us."

"'Miss Angela *gave* us,' Willie. Open your mouth." I looked at Ellie and said, "You too, little missy."

They both opened wide, and all I saw was chocolate all over their teeth and tongues. I was hot like lava. I turned around to look at Angela, who was so busy gossiping with her customer that she didn't even notice what was going on. You'd think she'd take a damn break with that mess on a Sunday.

I walked up to her and said, "Excuse me, Angela . . . may I see you in the back room for a minute?"

"Sure, honey." She looked at her client. "'Scuse me, Vernessie. I'ma be right back."

I said to Vernessie, "Sorry . . . just need to borrow her for one moment, girl."

"No problem. I'm good," she replied.

We got in the back room, and I asked her, "Did you give my kids candy?"

"Yeah, I got summa those little mini Snickers bars in my bowl. I only gave 'em one each. They small little pieces o' candy."

"First of all, it's ten o'clock in the morning. My kids don't eat sweets this early in the day. Second, you didn't ask me if they could even *have* candy. Why would you feed my kids junk food, or any kind of food, without asking my permission first?"

"Well, I'm sorry, honey. I didn't think it was no big deal. Kids like candy. I was just bein' nice, offerin' them a little treat while they was waitin' for you. I ain't tryina cause no problems, child."

"Okay, well, then here's what—in the future, if you wanna offer my kids food, you need to check with me first. I don't care what it is. The only people who can feed my kids without my permission are my husband, my parents, and the people at the kids' preschool, because they all know what and when to feed them. Are we clear?"

"We sho' are." She said that like she was holding back a load and a half of attitude.

"Good. And since I have you back here, have you seen the bottle of conditioner I had sitting on this shelf . . . the one I told you I was gonna give to my mama?"

"Oh . . . that was for yo' mama?"

"*Yes*, Angela . . . where is it?"

"Well . . . I opened it this mornin' and used some of it on one'uh my customers. I thought it was for us."

God . . . damn . . . her!

"How could you think it was for us when I told you yesterday it was for my mama?"

"I didn't think you meant the whole bottle was for her. I thought you was gon' pour some in a little container and give it to her. I thought you said it was for us to sample, too."

"Now, you know good and well you didn't hear me say that."

"I mean, no . . . but that's what I thought you meant. You said it was a sample bottle, so I just figured—"

"Angela, know this about me—I'm gon' always say what I mean, and mean what I say. Period. The next time I say something, don't read into it what you figured or what you thought. You got that?"

"Yes, ma'am."

"Good. Now, where's the bottle? I'm taking it with me."

"Over at the sink."

I pushed past her, leaving her to trail behind me from out of the back room. I stormed over to the sink, snatched the bottle, said a sharp-toned "Come on, kids, let's go," didn't say good-bye to Vernessie, and stomped out of the shop with my babies trotting on the side of me, damn near tripping over themselves trying to keep up.

All I kept thinking all the way to my parents' house was *Lord, please bring Tiki home* and *How did I get stuck with such a stupid bitch?*

When we got there, Mama met us at the door. I was so perturbed about Angela that I barely spoke as I brushed by her with the kids in front of me;

then I said, "Here, Mama. Angela opened it, but the rest is yours." I handed her the bottle of conditioner; then I took off the kids' coats.

"Well—thank you . . . and hello to you, too, missy. What kinda greeting is that?" Then she turned to the kids and said, "How's Grammy's babies today? Come gimme some sugar."

"Hi, Grammy!" they both said at the same time as they made their way over and into her arms.

"Sorry, Mama. Angela pissed me off again today. She's really wearin' my nerves thin."

Mama told the kids, "Y'all go on in the kitchen. I put some snacks out for you."

Willie said, "Grammy, did you make sammiches? 'Cause that's what we want."

Ellie jumped in. "I didn't say I wanted that—*you* said that! You can't tell Grammy what I want! I want cheese 'n' crackers!"

"It's the same thing! It's like bread with . . . somethin' in the middle!"

"Crackers is not bread, Willie! You're stupid! And it's not '*sammiches*,' it's sam-*wuches*!"

I said, "Hey! You guys *stop yelling*, first of all, and second, Ellie, I told you about calling your brother stupid. You got one more time and it's gon' be me and you and a belt."

Mama said, "Okay, y'all two get in the kitchen. There are *sandwiches*, which is how you say *that*, my dears, *and* cheese and crackers. Grammy knows what her babies want. Now git. I need to talk to your mother for a minute."

They scurried off to the kitchen with Willie

saying to Ellie, "You better stop callin' me that. You gonna be in trouble next time."

"Shut up . . . *stupid.*"

"Hey! Stop it!" I called after them, more annoyed than usual.

Mama said to me, "Okay, *you* sit down. What is the *matter* with you today?"

I plopped down on the couch. "Angela is the matter with me today."

Mama sat down next to me, set the conditioner down on the coffee table, sighed, then said, "Well, surprise, surprise. What the woman do now?"

"Why you say it like that?"

"Because every time you mention her name, it's attached to some negative attitude or comment. So what she do this time?"

After I told her all about the candy and conditioner incidents, she said, "Lemme ask you somethin'. How much do you know about Angela?"

"What's that got to do with anything?"

"I'll ask the question again. This time, answer it insteada givin' me lip. How much do you know about Angela?"

"I don't know. Not very much. Some stuff. Why?"

"Daughter, you're a piece o' work, for real."

"Mama, I don't understand what you're getting at."

"What made you hire her?"

"Her credentials. She's amazing at what she does."

"Is that all?"

"All what? Why else was I supposed to hire her? She does great hair—that's what I hired her to do in my shop."

"Did you interview her?"

"I asked her about her work, if that's what you mean. That's what you do when you interview someone, right?"

"So you hired someone that you know nothing about, other than the fact that she's good at doing hair?"

"I suppose. Mama, I'm irritated. Can you *please* make your point?"

"When you guys talk, what do you talk about?"

"We don't really talk all that much, except about hair. There isn't time for much else—we're supposed to be working."

"Oh, I beg to differ. You had plenty of time to talk to Tiki while you were at the shop working."

"That was different. Tiki and I are friends."

"Exactly."

"So what . . . now I'm supposed to try to be friends with Angela like I am with Tiki? Is that what you're saying? 'Cause that's not happening. She's *nothing* like Tiki. I don't see a friendship in our future."

"So you've just pretty much decided that, then."

"Pretty much, yeah."

"So, again, what do you know about her?"

"She's been doing hair for, like, twenty-some years. She's from L.A., Inglewood, I think. She's forty-five, lives in Piedmont, and had a shop once, a long time ago, but it got burglarized so many times that she finally closed it down and started doing hair out of her kitchen."

"Is that all you know about the woman, really?"

"Basically. Oh, and she has two daughters. One lives out here and the other one lives in Seattle."

"Lemme tell you what your problem is. You hired

a woman based solely on her credentials, and you never bothered to ask any other questions about who she was or what kind of life she's led. When you hire someone to work for you, *with you,* those are questions you need to ask, as well as how qualified they are. The people you hire should be good at what they do *and* be compatible with you on a personal level. What's the point in hiring someone who's good at the job, but you can't get along with? You're running a business, Katrice. You can't always have your 'girls' working with you. It's fun and it's nice, but it's not always realistic. You and Tiki had something great, but now she's moved on with her husband. Okay, so you made a choice to hire someone to take her place. Someone *new.* Someone with a whole new personality and style. No, she's not like Tiki. Deal with it. She's not supposed to be. She has her own good qualities that you've chosen not to find out about, all because you're upset that Tiki's gone. I've talked to Angela several times on the phone, and, personally, I like her spirit."

"Great. So now everything's *my* fault?"

"Katrice, I love you more than life itself, but you're judgmental, you have very little patience with people, and you hate change. And . . . to be honest . . . sometimes you're kinda prissy. Snooty, if you will."

"Mama. I'm offended. Where's all this coming from?"

"You remember that time when you were twelve, and you fell asleep with that wad of gum in your mouth, and when you woke up, it was all in your hair? It was so bad that Marie Louise had to cut it out. But she cut your hair in that really cute style, and you pouted about it for weeks. Everyone loved it—they complimented you on it and everything. The only person who had a problem with it was you. When I asked you why you didn't like it, do you remember what you told me?"

"Not really, but I'm sure you're gonna refresh my memory."

"Of course, I am. You said, 'It's not that I don't like it, I just want my other hairstyle back. I liked it the way it was. I don't want a different one.'"

"What's wrong with that?"

"What's wrong with that is you're still that way today. Just as rigid as you wanna be, and still don't like to accept change, even if it's a decent one. You've never been one for giving new things a try. Katrice always has to have things the way she wants them, and when they're not, it's Pout City till the cows come home."

"Geez, Mama. I didn't know you had such a dim view of me."

"It's not a dim view—it's just who you are. But you don't hafta *stay* that way. Just grow a little. You're a wonderful woman with outstanding qualities. Pouting is very unbecoming, though, and you do that quite well."

"So I pout and I'm snooty. *Fabulous.* Thanks."

Mama laughed at me, then pulled me close and kissed my temple. "As they say in your generation, it's all good. You da shit."

"Mama, please don't attempt to use gangsta lingo. *That* is unbecoming for *you.*"

We laughed together; then she said, "Seriously. Give Angela a chance. Get to know her. *Talk* to her.

I know she does things that irritate you, and she's got a different way about her. But if you learn more about her, you might understand where she's comin' from. It's all about communication and clarity, baby. Communication and clarity."

"Well, thanks for the bubble-busting talk, Mama. I'll be sure to watch out for future pouting actions and drop down a few notches on the snooty meter so I don't turn anyone off."

"Oh, girl, stop bein' so sensitive. Everyone has things they need to work on."

"I guess."

Then she looked at me out of the corner of her eye. "So, that Royce fella been back in the shop lately?"

I had already filled Mama and Daddy in on what happened; you know I couldn't leave them out of the loop. I might need them for advice later on.

"No, and I'm hoping he won't come back. I don't need the stress. It took Weston and me all week to get back on track after that blowup we had. I can't believe this mess is starting all over again."

"Well, you just make sure *you* mind your p's and q's. Don't let him get too close to you. However long he's in town, you can be sure he'll wanna see you as many times as he can manage to squeeze in. You can't trust him, Katrice. I hope you know that."

"Yeah. I guess you're right."

"Oh, baby, I *know* I'm right. I been knowin' men like Royce since before you came along, and, believe me, now that he's had a dose of you, he's thinkin' about gettin' a refill. Mark my words."

"I don't really think it's like that. He's into some

other woman somewhere else. I think he's trying to have a relationship with her, whoever she is."

"Child, do you think just because he's interested in some woman in another state that he wouldn't try to see if he could make something happen with you before he goes back to her? He's a *snake,* Katrice. Look what he did at the wedding. He didn't care if you had a man or not. He was only interested in what he wanted at the time."

"Yeah, but—"

She gave me her famous I'm-not-playing-with-you glare. "Yeah, but nothin'. Stay away from him, Katrice. I mean it. If you don't, you'll be sorry."

And on that note, she patted my thigh; then she got up and went to the kitchen to entertain her grandbabies.

10

WESTON

It took a minute, but me and Katrice finally returned to a pretty normal routine. Of course, the fact that she cleaned out the clog in the Dangerous pipe like never before helped a *whole, whole* lot. Man, did I pick a winner in the oral-sex department. I don't even wanna know when and where she learned to do some of the tricks she did to me that night, but I'm sure glad she was paying attention in class. But, anyway, off that subject, because I'm getting hot around the collar thinking about how she put it down—after that, things picked up between us. We started talking and laughing again, and we needed that. I know I'm making it sound like we were on the outs for months, but you have to realize that four days of funk between the person you share a home with—not to mention the same bed—can really make things uncomfortable, especially when you have kids. You can't even be mad at each other in peace—if that makes any kind of sense—because you're too busy trying to hide the beef from your children. I was just glad we moved on and started loving each other again.

I tried my damndest not to ask her if Royce had been back in the shop. The smoke had just cleared up, and I didn't wanna set off another explosion by making her think I was completely insecure about the issue—which I was—but that's not the point. She didn't need to know that. I just hoped that if he did come back, she would be honest and tell me. But she wasn't acting out of the ordinary and she didn't seem shaken up, so I figured, for the moment, he was minding his own business.

I was chilling in the living room with the twins, watching *Martin* reruns and falling out laughing at them like I had never seen them before—knowing I could almost recite the damn dialogue, word for word, because I had seen the episodes so many times—when the house phone rang. Katrice was doing laundry, so I got up to get it.

It was my mama. I hadn't talked to her in a couple of weeks and had been meaning to call her, but with all the Katrice-Royce drama, I got sidetracked and forgot to get with her that week. So I was glad she called . . . at first. But about ten minutes into our conversation, I wished she had forgotten to call *me*.

She said, "So, anyway, there's . . . something else I called to talk to you about."

"Oh. Okay, wassup?"

She started clearing her throat and taking in these deep, heavy breaths, like she couldn't get enough air or something. It was starting to irritate me because I know my moms, and when she starts clearing her throat over and over, it means she's stalling with her words. This usually means the next thing out of her mouth isn't good.

"Mama, stop doin' that. Stop clearin' yo' throat. I know what that means. You got somethin' bad to tell me."

"Okay, well, just wait a minute—"

"*Nnnoooo* . . . you need to say what'choo tryina say and stop stallin'.'"

"Well, Weston . . . your father is . . . well, he's depressed . . . about some things."

"Depressed about what? What happened?"

"He's . . . going through a bad patch right now, and he's just not dealing with things very well."

My eyes darted around the room in puzzlement. Moms was starting to scare me with all the cover-up talk. "What things is he not dealin' well with? And what does a 'bad patch' mean? I just . . . I need you to stop mincin' words and come wit' it. You got somethin' to tell me about Pop, so just say it."

She got so quiet on the other end that I thought I had lost our connection.

"Mama? Mama, you still there?"

In the heaviest tone I had ever heard, she said, "Yes. I'm here."

I felt my skin start to crawl. "Mama . . . what's wrong wit' Pop?"

"Are you and Katrice busy right now, baby? I know it's almost the kids' bedtime, and I know how you both like to read to them before you turn off the lights. I can call you back tomorrow."

"No—hey—Mama, ain't gon' be no callin' back.

You gon' sit here on this phone and tell me what's goin' on wit' my father . . . *now.*"

She swallowed so hard, I swore I heard the spit trail down her throat before she said, "Weston . . . after your grandfather died year before last, Sonny took it very hard. You know he and his father were like best friends."

"I know that, Mama. What . . . he's still havin' a hard time adjustin'? Is that what he's depressed about? I mean, 'cause I can understand that."

"Well, yes and no." She sighed and made a funny tongue-to-teeth sucking noise with her mouth before she went on. "Your father . . . afterward, he had kind of . . . well . . . a setback."

My mind raced. *Oh God oh God oh God oh God oh God . . . please don't let her say what I think she's about to say.*

"And . . . he sort of . . . fell off—"

"Mama, *please* don't finish that sentence. *Please* don't. I can't hear that from you."

She didn't say anything. All I could hear was her choppy on-the-verge-of-tears breath. I wished I had gotten off the phone with her thirty seconds prior. She was about to hand me one of my worst fears on a hefty-ass plate, and my nerves were shot at that point.

But since the story was halfway on the table, she went ahead and confirmed what I already knew. "He . . . started using again. He had a stint that lasted a couple of months. He was . . . shooting—"

Breathless and devastated, I let out, *"Mama,"* and felt my heart cave.

We both let the sound waves pass between us for a minute while I felt the blow she had just dealt me course through my body, and she tried to figure out how to finish killing me softly.

"He, uh . . . he went back into rehab after that . . . here, in Chicago, for about six months. He came to me and asked me for help, said he didn't wanna shut me out again like he did the first time."

"*What?* Why didn't you guys tell me any of this?" Then I thought back to a conversation that I had with Pop about a year earlier that all of a sudden made perfect sense. "Hold up—is that why Pop called me and said not to try to call him 'cause he was havin' some beef wit' the phone company and his service was gon' be cut off for a while, and he said he'd call me when he could? Was he lyin' to me 'cause he knew he was goin' back in?"

"Well . . . yes. He was, but—"

"And all those times he did call me durin' his so-called phone service problems, where was he callin' me from? Rehab?"

"Yes. But, Weston, he—"

"And he was all up on the phone wit' me, jaw-jackin' like wasn't nothin' wrong, tee-heein' and ha-ha-in', talkin' 'bout how everything was goin' good. And you just let him betray me again like that, after everything we went through back in the day? You hurtin' me right now, Mama . . . deep down in my soul. I can't believe you didn't say somethin' to me. You *know* how I feel about stuff like this."

"Weston, I need you to stop fussin' and listen to me for a minute. I hafta finish telling you what I need to tell you. I'm sorry we kept everything from you, but, baby, we had it under control, and there wasn't anything you could do about it in the first place. Sonny had a slipup, and we took care of it . . . together. It wasn't about betrayal, honey. It was about you having a wife and family to focus on, and not needing any extra stress. I know you. If we had told you, you woulda been on the first plane to Chicago, bustin' through doors and makin' a big to-do like you always do when you wanna be a savior. There wasn't any saving for you to do at that time. You needed to be where you are right now. With your wife and three kids."

"So I don't get it . . . I mean, is Pop okay? You said he's depressed. Is he still clean? Why you tellin' me about this now if it was all taken care of?"

"Because . . . Weston . . . there's a bigger issue at hand right now."

"Bigger? Damn, Mama. What the hell is goin' on out there?"

"Sonny went to the doctor for a checkup about three weeks ago . . . it was long overdue. . . ."

She paused, hesitated, then started that damn throat clearing again. Just when I was about to inform her of my increasing impatience, she bowled me over with words I thought I would never have to hear in this lifetime: "Baby, your father is HIV-positive."

The phone slid out of my hand in slow motion, I choked on my breath, and then I dropped to my knees.

11

KATRICE

October 3, 2007, 9:49 P.M.

I'm still at a loss for words about what Weston found out about Sonny on Sunday night. My heart is aching so bad for my husband right now. He's in an absolute state of despair, one that I've never seen him in before. He hasn't eaten a single thing since right before Lorraine called and broke the news to him. I'm so worried. He canceled all his clients' fitness appointments and told them he had a medical emergency, and I don't know when he plans on going back to work. I'm not asking him, either. He's barely said a hundred words since that night, and the kids are upset because they think he's mad at them. He's barely paid any attention to them the last three days. They don't understand what's going on; all they know is their daddy is not laughing and playing with them, and they think that means they've done something wrong and they're in trouble. Poor Ellie. She asked me today what she did to make Weston mad. When I told her she didn't do anything, she said she must have, because he didn't watch the cartoon channel with her like he does every night. Then she started crying and asked me, if she drew him a picture, would it make him not be mad at her anymore. She's so sensitive. She gets that from Weston. I told her he wasn't mad at her, but she could still draw him a picture because it would make him feel better. And, of course, Willie thought he was in for a spanking. Ever since that incident last year when he acted so raunchy one night that Weston actually pulled off his belt and swatted him in the ass to make him stop, he thinks he's about to get spanked at least every couple of weeks, even if he hasn't really done anything. I don't know what's gonna happen now. This is terrible. I tried to explain to Weston that just because Sonny's positive doesn't mean he's gonna die anytime soon. He wasn't trying to hear that, though. All he knows is Sonny is terminally ill. And he's coming apart at the seams because of it.

Well, Mama was right about me being snooty and judgmental, and about me needing to get to know Angela, and today's conversation with her proved it big-time. I can't believe I've been such a bitch to her. I still feel crappy, now that I know what I know about her. It's a good thing Mama put me in my place, because if she hadn't, I can't say I would've done what I did today. I think me and Angela are gonna be okay. We might not be BFFs, but we can definitely start fresh, and I think I can learn to get used to her with a little extra effort on my part.

Here's a news flash: Royce had the nerve to pop his ass up in the shop today, after two weeks. I thought I was home free since I hadn't seen him again since that first day. I even thought he might have gone back to Maryland. Turns out I was wrong. But today was a new dawning for *me, because I did something I haven't had the strength to do until now—I turned him away. Flat out. I didn't even have to think once about it. Something about everything that's going on right now with Weston and his family, and the fact that we just went through that Royce crisis last month, made me realize I really do need to shake him completely. There is far too much going on for me to be associating with him, even on a mild level. The last thing Weston needs right now is me making him feel worse by engaging Royce in any kind of way. Not that I would even tell him about Royce being at the shop at this point, because he's already losing it, but I would feel like a slime-ball if I got caught up with him, knowing the trouble it could cause and the hurt it would bring to Weston if he found out. All it would take is one person who knows Weston to see me talking to Royce in the shop, and it would get back to him before I could get the information to him myself. So, hell no, I'm not hurting my husband anymore. This Royce thing is over. For real. I might be attracted to him, but that's too bad. What I have with Weston and my kids is real, valuable, and sacred. So Royce Phillip Jordan III can officially kiss my black ass and take his back to Maryland, where he belongs.*

When I got to the shop on Tuesday morning, I spoke to Angela, and she spoke to me, but it was different. Her tone was real flat, and she didn't even look at me. I didn't really care; I had the Weston issue on my mind, anyway, so her not being in the mood for chitchat was just fine. I went in the back to start getting ready to set up my area and was mentally ready to be on shutdown myself, because all I could think about was how I was gonna help Weston get through the ordeal with his family.

When I came out from the back, I noticed Angela was still really quiet. She was prepping her area, but she wasn't doing it like she usually did. There was no rap music playing, she wasn't talking on her cell, and for once, she wasn't doing something to make me wanna kick her.

For about five minutes, I went about my merry way, but then I thought I heard sniffing noises coming from her. At first, I didn't say anything because I thought she might just have a little cold or something. But when I peeped her wiping her eyes a couple of times, I knew something else was wrong.

I made my way toward her and carefully asked, "Angela? Are you okay? Are you crying?"

She tried to pull herself together and pretend she wasn't that bothered. She shoved a Kleenex up to her nose, turned away from me, and said, "Oh— mm-hmm—I'm fine. It's okay, honey."

"Well, something's not okay, or you wouldn't be crying. Can I . . . help you? I mean, is there something I can do?"

She tossed the tissue in the trash and gave me a fake everything-is-fine smile. "Oh, no. I'll be all right. But thank you."

I thought about what Mama said that day about my needing to talk to Angela and get to know her. I figured that was as good a time as any. So instead of letting her sulk, I said, "What time is your first client coming in?"

"Nine-thirty."

"Okay. Well, we got twenty minutes, so let's sit down and talk for a few."

I headed over to a dryer seat, and she followed. Once we sat down, I asked her, "Now, what's got you all off track today? I mean, damn, you even shut your boyfriend Jay-Z down. What's up wit' that?"

She giggled a little and then finally opened up. "Well . . . today's my grandbaby's birthday, and . . . my daughter ain't speakin' ta me, so I can't even call and say happy birthday. She turned three. Her name's Essence."

"What do you mean she's not speaking to you? Why?"

"We fell out a coupla years ago, and she ain't tryina have nothin' ta do wit' me no more. Told me I couldn't see my grandbabies and said don't be callin' her, either."

"What? That's terrible. How many grandkids do you have?"

"Three. Lena, my daughter, she got three girls. My other daughter, Kelly, in Seattle, she don't have no kids."

"Well, when's the last time you saw any of them?"

"The day I put Lena outta my house. I was basically takin' care'uh her kids while she was out runnin' the streets wit' her friends and gittin' high all the time—smokin' that reefer—and she ain't have no job or nothin'. This when we was livin' in Inglewood. And I got tired'uh her takin' advantage'uh me. I couldn't even try ta have me a life 'cause every time I looked up, she was runnin' out the door, talkin' 'bout, 'I'll be right back, Mama.' Then I wouldn't see her for two, three, sometimes fo' days. She wouldn't call or nothin', so I didn't have no choice but ta watch the kids. I had me a little hair shop—you know how I had told you about that—"

I nodded.

"And you know it kep' gittin' broke into all the time. Well, anyway, the last time it happened, I seen her boyfriend lurkin' 'round afterward, and I started figurin' it out. She had a buncha gangsta-type friends she was hangin' out wit', and wasn't none of 'em doin' nothin' positive. I put two and two together and realized it was her crew that was breakin' in, stealin' money and products. After that, I was through. I told her she had ta go, and she had ta take the kids wit' her. It broke my heart ta put my grandbabies out, but I had ta do it. If I didn't, I'da ended up raisin' 'em myself, and much as I love my grandkids, I just couldn't do it. I already raised four kids—"

"Wait—I thought you only had two kids—your daughters."

"No, I had four. I also had two sons, but they died back in 2000. They was on they way drivin' out ta Ohio ta visit they daddy, and Demarcus fell asleep at the wheel and they went flyin' off the road and crashed into a tree head-on. Him and Marcell was killed instantly."

I was heartbroken for her. "How come you never told me any of this? I'm so sorry. I feel so bad—"

"Oh, honey, wasn't nothin' you could do. 'Sides, I ain't wanna burden you wit' all my problems. I just come here ta do my job, that's all."

"So what happened with your daughter?"

"Well, when I put her out, she told me she would never speak ta me again. Then on top'uh that, she said I couldn't see or talk ta the kids no more, either. She said if I was gon' put her and the kids out like that, I didn't give a damn about them and

I must not wanna be part'uh they lives, and she stormed out.

"Then about a month later, my sister, Virginia, called—I call her Ginny—and said Lena and the kids had showed up at her door—she live out in Vallejo—and was askin' if they could stay wit' her. I told her what had happened, and Ginny told Lena she couldn't stay wit' her—unless she got a job and got herself together. Then after that, she was gon' hafta find her own place wit' the kids.

"So then, about four months later, Ginny calls me up and says Lena dun moved out ta San Pablo wit' the kids. She had got her a job workin' at the DMV and was doin' better. I was lonely wit'out her and the kids around, and since I had closed down the shop, I really didn't have no reason ta stay in Inglewood. You know I was doin' hair outta my kitchen, and I said, 'Hell, this ain't about nothin'. So I decided ta sell my house and move out here. I figured since Lena had got herself right, maybe she'd start talkin' ta me again and let me see the kids. So I went on and sold my house and moved ta Piedmont so I could be closer to 'em, just in case she came around and decided ta let me back in they life.

"So when I got out here, I got Lena and the kids' number from Ginny, and I called her up. Well, then she got mad and damn near cussed me out, said don't call her no more, and then hung up on me. The next time I tried ta call, she had changed the number. I called Ginny, and she said Lena was mad at her, too, for givin' me the number, and wouldn't give *her* the new number ta reach her at."

She started crying again, and I just felt like the worst bitch ever.

She continued, "So I ain't seen none of 'em since 2005, and I miss my daughter and my grandkids. They the only reason I'm livin' out here."

"I'm really sorry. I don't know what to say. I had no idea you had so much going on. I really wish I had known before now. Are you gonna be okay today?"

She wiped her eyes. "Yeah. I'm gon' make it. Long as I can do some hair ta keep my mind off thangs, I'ma be all right." She looked at the clock. "*Oooo,* I better get cleaned up and get ready for my client. But I sure do appreciate you listenin' ta me, honey. Feels good ta talk about it a little."

We both got up, and I said, "Ummm, I wanna tell you that I'm sorry I haven't been very nice to you since you've been working here. Honestly. It's just been hard for me . . . adjusting to my old partner being gone."

"Child, don't worry 'bout it. I know you been sufferin' over it. Eleven years is a long time ta work so close wit' a person, 'specially if y'all was good friends, like you and Tiki was. I know you just missin' her—you don't mean no harm. Don't nobody know better than me how it feel ta lose people ya love."

I felt so bad about the way I had been treating her that all I could do was just stand there and look at her, ashamed.

She saw that I was at a loss for words, smiled at me, and said, "Child, come on here and gimme a hug, now. We gon' both be all right."

I hugged her and said, "Thank you for understanding. And seriously, if you need anything, just let me know, okay?"

"I'll do that. Now lemme git on over here and turn on my boo, Jay-Z, so I can git myself together."

We both laughed, and then went back to work in our areas.

Around twelve forty-five, as I was cleaning up after cutting a woman's hair, Royce came strolling in all decked out in a denim Rocawear outfit. As usual, he looked superfine, and he smelled heavenly; but my pussy definitely was *not* throbbing. The only thing physical that happened with me was that my heart kind of jumped when I saw him, partly because yes, he is that fine; but mostly because he surprised me when he walked in. Again, it had been two weeks since his first visit, so I really wasn't expecting to see him anymore.

Angela was there, and she was doing a perm and was over at one of the sinks talking to her customer while washing the neutralizer out of her hair. I was between clients and was waiting for my one-fifteen to come in for her weave.

He walked up, all confident, smiled, and said, "Hey, beautiful. I been tryina get back here for an appointment, but I been real busy these last coupla weeks. You got time to shave me?"

I looked at his hair, which had grown in some, but it didn't look bad at all. He could've kept it the way it was and been just fine.

I surprised myself when I looked dead in his face and said, "Actually, no. I don't have time. I have someone coming in at one-fifteen, and I need to get ready for her." I was totally professional, and barely friendly.

He looked somewhere between confused and disappointed by my response, and for a few seconds, he didn't say anything. I just continued to look at him, but only in a business kind of way.

Then he said, "Oh. Okay, well, what about after that? I got somewhere I need to be this evening and I wanna look sharp as a tack. A cut like the one you gave me would definitely make that happen. I can come back in a coupla hours if you need me to."

Then he looked at me in a halfway-seductive fashion.

It didn't move me one bit.

"Nope. After that isn't gonna work, either."

"Oh. You all booked up for the day?"

I just kept surprising myself. I told him, "No, I actually have about an hour free after my next appointment. But I'm not gonna cut your hair again."

He actually had the nerve to look hurt. "Why not?"

"Because while it was nice visiting with you last month, it doesn't need to keep happening."

"What's gon' happen? You just gon' cut my hair, like last time."

"No. I'm not. I think you need to find someone else to do it. I'm not the only shop in town. And if you just *have* to get it done here, Angela can do it for you just as good, if not better."

He was totally perplexed. "I don't understand. What's the problem? You mad at me or somethin'?"

"Not at all. I just don't think it's a good idea for us to keep our lines of communication open anymore."

"Damn. What happened? I mean, did I do something? Did I *say* something last time I was here that upset you?"

"No, not really. I just have a lot going on right now, and I don't need to add to the pot by continuing to chop it up with you."

"'Chop it up'? Dang. Like that?"

I looked at the clock. "Yeah. But look, I gotta get ready for my client. Sorry, Royce, but you're gonna hafta find someone else to take care of your shaving needs. Um, excuse me. I need to head into the back. I don't mean to be rude, but I gotta end this conversation and finish what I was doing. Okay?"

He just stood there, speechless.

About five seconds later, he said, "Man . . . all right, then. Well, you take care, Katrice. I'ma . . . head on out. Sorry if I upset you."

"You didn't. Take care, Royce."

I turned my back on him and walked away, more proud of myself than I thought I could ever be. I didn't even wait to see how long he stood there before he left. I went into the back room and continued taking care of my business.

12

ROYCE

I didn't know *what* the hell happened. But what was clear was that someone or some *thing* got to her and made her turn on me like a caged circus cat. I was actually dumbstruck behind her attitude toward me. It's hard to get me dumbstruck, especially where a woman is concerned. She treated me like a Joe Schmo off the street that she was totally unfamiliar with. That had me baffled as hell.

After I left, I started thinking that maybe two weeks was too long to wait between visits. Maybe I gave her too *much* space and time. Maybe I miscalculated my moves and laid the wrong plans out. Maybe I should've swooped on her like I thought about doing when I was first putting the plan together. Sometimes if you give a woman too much space, she has time to start rethinking the situation. She might have ten or twelve conversations with her girlfriends about you, and they'll mull things over a thousand different ways. Next thing you know, she's all switched up and acting like you never mattered to her. You gotta beware of those girlfriend conversations. They can really do a brotha in, big-time. You and your woman might be all good, might never have had any kind of beef, and then one day she goes and spends the day with her girls. When she comes home, she's on some kinda mental trip that you have no inkling about how to get her back from. That girl talk is a door closer for real.

I figured that was exactly what happened. She probably got together with her crew and laid everything on the table about how she felt and what we talked about. They started male bashing, like most women do in girl talk, and the little bit of hold I had on her started dwindling away with every sentence her girlfriends spoke. It only takes a couple of hours of a girls' night to ruin a man's relationship with his woman. Or at least put a hell of a damper on it.

At any rate, what happened at the shop got in the way of all my plans. I definitely wasn't expecting to encounter that kind of obstacle—at least not so early on. I mean, damn, I had only seen her once. I didn't even get to work my magic and charm in a few good conversations with her. I had expected to at least get her to a point where she felt close enough to me that even if the girls did try to sway her, she would be sprung enough that they couldn't poke a hole in the balloon of feelings she had developed. But somehow they managed to get in her head and make her go the opposite direction.

I have to say, though—and this is gonna sound crazy—but the fact that she was so stern and strong and confident in that moment was so goddamn sexy, I almost couldn't stand it. Even though she was kicking me to the curb, it was still turning me on to the nth degree, because it showed me that she had some kind of willpower. One thing I don't like is a weak woman. You know, those types that fall for you *too* easy—and they don't resist at all. No matter what you say or do, it's all good because they want you that bad. They don't present you with a challenge. There's no work to do. They don't wait for you to call them; they call you all the time. They don't wait for you to ask them out; they just take matters into their own hands and start asking for dates, left and right. They use Women's Lib as an excuse, that it's-okay-to-assert-yourself-and-ask-a-man-out–type stuff. Bump that. We're not fond of that course of action. Really. It's flattering and all, but in the end, those women are not the ones we generally choose to be with. We already know they're gonna take over everything and leave us with nothing to do but dick 'em down. They'll make sure they assert themselves in that arena, too. Start *demanding* that we put it on 'em. Oh yeah, they'll pay for us all the time; buy us gifts—even when it's not our birthday or Christmas; go out of their way to travel across the states to visit us—and shell out their own hard-earned money to do it, instead of letting us send for them—like we *will* do when we really wanna see a woman. They'll lend us their cars at the drop of a hat so we can go do some stupid shit, when they know they need to use it for themselves to take care of their own important business and let us fend for ourselves; and they'll damn near move us into their apartment in the first month of knowing us, without us having to even ask. It's crazy. The thing is, some of it we like—but only because it's flattering and it'll get us unlimited sex. But at the end of the day, next to none of those women will get an engagement ring from us, simply because, sad to say, we know those women are spiritually weak. Don't twist what I'm saying. A man wants a woman to have his back, but not if she's gonna forsake her own. That's just unattractive altogether. We don't fool with those women for long, no matter how good her pussy is.

Katrice showed me in that moment that she wasn't gonna be an easy conquer. Even though it hurt me that she was brushing me off, it fueled my fire that much more. I knew then that she had the strength to stand up to me, and if need be, take care of herself first. That's the kind of woman I want. The kind I *need*. I can be an aggressive bastard, and I need a woman who can put me in my place and let me know not everything I wanna do is gonna happen. Even though she gave it up that night in May, she didn't do it right away. She fought me on it. She called me out about the past. She wanted answers. She got pissed off. She lit into me. She even removed herself from the scene so she could go assess the situation away from me. She didn't jump into my arms as soon as I said I wanted her. I took notice of all that. It only made me like her even more.

When she refused to shave me, the look on her face was so serious and businesslike. She was so fine, I almost couldn't hear her shutting me down. She had on a pair of formfitting jeans that showed me *everything* that had developed since '99. The sleeveless silk blouse she was wearing was unbuttoned *just* to the point of showing that unbelievable cleavage of hers; and her arms were so gorgeous and toned, I wanted to take a bite out of one of 'em. She had something different on her lips that time—some deep wine-colored gloss that had 'em looking so luscious, I wanted to shove my dick in her mouth. And her *feet*. She had on some open-toed heels that showed off her perfect little toes, which were painted this real dainty lavender color, and I wanted to do a repeat of the hotel and spray whipped cream on them bad boys and suck 'em right off her body. Her hair was still in the same bob, but she had it parted on the side so there was more hair on the right than left, and it was falling on her face real sexy, kind of over her right eye. Lord. It should be illegal for a woman to be that fine.

So after she left me standing there, I'll admit, I was shocked and a little disjointed mentally by the whole experience, but I still wasn't through. She might have sent me on my way that day, but all that did was make me more determined to devise a better plan of action. I decided to lay low for a while and let whatever her girlfriends said to her hopefully have a chance to settle in the back of her mind—far enough so that when I came back to check in on her, she'd see me in a different light.

No, the game wasn't over. Not by a long shot.

Karma

That thing called Karma
will follow you,
so watch what you say
and watch what you do.

You may have said sorry.
You may have regret.
But you've yet to pay.
This you can bet.

Now that it's over,
and all have forgiven,
you hope to get back
to that fun and good livin'.

But hold your horses.
Stop—not so fast.
You can't disregard
things done in the past.

Karma will be there
to teach you a lesson.
But when it will strike,
you'll surely be guessin'.

It may be today
or sometime next week.
Could be years from now
that your payback will peak.

Here's something else
about Karma to know.
Those thoughts that you have
are part of the show.

Before you ran out
and did things that you shan't,
those words in your head
had begun to rant.

They taunted and pushed,
and you tried to ignore.
It was good versus evil,
a full-blown war.

But in the end
you gave into
the devil inside,
and now you rue.

No, you can't hide.
You can't turn and run.
There's a price to pay
for what you have done.

So watch what you say,
think, and do.
Then that thing called Karma
will be good to you.

13

WESTON

I was so destroyed after my moms told me about Pop that I just shut all the way down. My soul literally ached. I couldn't even eat. I think three or four days went by, and all I had was maybe an apple and part of a leftover Subway sandwich I had bought several days prior. It wasn't until about Wednesday when I ate that. My kids all thought I was mad at 'em. I called off from work. I missed a meeting with Dr. Owen because I forgot about it. Fortunately, he was cool about the whole thing. I told him, like I told everybody else I canceled on and forgot about, that I had a medical emergency. Medical emergency. Yeah. Of the worst kind.

Katrice tried so hard to comfort me, but I wasn't at a comforting stage yet. I just wanted, *needed,* to be left alone to let the news really sink in, and so I could figure out what the hell I was gonna do. Not that

there was anything I *could* do. But my wife knows me
inside and out, so after a couple of attempts to make
me feel better, she gave up and just let me be. She
took over all the household stuff and dealt with the
kids on her own. She told them I wasn't feeling
good, but that pretty soon, I'd be well enough to play
with them again. That made them feel better, and
they finally stopped worrying about being in trouble
or me being mad at them. For an entire week, she
didn't ask me to do a single thing. She just showered
me with the affection that I love to get from her, and
asked me if there was anything *she* could do for *me*.
She took care of calling Yolanda and Thomas and
letting them know what was up; and she even took
Lydia and the twins to the movies and to Chuck E.
Cheese's in my place that weekend since I was too
tweaked in the head to go. At night, in bed, she just
wrapped herself around me, stayed quiet, and didn't
ask me any questions; all she did was tell me she
loved me. She made sure there was plenty of food to
eat for when I finally did get my appetite back; she
made sure the kids were extra quiet and didn't try to
bother me; she never once asked me about my work
situation and when I was due back. She just let me lie
around the house and mope, which is exactly what I
wanted to do, and she knew it. I'm telling you, I love
that woman so much, sometimes it almost drives me
out my mind. Without her, I might as well hang it up.

I finally called and talked to Pop after about a
week and a half went by. I wanted to talk to him
sooner, but I just didn't know what to say. It was all
too unbelievable. As a matter of fact, I spoke to
everyone else in the family before him. They all had
accepted the situation and were just focused on

doing whatever Pop needed so he wouldn't go crazy.
When I finally did talk to him, he actually sounded
halfway okay. We stayed on the phone for over four
hours, just talking about all kinds of stuff. I was so
glad Katrice made me talk to him at the reunion
back in '98, because I know me. To this day, I probably still wouldn't be speaking to him; and if that
were the case, and Mama had called and told me
that, I probably would've committed suicide. Seriously. The guilt of not patching things up with him
would've eaten me alive. Knowing he was gonna die,
and the fact that I let twenty years go by without
working everything out with him because of my
stubbornness, would've been too much for me to
deal with. Just another reason I'm glad I found
Katrice. You can't get through life without people
like her to push you to do the right thing sometimes.

   Anyway, even though I talked to Pop and we got
a chance to have a good heart-to-heart session, I
knew he was still real depressed about his situation,
and that made *me* continue to be depressed. I went
back to work, but I was out of it most of the time. A
few of my clients even had to remind me about certain things I said to them during our fitness discus-
sions, because I just wasn't retaining info very well.
I finally told Dr. Owen what the real deal was, and
asked him if we could hold off on our business ven-
ture for a while until I had a chance to get my head
straight. He said that was fine, and he was sorry to
hear about Pop. I told him I would keep in touch
and let him know when I was back on my feet, so to
speak. I felt real good about working with him, and
he liked me a lot. Every time we met, we ended up
talking about other stuff that had nothing to do

with our project. I knew I really wanted the partnership to work out with him.

I tried to get back in the swing of things with Katrice and the kids, but it was difficult. Katrice knew I was struggling, so she didn't make things any harder. She told me to just focus on the kids and reassuring them that I was still there for them, and not to worry about her. My amazing wife. Ellie drew me a picture of what was supposed to be me smiling and standing in some grass with the sun shining over my head. She said she drew me a happy picture, since I looked so sad all the time. Then she jumped in my lap and gave me a big hug and a kiss. She told me she loved me, and that if I wanted to be sad still, it was okay with her, and she would draw me pictures until I felt all better. I almost dropped a few tears behind that. My eyes actually got misty on me. But I didn't cry because I didn't want her to think I was upset. Willie had me in silent stitches. He told me he would make sure that while I was sick, he wouldn't do anything bad to make me pull out the belt and spank his butt. He would take care of Ellie so I could rest, and he'd even leave her stuff alone. I wanted to howl when he said that! The only reason I didn't—and it was hard not to—was because he was so serious about it. I didn't wanna laugh in his face and risk hurting his feelings. I just said okay and told him I appreciated it, while I held back my laughter. Man, I love my kids. And Lydia. Boy, she's a stone-cold trip. She *kills* me with some of the things she says. I called her up one night to check in on her and see what she was up to, since I flaked on taking her and the twins to the movies that one day, and she told me that she was fine.

Then she made me fall off my seat when she said that I should just take care of myself, not worry about her. When I was feeling better, I could pencil her in so we could spend some time together, but that I should call to let her know when that was, so she could check her schedule. I about *died* laughing at her! I asked her where in the world she got that penciling-in stuff, and she said she heard it in some movie Yolanda and Thomas were watching a few nights prior. Never in a million years did I think my own kids would be able to supply me with such entertainment.

About three weeks after the conversation with my moms, I was tired of sitting in the house sulking, so I called up Eric and Thomas and told them I needed to go have a couple of drinks and just get outta the house to clear my head. They said cool. Thomas called his brother, Gerald, and we all met up at Kimball's in Jack London Square, one Friday night. We didn't hang out as much anymore because we all had wives and kids—even though, technically, Lydia is mine—but Thomas is still her stepfather—so it was good to take a break with the guys and go talk shit, knock a few back, and look at all the women we were thankful we *weren't* involved with. And, yeah, check out a little eye candy, too. No harm in that.

I told them what was going on with Pop and how I had been twisted in the head behind it, and they all understood and felt for me. I never bothered to tell any of them about the Royce mess, because that was a subject that was still real touchy for me. I wasn't ready to bring them in on that just yet. Even though Eric and Thomas already knew the history, I still didn't feel ready to lay the new chain of events out there. Gerald didn't know the first thing about Royce and Katrice; he and his wife, Brinda, moved to Oakland in '03 when they relocated from L.A., so he was totally in the dark. He was real cool, though, and he was a trip to talk to. He and Thomas looked exactly alike, except Gerald was a shade or two darker.

I was getting *seriously* lit on Hennessy shots, and everyone else was drinking beer after beer—and talk shit, we did, indeed. I was glad to be out doing something to take my mind off my circumstances. The music was bumping, the liquor was hitting me just right, and I felt halfway decent for about thirty, forty-five minutes.

I swigged the last of my eighth shot and slid my glass toward the bartender for a refill. I heard a bunch of loud-ass dudes yelling and shouting, so I turned my head to see what all the commotion was about. Over at the other end of the bar toward some tables, within the group, I saw a familiar face. I did a double take to try to get a better look, because I wanted to make sure it was who I thought it was; but there were three other dudes blocking him, so I couldn't really see all that good. Finally two of them moved and I got a better view of him. It was definitely who I thought it was, which was perfect, because I had been hoping to catch him for a minute. But I kept staring.

Gerald asked me, "Man, what'choo lookin' at over there? Who business you all up in?"

I waved him off and started getting up. "Hol' up, dude. I see somebody I need to go talk to right quick."

Eric and Thomas turned around to look where I was looking.

Thomas said, "Ay, you want'cho drink refilled or what?"

I had already started slowly making my way toward the crowd. I turned and told him, "Nah. I'm good. I'ma step on over here for a minute. I'll be back."

They all shrugged me off and went back to drinking and talking.

As I crept up on the group, I checked the scenery a little to see who was standing around and what people were doing. I checked the spacing in the area. I peeped out security posted in all the corners, but none of them were really paying any attention to what they were supposed to be paying attention to. A couple of them were talking to women, and a few others were watching the big-screen TV. But nobody was checking out the group.

I walked up behind one of the dudes and stood there for a few seconds. He moved backward and bumped me by accident, turned around and said, "Oh, I'm sorry, man. 'Scuse me."

I said, "No problem."

He moved aside, which was as good as I wanted it, because he gave me the opening within the crowd I needed to look at the guy up close. Once I fixed my eyes on him, that's where they stayed. He was laughing and talking with about four other dudes, and there were about five women huddled near him, cheesing like their horny asses just had their teeth cleaned. I stood totally still. So still that it started distracting the group, because it was obvious I was interested in something—or some*one*—in the area.

All of a sudden, the guy looked at me. He saw I was eyeballing him, so he eyeballed me back, but with no particular expression.

I raised my right hand and did a sideways four-fingered beckon, letting him know I wanted him to head in my direction.

He smiled at me, walked about eight steps across the floor, stood right in front of me, and said, "Ay, wassup, dude? How you doin'?"

"I'm coo'."

He kept smiling, but he was confused. "All right, then. So wassup? Do I know you?"

"Yeah. Indirectly."

He was still smiling, but some of it faded away in his bewilderment. "Oh."

His head doggy-cocked to the side, and he studied my face, squinting and taking in my features, trying to figure out how we knew each other.

I just stood there and waited for his punk ass to ask the next question.

After about five seconds, he couldn't figure it out, so he gave up and asked, "You sure we know each other? You don't look familiar to me."

"We have a mutual acquaintance."

"Oh . . . really? Who's that?"

I took in a deep breath, and I felt all the Hennessy bubbling in my cells making me feel warm. I let the breath out real slow and then expanded my chest. "I believe you know my wife."

"Is that right? Who's your wife? Oh—by the way, I'm Royce, man."

And that arrogant muthafucka put his hand out for me to shake.

I looked down at his hand, then back into his eyes. "My name's *Weston* . . . Porter."

His whole body froze. First shock filled his eyes; then right after that, a look of hatred took over and he snatched his filthy hand back; his glower never left mine.

I didn't move a muscle.

Neither did he.

We stood eye to eye in total silence; it was like we were two pit bulls about to throw down.

He was almost as tall as me, but I still had him by about an inch. His physique was similar to mine. His chest was solid, and his frame was sturdy. He kept in shape. No fat on his body. Big, muscular hands. Thick, firm legs. Strapping arms. Dense neck. Broad-shouldered. Two hundred twenty pounds of might to my two hundred thirty. A force to be reckoned with.

But not as big a force as me. Not with how heated I was. Not with the wrath I had that was injecting me with the power to do the damage I had always wanted to do to him. Whatever he felt didn't even matter, because it couldn't match the amounts of detestation and fury that I had pent up in me for the eight years leading up to that point. I thought a hundred times a day about that moment. I actually used to pray for a chance to be able to let loose on him. He tried to thieve the heart of the one woman I knew I would ever consider spending my life with—and I was willing to bet my last dollar he was back to try to do it for a second time. My adrenaline was off the goddamn charts.

His face was exactly like I remembered. And I was about to make *sure* he didn't leave the club in one piece.

He took five real slow steps backward. "Soooo . . . that means . . . your wife would be . . ."

At the same time, we both said, "Katrice."

And then there was nothing but silence between us.

But just us. Everyone else was still talking and laughing, not knowing a 187 was about to be in progress.

Before I knew it, my feet had levitated off the floor. At least that's what it felt like when I found myself three feet in the air, diving through the crowd at him.

We tumbled, me on top of him. When I knocked Royce over, we took at least four people down with us, all of them toppling over like rickety dominoes. The women screamed and shrieked. I heard glass shattering, chairs and stools breaking, and men hollering. I felt body parts knocking against my head. We crashed to the floor; then we slid into the bottom of the bar, courtesy of all the previously spilled liquids. The back of Royce's head slammed into the wall, and I was right there on top of him. He tried to struggle, but I was way too strong for him.

We didn't say one word to each other. We didn't need to. We knew what—and *who*—we were fighting for.

I shoved my hand up to his throat, pinned his head to the wall, wrapped my fingers tightly around his jugular, and squeezed with everything I had. I tried to wiggle my thumb down and lodge it in his windpipe, but he kept moving his neck just enough so I couldn't get it there. He was strong, too. I had my work cut out for me.

With the weight of my body mashing him into the floor, he couldn't get his arms into a position to hit me.

There was so much other commotion that security didn't even realize there was a fight going on at first.

Then I heard a dude yell, "Ay, he 'bout ta kill this nigga!"

Someone else hollered, "What the fuck just happened?"

The four people we knocked over scrambled off the floor and scurried away from our scuffle.

No one jumped in to try to stop the fight.

Royce gagged; then, in a split second, he managed to maneuver his right arm away from my crushing torso. The bastard worked a slab of glass into his hand from the floor, where someone had dropped their drink during the tumble, reached over, and sliced the left side of my face open from the top of my cheekbone to the tip of my chin. I yelped, and the shock from the cut made me instantly let go of his neck; then blood started gushing and sliding down my face like a small river. As soon as I let him go, just like one of those UFC dudes, he used all his strength to knee me in my stomach; then he smashed me in the temple with his rock-hard fist, and I fell backward off him and rolled about four feet.

By that time, the crowd was large, but security couldn't get through because there were so many people surrounding us. Plus, you know looky-loos love a good fight—so, really, they weren't trying to *let* security through. The club was jam-packed by then, and with the earsplitting music, people shooting pool, twenty different volumes of talking and laughter, and, of course, five TVs going at the same time, it was a madhouse in there.

My face was on fire with pain, and now the blood was literally pouring down my cheek and onto my clothes, but I didn't have time to worry about that. I had to get my black ass up off the floor before Royce had a chance to start stomping on me, which I was 100 percent sure was gonna be his next move. I figured I only had about five seconds to get up, because he was still dizzy from me choking him, so we both took the opportunity to find our way to standing positions; then it was right back on.

I heard the bartender shout, "Y'all muthafuckas, git outta here wit' dat shit! Y'all not gon' be fuckin' up my bar tonight! Somebody git these niggas outta here!"

Finally I heard a security guard yell, "All y'all, git outta the goddamn way! Let us through!"

But security didn't have a chance to break through the crowd, because after we both got up, the bullfight began.

I was woozy from the temple shot, and my balance was off. Royce rushed me like Jack Tatum, and once again, we went careening through the crowd, except this time we went the opposite direction, and we tore through about twelve bystanders *and* the four security guards. They all collided to the floor, and with that went more drinks flying, glasses breaking, chairs coming apart, and women screeching.

But me and Royce soared through the air and landed on a table. I landed back-first, and he was right there on top of me trying to finish me off. As soon as my back hit the table, I heard a loud crack; then I heard the legs pop, and me, Royce, and the table collapsed to the floor. Then we brawled like Ali and Frazier. He stole on my right eye, and his fist felt like a hundred-mile-an-hour fastball. I socked him in his jaw so hard, one of his teeth jumped outta his mouth and flew across the room. He used the tip of his elbow and cracked down real hard in the middle of my chest cavity and knocked the wind outta me. But I held it together and smashed his ass so hard in the nose, I felt his bone shatter on my knuckles; then blood shot out like a water hose. He tried to keep me down by shoving his knee into my neck, but I sent a right hook up to his chin, and his head snapped back and he fell off me.

It's a trip how sound really does travel, even in the loudest situations, because I actually heard Eric shout, "Oh shit! That's Weston, y'all! What the fuck goin' on?"

I rolled on my side real quick and got up before Royce had a chance to get his bearings. I stomped him in his shoulder about four times; then I started kicking him in his ribs with my right leg. But since my left leg wasn't in motion, he found a way to reach over and karate-chop me in my kneecap— right in that spot where the doctor checks your reflexes—and that knocked me off-balance and brought me back down. I fell forward and busted both my lips open when I hit the corner of another table on my way to the floor; then I landed across his body. He pushed my legs off him and we both scrambled; he rolled to the side and I crawled forward. I used the table to pull myself up, and when I looked back, that dirty bastard was already up on his feet again.

I had to keep my eyes on the prize. This dude could throw 'em; he had skills I had never seen before, and I knew if I let myself get caught, even for a second, he might do to me what I planned on doing to him.

Another crowd formed around us that was even bigger than the one we had just busted through. We didn't waste any time getting back to business. Both of us were tore up—breathing hard, bleeding, staggering, damn near blind, and crippled, but it still wasn't over. Round three of the Porter-Jordan fight was about to get started.

Not five seconds went by before we were back in each other's faces again, but this time we stayed standing while we boxed, toe to toe. More left hooks and right hooks were thrown; more blood was shed; and fracturing and breaking of bones continued to take place. Security started trying to push their way through the crowd again, but then the show got real raw.

Royce came with a swift move, got me in a head-lock, and tried to pull me down to the floor. But then he said words he shoulda never in his black-ass life said to me: "You punk muthafucka! I'm 'bout to lay yo' bitch ass out so I can bounce up outta here and go have round two wit'cho *wife, nigga*! Them *juicy-ass lips* sho' felt good wrapped around my *dick* eight years ago!"

I saw ninety-nine different shades of red, and at that point, all I had was murder on my mind. The next thing I knew, I brain-locked on him. I tackled him in his midsection and rushed him backward. We tore through the middle of the floor, knocked over a few more people and chairs, and then I used every bit of force I had to try to bring him down so I could stab his ass in the heart with my pocketknife. But right before we were about to go down, I heard Gerald holler, "Fuck! They 'bout ta go through—"

And then our locked bodies went crashing through the large window by the door.

Royce went back-first, and I stayed attached to him.

We flew out onto the sidewalk, and the glass show-ered down on us like pieces of hail.

I heard multiple cop car sirens blaring as they barreled up the street and all skidded to a halt.

Royce landed with a back-cracking thud; then his head hit the curb real hard. I bounced off him and jumped up, still blacked out mentally on what he had just said to me. I stood over him and then stomped him in his dick about six times; then I started kicking him in the head repeatedly, like a horse gone mad. I just kicked and kicked and kicked until finally about three cops tackled me and took me down.

But then something deep started happening. Royce's body started shaking, twisting, and jerking. His eyes started rolling back in his head. Then he started foaming at the mouth. A second later, his body started flapping every which way. I couldn't believe my eyes. He was having a seizure.

By that time, everyone was piled outside, screaming, shouting, hollering, and trying to see what was happening.

Then I heard the ambulance rounding the corner and coming to a screeching halt.

The cops had me pinned to the ground, and they started reading me my rights and cuffing me.

Royce was still seizuring, and the paramedics swarmed over to him to try to stop it.

It seemed like nobody but my boys gave a damn that I was hurt, but with Five-O all over me, they couldn't help a brotha.

I heard Gerald, Eric, and Thomas all talking to me at the same time, but between my rights being read and Royce's voice echoing in my head about Katrice sucking his dick, nothing else got through to me.

The cops got me up off the ground and started dragging me away. I was drenched in blood. My ribs were so busted up, I could feel 'em moving, and I could barely see out of my right eye.

I looked at my boys and shouted, "One'uh y'all call Katrice!" I looked down and noticed my keys had fallen out of my pocket during the arrest, and I yelled, "Eric, come git my keys right here and drive my shit home!"

And the police they shoved my broke-down ass in the back of the car and skidded off.

14

KATRICE

October 20, 2007, 2:47 A.M.—in the car, writing this five minutes after leaving the hospital, about to scream!

I am so fuckin' mad at Weston right now, it's not even funny! I can't BELIEVE what he did! What is WRONG with him? It's a good damn thing I don't hafta work today, 'cause now I gotta spend it cleaning up the goddamn mess his stupid ass made! I mean, what the HELL was that? How are you just gonna go to a club and try to kill a man? Why do men act ignorant like this? Then weeeeeeee gotta stay behind and fix everything! Weeeeee gotta take care of the kids! Weeeeee gotta make the phone calls and tell everybody how your stupid ass acted so retarded that you got thrown in jail! How embarrassing is THAT? And what am I gonna tell my kids? Seriously! What am I supposed to say to them? Oh, sorry, kids, but Daddy went out last night and tried to kill somebody all because I slept with him eight years ago and his ass can't get past it? Is that what I'm supposed to say to my babies? 'Cause in about five hours when they get up and Daddy isn't here to play and talk and make them breakfast, guess who's gonna hafta figure out a way to explain it? That's right—meeeeeeeee!! And when they start crying and screaming and calling for their daddy, guess who's gonna hafta figure out how to comfort them when they don't want me, they want him *? Right! Meeeeeeee!*

And let's not even talk about Royce's stupid, arrogant ass! Why did he hafta come back here, anyway? And what the hell did he say to Weston? 'Cause now he's trippin' off some dick-sucking thing, and I don't have the slightest idea what the hell that's even about!

I'm through with both their asses!

My doorbell rang at one-ten in the damn morning. Then, right after that, my cell rang. I was knocked out. I woke up, looked at the phone, and saw Thomas's name pop up. I sat straight up in the bed, scared to death, because I knew Weston went out with Thomas, Eric, and Gerald; and Weston wasn't home yet, so Thomas wouldn't have any reason to be calling me unless something was wrong. I opened the flip and didn't even say hello.

"Thomas . . . why are you calling me?" I asked cautiously.

"Um . . . can you . . . come open the door? We outside."

"Who's *we?*"

He hesitated. "Me, Eric, and Gerald."

I paused, then closed my eyes before I asked, "Where's Weston, Thomas?"

"Can you just come open the door, please?"

"Hang on."

I closed the flip. Then my stomach churned, and I felt my guts about to fly out of my mouth.

I swung my legs over the side of the bed and sat there for about ten seconds before I got up. I was paralyzed with fear.

I finally got up, quickly threw on my T-shirt, sweatpants, and slip-on tennis shoes, and went downstairs. My legs shook with every step I took.

When I opened the door, the three of them were standing there, looking both ashamed and scared.

My eyes scanned each of them slowly. None of them would look me in the eye.

I finally stopped scanning on Thomas.

"Thomas?" I said calmly.

He looked at me like he was a schoolboy about to be expelled. The other two looked away, like they were accessories to whatever was going on.

"Where . . . is my goddamn husband?" I said that even calmer.

I knew Weston wasn't dead, because if he were, the police would've been at my door; so while I was sure I didn't have that issue to deal with, I was positive what I was about to find out was gonna change my life.

"Well, right now, he, uh . . . he prob'ly at the hospital."

I nearly fainted.

Then I felt myself getting mad.

"Get in here. *Now.* All of you."

They filed in, still not looking at me, and I shut the door behind them quietly, but with authority.

The reason I wasn't hysterical is because I could tell by the look on all their faces that whatever was wrong had to do with some bullshit. If Weston had been in an accident, they would've gotten right to the point; and they most definitely would've been missing the shameful looks on their faces.

I had experienced this kind of mess countless times growing up when my brother P.J. was always getting into trouble, and his friends inevitably ended up being the ones to break the news to Mama and Daddy in the middle of the night. P.J. got in so many fights in his late teens and early twenties, it was ridiculous. It seemed like he could never go to a club or just out with friends without getting involved in something ignorant. The next thing we knew, one or more of his buddies was at the door telling us what happened. Then Daddy would be on his way down to the police station to pick him up. The expressions on Weston's friends' faces were replicas of the ones I used to see on P.J.'s friends.

I turned from the door, glared at them, and said, "Now. One of you has two seconds to start talking."

Eric shocked the shit outta me when he blurted out, like he had Tourette's syndrome, "Weston got in a fight at the club wit' that dude Royce and I think he tried to kill him."

My mouth flew open, and my words got stuck in my throat.

Before I could get myself to say anything, Thomas added, "We didn't even know what was goin' on till it was too late."

I finally pushed some words out. "Too late for *what*?"

Gerald spoke up. "They crashed through a window together, and then Weston started kickin' him in the head. The cops swarmed in and arrested Weston. He gotta be at the hospital, though, 'cause he was—well, I ain't even gon' *tell* you what he looked like."

Barely breathing, I threw my hands up and plastered them to the sides of my head; then I released my words in choppy whispers. "Wait—stop—stop—back up—just . . . stop for a second—"

Everyone froze.

"Just—lemme breathe for a second."

I found some air and took it in slowly, not wanting to hear any more of the story, but knowing I had no choice.

Then I asked, "Is Royce . . . dead?"

Thomas said, "I don't think so."

"You don't *think so?*"

"No . . . but he had a seizure out on the sidewalk, though. So I don't know *what* happened when the ambulance took him away."

"*Whhhaaaat?* Wait a minute. This is—I can't deal with this." I went to sit on the couch so I wouldn't crumple.

They stayed standing while looking at me, like they were scared they'd to rush *me* to the hospital.

Before they could start talking, I said, "Eric, you said it was Royce. How do you know that?"

He looked like he didn't wanna answer the question.

"*Eric?*"

He gave in reluctantly. "When I finally saw it was Weston fightin', I peeped out the dude and . . . I remembered him from . . . you know . . . the hotel."

I started getting a migraine. I had forgotten that Eric knew what Royce looked like.

"Goddammit! Why didn't you guys try to stop it?"

Gerald said, "We *couldn't*. It was too much goin' on. By the time we saw him, the crowd flocked around so fast, we couldn't git through. Security couldn't even git through. Next thing we knew, they asses was on they way out the window."

"How did the fight get started? How the hell did Weston even know it was Royce? He doesn't know what he looks like. Eric is the only one who knows what he looks like other than me. And that I know of, Royce doesn't know what Weston looks like."

I thought about the day I turned the picture of Weston and me over when Royce walked in the shop; so I knew if he did know what Weston looked like, it wasn't because of me.

Nobody said a damn thing.

I was hopping mad. So I wouldn't wake the kids, I yell-whispered, *"Answer me, dammit!"*

Gerald finally said, "Well, I don't know who knew what who looked like, but I think . . . Weston mighta started it."

"And you think that because . . . ?"

"This one dude said he thought he saw Weston jump Royce all of a sudden."

I needed answers, clear ones, because I was confused; and the only person I knew who could give them to me was Weston.

"Okay—you know what? That's enough. Which hospital did they take him to?"

Thomas said, "Prob'ly Kaiser, since we was only in Jack London Square."

"Where the hell is Weston's car?"

Eric said, "I drove it here."

I stuck my hand out. "Gimme the keys."

He handed me the keys. I snatched them, shoved

them in my pocket, and looked at the three of them, so mad I almost couldn't see straight. "Who else drove?"

Thomas said, "Me and Gerald are in my car."

Eric said, "I rode wit' Weston."

"Well, I'll tell you what. All three of you stay your asses here and look after my babies till I get back."

Eric asked, "Why we *all* gotta stay?"

I shot him a look that said if he uttered one more word, I was gonna knock him out.

He got the message. "A'ight, then."

When I got to the emergency room, I rushed in and asked if they had brought Weston there. Sure enough, they had. The two cops who were guarding the doorway let me in after I identified myself, and when I got to the room and pulled back the curtain, I couldn't believe what I saw. He was sitting on the side of the bed, and he looked like a monster. The left side of his face was covered in a blood-soaked bandage from his cheekbone all the way to the bottom of his chin. His right eye was black-and-blue and almost completely closed. His lips were all busted and swollen; his nose was blood-encrusted and bruised. His ribs were taped; his right shoulder was bandaged. Every one of his knuckles were red and puffy; he had a gash at the top of his left eyebrow. His arms had small cuts and scratches in a zillion places; and on top of all that, he smelled like nine bottles of alcohol. I almost cried on sight, but I was too mad to let myself go there. Somehow I knew Weston was the cause of everything, and I was about to get to the bottom of it.

I walked up to him, and at first he looked at me; then a second later he looked away. His vibe spelled "guilt" in bold, capital letters; and I could tell I was about to get madder than I already was. I was glad there wasn't anyone in the bed in the next stall, because I was ready to light into his ass big-time, and an audience would've made that difficult.

I couldn't even bring myself to give him any sympathy. I was just too damn mad. Asking if he was okay would've been stupid, because that was already clear.

After I stood in front of him for about fifteen seconds, saying nothing, and he sat there, doing the same, I finally said, "Weston . . . would you care to explain to me . . . what the *hell* went down? Because, see, your friends . . . they can't seem to give me the whole story. But I'll tell you what I do know—you're lookin' *mighty* suspect right about now. So I'ma need you ta git ta talkin' *right . . . this . . . second.*"

From between his split lips came, "Me and Royce had it out."

"Yeah, so I've been told. Now gimme the how and why."

"I saw his ass . . . and I just . . . jumped on him. Then we started rumblin'."

Out of his one good eye, he looked at me like that was the beginning, middle, and end of the whole story.

"What the *hell* were you thinking? I mean, how did you even know it was him? You don't know what he looks like."

He looked away from me.

"*Hel-looooo?* What the *fuck,* Weston?"

He mumbled, with his head down, "I knew what he looked like."

"Wait—excuse me? How would you know that? What've I missed?"

He looked up at me sheepishly. "From yo' . . . I saw him in yo' high-school yearbooks."

"My *what*? What're you talking about? When?"

"When you took the kids to visit Joan-Renee . . . I was bored . . . and I did some work in the garage— you know—I mean, I was just out there cleanin'."

I put my right hand up and shut my eyes for a second, opened them again, then said, "Wait—stop— two things. First of all, that trip was last summer—like, June 2006 summer."

"I know that."

"Yeah—okay—and second, those yearbooks are buried ten boxes deep."

"I know that, too."

"Okay, so tell me why in the *fuck* you were scrounging around in the garage, digging up my old, dusty-ass yearbooks that you've never *once* mentioned being interested in looking at. Those things have been packed away since I was in my early twenties. Hell, *I* don't even look at the damn things anymore."

"Katrice . . . calm down, lower your voice, and can you please stop cussin' at me? We in a public place."

"That would be an emphatic *no* to *all* of that! Goddammit, Weston—I'm so livid with you right now, I almost don't even wanna *look* at you! Now hurry the hell up and tell me about the yearbooks!"

"I was rearrangin' and straightenin' up around the garage and I started movin' the boxes around and some of 'em fell over. The one wit'cho year-books was one of 'em. I started pickin' stuff up and

ran across yo' freshman book. I realized I had never
seen any of 'em, so I pulled 'em all out and sat
down and started lookin' through 'em." He paused
before he said, "Then I remembered Royce woulda
been in yo' freshman and sophomore books—and
I got kinda curious about what he looked like. So I
found him."

I was completely beside myself, and my mouth
was hanging open.

"Please . . . tell me you're joking right now."
Silence.

I said my next sentence superslow, as if the absurd-
ity of the whole concept were sinking in as I spoke it.
"Soooo, last June . . . you saw . . . a coupla pictures of
Royce . . . from, like . . . twenty years ago . . . and
they've . . . what . . . been etched in your brain *ever
since*?"

He cleared his throat, swallowed the dryness,
where saliva was supposed to be, and rubbed his
busted ribs before he said, "I guess you could say
that."

I stared into his left eye, ready to give him a
second ass beating for the night.

"You *guess* I could say that. Is that it? I mean, is
that the best answer you can come up with?"

His tone was totally blank when he said, "Yep. For
right now."

He was talking to me, but it was like he was distracted or something.

I squinted and looked deeper into his eye. There
was dishonesty floating around in it, but I couldn't
put my finger on what he was keeping from me.

I had never been so disgusted with him.

"I don't believe this. You're obsessed. I mean, I

thought I had issues in that department, but clearly you've got me beat. This is *absolutely stupid*. Just stupid! You attack a man who I already told you was of no threat to you, and now—"

"Did you suck his *dick*?"

I almost fell over. *"What?"*

"Did you suck his dick that night?"

I kept my voice down, but I went all the way off on his ass. *"Oh . . . my . . . God . . .* tell me you did not just fix your lips to come at me with that *ignorance*! You almost *kill* a man tonight, and that's what you're worried about? Some shit from eight years ago? Are you serious? Is this really where we're at? 'Cause if it is, *sweetheart,* you really need to rethink your priorities! You have a wife and two *goddamn* kids that you won't be coming home to tonight, and another child across town! You're looking at some *seriously* hefty assault charges—*if* not attempted murder— and you're sittin' up here askin' me some stupid-ass shit about suckin' *dick*? I should *push* your black ass off this fuckin' bed for asking a question like that at a time like this!"

He just sat there, staring right through me, and didn't say one word.

Five seconds later, the two police officers interrupted us.

"Ma'am?" one of them said cautiously.

I spun around. "Yes?"

"Need to have you step aside, please."

I was totally horrified. "Wait . . . what's happening?"

The other officer said, "Need you to stand up, Mr. Porter. And put your hands behind your back."

Weston got up slowly, while holding his ribs; then he obliged.

Panicked, I asked, "Wait . . . you're taking him right *now*?"

The second officer didn't answer. He just started gently putting the cuffs on Weston.

The first one said, "Yes, ma'am."

Scared out of my wits, I asked, "What are the charges?"

He said, "Well, right now, we got battery, and possibly attempted murder. But if Mr. Jordan doesn't wake up from that coma—if he dies—then we're lookin' at murder."

My heart fell into my stomach. "He's in a . . . coma?"

"Yes, ma'am."

Weston and I looked at each other.

He mouthed, "I'm sorry" and "I love you."

Then I stood there with tears in my eyes, watching the back of my husband's tattered and bruised body as they took him away.

15

WESTON

I already knew Katrice was gonna light my ass on fire when she got there, so I was ready for it. I could just imagine her reaction when my boys showed up at the house breaking the news to her about me and Royce. Once Eric saw me, I knew he'd know who I was squabbin' with. He never forgets a face—no matter how brief his encounter with a person is, or how much time has passed since it happened. Once Eric gets a close-up look at someone, they go into his memory bank for life. So I was already knowing that by the time she got to me, she'd know me and Royce had tore up the club.

I wanted to apologize to her for causing so much trouble, but I couldn't do it. It took me eight years to finally understand something: how a person can be sorry, but at the same time *not* sorry they did something that hurt somebody. Back in the day when me and Katrice had it out about her and Royce, she basically told me the same thing. She was sorry she hurt me, but deep down she wasn't really sorry she did what she did, because it was something that had been eating at her for ages. I didn't really understand how she could come at me like that and expect it to make sense; but after I released all that anger on Royce, I finally felt exactly what she felt. I mean, it hit me deep in my core. It was the biggest relief I ever felt in my life. I never really wanted to hurt anybody that bad before. That issue with Pop was different, because I wasn't harboring violent rage toward him, really. Although, for a second at the reunion, I was almost that mad. But what I felt about Pop was more on the betrayal and hurt tip. Like I felt with Katrice. It's a different kinda anger. When I get mad like that, I just don't wanna deal with those particular folks anymore. But my rage toward Royce was something I had never felt for anybody before. That was on the disrespect tip; and everybody knows when a man feels disrespected, that's the worst kinda anger he feels. He might be ready to kill up a whole room full of folks, all because one dude stepped outta bounds with him. That's one of the number one reasons men fight. Disrespect. And don't let it be that he got disrespected because of something having to do with his woman—especially if he's deep in love with her— because then you can be *sure* it'll be on.

I know she thought I didn't give a damn that I was about to go to jail, but I did. That's part of the reason I was so quiet, and why I just let her rip into me. After I got stitched and bandaged up and had a chance to sit there by myself while the doctors went and finished up some paperwork on me, I thought about my kids waking up the next day, looking for me, and my black ass would be laying up in somebody's funky-ass jail cell, instead of home, where I needed to be. I thought about the fact that I wouldn't be able to roll around on the living-room floor with Willie while I taught him how to wrestle. It hurt me that my Boo Boo, Ellie, would probably cry if I wasn't there to watch the cartoon channel with her, because that's our little thing, our father-daughter time we spend together. I love cartoons. I always have. I don't care how old I get, it's gonna be me and some cartoons for life. Ellie's just like me. She can't wait to get to the TV to watch her 'toons. So that's my bonding time with my baby. Now it was all over. I thought about the fact that I was gonna miss Lydia's eight o'clock call every night so we could have our daily father-daughter chat before she went to bed. That's an important part of our day, since we only see each other a couple-few times a week. I want her to know that even though she doesn't live with me, she's still my baby girl, my firstborn. Even though Thomas is my dawg and I trust him with my life, and I know he loves my daughter like one of his own, I need her to know that *I'm* her daddy. I mean, she knows that, but I just don't ever want her to get it twisted. Then, of course, there was the fact that I wouldn't be laying in the bed next to my wife. I can hardly wait to be near her again, when I'm gone all day at work. I love touching her. I love looking at her. I love for her to touch *me*. I love her voice. Her smile. Her body. Everything about her. I kept thinking about how the hell I was gonna get through the days without her. It started scaring me at one point. Then when she came up in the hospital, mad as hell, and I looked in her eyes and saw the pain underneath it all, it hit home that I was off into something that I had no idea how I was gonna get out of.

I didn't know *what* I was gonna tell my boss, my clients, and, most of all, Dr. Owen. I had a top-notch reputation at 24-Hour Fitness. I was one of their best trainers. I was in high demand all the damn time. My pockets stayed fat because I had so many clients. I had a good thing. I had to think about what I was gonna tell my supervisor, Steve. What would my clients think when they found out my ass went from goody-goody citizen to convicted felon? Would they even wanna work with me anymore, or would they all of a sudden be scared of me, like I would just be going around attacking people for no reason? Me and Dr. Owen were on our way to something good. I had my money ready to do my thing with the physical-therapy gym. My credit was spotless, and I was all set to get whatever loans I needed to help me along so I could open me a high-class establishment. I was ready to really make a name for myself in the fitness world, while I was helping people get their heal on after whatever—car accident, surgery, sports injury. I was on my way to really having a comfortable life with my family. My plan was to move us into a bigger house by the end of, at least, 2008, maybe 2009, because me and Katrice had already been talking about having another baby. Really, we talked about rounding our family out to four kids. We wanted to wait till the twins started grade school to try for our third child, though. So all I could see was all my plans going down the tubes after I lost control at the club.

If I don't know anybody else, I know my wife; and

I knew she was gonna ask me how the hell I knew what Royce looked like. I figured it would come up, one way or another, so I was ready for that line of questioning, too. But I didn't tell her the whole truth about it, because she was already looking at me like I had lost my natural mind; so I just let the rest of the yearbook information go out the back door and hoped it would stay there. That day in the garage, that was all true. I don't know why I never thought to check out her yearbooks before then. I guess, because we had so much going on—like with the kids and work and stuff—it never really crossed my mind. But I didn't have anything else to do while she was gone for four days with the kids, and I wasn't used to being alone in the house, so it started rattling my nerves. I figured if I kept busy with some type of project, it would make the time go by faster.

So I went out in the garage and started messing around with some of that junk, since it did need a little reorganizing. When I moved the first set of boxes, I noticed some old pictures of Katrice sticking out of another box underneath. I went over and started pulling stuff out, and that box fell over. That's when the yearbook box came to my attention. I was having a moment, you know, since she was gone, and I wanted to be close to her in some kinda way. So I pulled out the old pictures and all her yearbooks and sat down and started going down her memory lane. Then I remembered about Royce being in her first two books, and my mind kinda snapped. I wanted to know what the dude looked like who fucked and ran the night of the wedding, and what the *hell* he had that would make her drop her panties like that; so I looked him up. It pissed me off that he was as good looking as he was, too. I mean, I shoulda known Katrice wouldn't give no play to a half stepper, but still. So I went on and checked out both pictures of his ass. I just sat there staring at his face and studying his features. But I wanted to get a real good look at him; I wanted to *really* know his face; I wanted it to be so clear in my mind that if I ever got the chance to do damage to him, I would be *sure* it was him. So I got the bright idea to take the pictures in the house and scan 'em onto my flash drive and blow 'em up to a bigger size so I could see his features better. I wanted every nook and cranny of his face to be clear as a bell. Once I did that, I took the books back to the garage and finished fixing it up, like I had started doing in the first place. After that, I went back in the house, opened up the file on my drive and studied his face again. I tried to picture him in as many different ways as possible, just in case over the years his look had changed drastically—with a bunch of hair on his head, with no facial hair, not smiling, with gray hair, with more weight on his face, with less weight on his face—any feature I could think of that would make it harder for me to recognize him. I tried to imagine him . . . so I'd be ready for anything.

I knew it was an obsessive move, but at the time, that's where I was at. It worked, too; because after I had looked at his picture every damn week for over a year, I knew there was *no way* he would be able to get by me if he was ever in my space.

Was I trying to kill him? *Hell yeah*—especially after that dick-sucking comment—which I don't know if I'll *ever* get past. I tried to kick his head so far open that his brains popped out and splattered and splashed all over the goddamn sidewalk. If the cops hadn't stopped me, that's exactly what woulda happened, because I had no intention of letting up until his ass was past dead.

But by the time I saw Katrice and realized how bad the situation was, especially when I found out he was in a coma, part of me wished we had just had a regular-old scrap, knocked each other around for a while, then called it a day and moved on.

Now the situation was on a whole other level, and I had no choice but to deal with whatever fate was thrown my way.

16

KATRICE

October 20, 2007, 7:05 P.M., entry part two

I was way too furious earlier to really finish what I was saying in that first entry; plus, I was in the car. I had to get that out before I got back here. Good thing I took my journal with me. Something told me I was gonna need it after I saw Weston.

I just re-read what I said in that entry, and what's amazing to me is that I barely remember writing it, I was that mad. But, anyway, I had other stuff I wanted to write about regarding the hospital visit, but at 3:00 A.M., that wasn't happening—hence, part two of this entry. Plus, the whole day has passed by now and I need to include that content, too.

Well, just like I thought, I ended up spending the whole damn day speaking on behalf of Weston's ignorant ass. I know I shouldn't be calling him names, but I'm still mad as hell. I had to get up outta my bed, leave my kids in the middle *of the night, and go rushing off to the damn hospital to deal with him. He looked so horrible, I could hardly stand it. But you know what was pissing me off? He acted like the situation was no big deal. Everything he said to me was just as nonchalant as if he was telling me he was going to the store to pick up some milk and he'd be right back. I couldn't figure out where he was mentally. And you know what else? I coulda punched his ass blind in his left eye when he asked me about sucking Royce's dick! What the* hell *was that about? I know it had to have something to do with whatever Royce said, because how else would he have known to ask me that question? I could kill Royce for that. But, hell, he's half dead right now. I'm scared, though. Because what if he doesn't wake up from that coma? This is just complicating things even more. I'm pissed at Weston, but I love his ass so much, it makes me feel sick sometimes. I don't know what the hell me and the kids are gonna do while he's locked up— however long* that's *gonna be for.*

I hated having to lie to them today about where Weston is, but I had no choice. How are you gonna tell two five-year-olds that their daddy is in jail because he tried to kill their mother's ex-lover? I don't even know why I just referred to Royce in that way, because we weren't lovers, per se. We had that one night, and that was it. I wouldn't call that being lovers. Well, whatever. Karma is a bitch, I tell you that. I thought I suffered all there was to suffer over this damn Royce situation, and that back in the day, I paid my cheating dues. But apparently I must have really messed up big-time, because this turn of events is definitely taking the karmic cake.

You know, when I was growing up, I had this whole idea about meeting my soul mate and us running off into the sunset. With our kids and our white-picket-fence home, we'd be all smiles and love, and nothing would ever happen to ruffle our relationship feathers. I wish someone had slapped my ass awake from that dumb-ass daydream, because real, true soul-mate love is HARD! I guess not the love part, but all the stuff that comes with being with your soul mate. Like, if your man gets fired and you live together, and now you have to pull his weight and yours, too; if he gets seriously ill and you have to take care of him; getting things back on track if you guys stop talking and stop having sex; if he starts taking you for granted; when things are messed up in his family and it affects his mental state—like Sonny having HIV; and, of course, if your man gets sent to jail. When you're in one of those fluffy relationships—that's what I call the ones that have no substance—those issues will make you pack your bags and head for the border. But when you're with your soul mate—like I am with Weston—you never even think of leaving that person behind one of those issues. If you did that, half of you would always be missing, because that's what soul-mate love feels like—that person is your other half. Now I know why people say, "She's my better half" or "My other half." Like right now. I feel like half of me is gone. Actually, I feel sick. I think I might need to throw up. I just realized that next month is Thanksgiving, and Weston probably won't be around for that. We haven't been apart during the holidays since we got back together in 2000. Where I go, he goes, and vice versa. The only time I've been away from him is last summer when I went to visit Joan-Renee; but I hadn't seen her in so long, that it was really an overdue visit. Plus, she had Scarlett, the new baby, in May, and I really wanted to see her and the new addition and the rest of the family. But being away for that four days, while it was fun, was really hard. I don't think I slept ten winks, even as comfortable as Joan-Renee's guest bed was, because Weston wasn't there next to me, with his leg thrown over me, like I had gotten so used to. I need him close to me at night,

*and when he's not, it makes me nervous. Like seriously . . .
I get nervous when he's too far away from me in the bed.*

*But, anyway, I really am feeling sick . . . for real. I'm
about to go barf. All this stress is wearing on my stomach. I
might hafta continue this entry later on. . . .*

When I got back from the hospital, the Three
Stooges were all laid out in the living room. Thomas
was sprawled out on the couch, snoring; Gerald was
reclined in Weston's chair, with his right shoe on
and the other dangling from his left foot; and Eric
was knocked out on his back on the big, fluffy rug
in front of the TV. As mad as I was when I walked in,
when I saw them, they actually looked so cute, I
smiled for two seconds. I do love all of them a hell
of a lot. And I know in half a heartbeat they would
lay down their lives for me, Weston, and the kids.
I'm so glad Weston has them in his life. They take
good care of each other, and not a lot of men have
friends they can say that about.

Anyway, I almost didn't wanna wake them up, because they looked so peaceful, but I knew they
needed to get home to their wives and kids. One
man not being home for his family when they got
up the next day was quite enough.

I tiptoed in and quietly woke all of them up.
Once they got themselves into focus, I told them
what had happened at the hospital, and that
Weston was gone.

Gerald said, "Sorry, Katrice. If I had known who
he was lookin' at when he got up and left the bar, I
woulda stopped him."

I smiled at him. I figured by that time, Eric and

Thomas had filled him in on who Royce was to Weston and me.

I told him, "Don't worry about it. It wasn't your fault."

Then Thomas said, "You gon' be okay today? You want me to take the twins home wit' me? They can stay wit' me and Yolanda for the rest of the weekend."

I could've jumped in his arms and given him the biggest bear hug ever. But I knew I needed to deal with telling Ellie and Willie something about Weston as soon as possible, even though I had no idea what that was gonna be at the moment.

"No, that's okay, T. I need to be with them today. I gotta find a way to break the news about Weston's absence to them. Plus, I don't wanna wake them up at this hour. But thanks. I appreciate the offer."

"Okay. Let us know if you change yo' mind."

And Eric said, "Ay, Katrice, you *know* if I had seen Royce's ass at the club before Weston did, I woulda had us be out before the fight had a chance to jump off. I didn't know he was there. For real. You *know* I wouldn't let my boy git caught up like that."

"I know. I'm not blaming you guys."

Then Thomas said, "Oh, uh . . . we ate some food out'cho fridge. We was *starvin'*! Who made that lasagna?"

I laughed. "I did, boy."

"That shit was on hit, fuh real. Ain't no more left, though. We tore it up. Ate it cold and right out the goddamn pan."

I cracked up. And I needed that laugh, too. That's part of the reason I love having them around. They can make me laugh when I'm feeling my absolute worst. The ironic thing is, half the time they're not even trying to be funny when they say the stuff they say.

"That's fine. Come on, Stooges, get up and go home to your wives before they put out the search party for you. Thanks for staying."

Eric said, "Well, it ain't like you gave us no choice. You was 'bout ta put'cho foot in my ass before you left. But it's cool, though. I'm just playin' wit'choo. You know I luh you, girl."

"And I love all you guys. Now get outta my house so I can get some sleep before my kids wake up. It's gon' be a long-ass day, and I miss Weston already."

They got up, and I kissed and hugged them all.

I told Thomas, "Tell Yolanda I'll call her later. You can fill her in on what happened, though. I got enough phone calls to make today, as it is."

"A'ight. I'ma holla at'choo later tonight, just to make sure you okay."

"Thanks."

I sent them on their way and sat down on the couch for a few minutes, holding back ten tons of tears. As much as I wanted to cry my eyes out, I knew if I started, I wouldn't stop. So I just sucked it up and eventually dragged myself back up to bed.

The moment I was dreading came at seven thirty-five in the morning. The twins came running into our bedroom and jumped up on the bed, like they do every Saturday morning, and started flopping around. But after they realized Weston's side of the bed was empty, they stopped cold. Together. That twin thing is really amazing. It's funny to watch sometimes, and other times it's kinda scary, because they're so in tune with each other that it's almost unreal. Even for a boy and a girl, sometimes they seem like one little person.

Willie asked, "Where's Daddy? Is he on the toilet again stinking up the bathroom?"

I wanted to laugh, but the moment was far too serious for that.

I sat up and pushed myself against the headboard to support my back.

"No . . . Daddy's not in the bathroom, Willie. You guys, come sit next to me for a minute. I need to tell you something."

They scurried up and plopped down next to me, Ellie on my left and Willie on my right. I felt a lump forming in my throat just as I got ready to speak.

"Daddy . . . had to leave *really* early this morning and go away to take care of some very important business, and what he had to do is gonna take a little while. He can't come back until he's all done with his business."

Ellie said, "What time is that gonna be? We hafta watch the cartoon channel."

I fought back the tears. Literally. I had to squeeze my eyes closed for a second so they wouldn't come pouring out.

Willie asked, "How come he didn't wait till we got up so he could say bye? Daddy always says bye."

"Well, it was *so* early that he didn't wanna wake you guys up, and he really had to go right then. But he told me to tell you he loves you both and he'll call every chance he gets. And as soon as he's all done, he'll be back to watch cartoons and play and do all the stuff you guys love to do together."

Ellie started crying. "But how come we couldn't go with hiiiimmm? I wanna go with Daddyyyyy."

Then Willie started crying, which always happens. Once one starts, so does the other one.

He wailed, "But *Daddy* said we could go to the park todayyyyy. Now we can't *gooooo*. Is he gonna be back tomorrow?"

Never in my life had my heart ached like it did at that moment. Never. The tears were about to fall, but still, I held them back. I couldn't let my babies see me crying, because then they'd know something was really wrong. I tilted my head back and blinked the tears away, took a few deep breaths, and then looked at my crying children.

"You're gonna go to the park with Daddy. You are. As soon as he gets home. But it's not gonna be tomorrow, sweetie. And, Ellie, you couldn't go with him because he really has to take care of business, and he wouldn't be able to play with you. Sometimes grown-ups have to go places without their kids so they can do important things. But he'll be back. I promise."

None of that helped, because they continued to cry. Weston had never missed a Saturday with his kids. Not once. No matter what. They understand what happens during the week—that Weston and I have to go to work and that we'll see them later. They're fine with being away from us during the day. They love preschool. But the weekends are different. He's always around, and so am I. We made a pact that weekends are for the kids, since we both work all day. Even though I work on Sundays, it's usually only for a small portion of the day so I can take care of my churchgoing clients. And even then, Weston's home with them, so they're fine with that. Sometimes I take them to my parents' for the day on Sundays, and they love that. But the sudden break in the Saturday tradition threw them for two loops.

I covered my face with my hands and prayed not to cry, at least until I could get them out of the room and into some type of activity that would quiet them down.

Finally I said gently, "Okay . . . okay . . . it's gonna be all right. Don't cry, you guys. Daddy wouldn't want that. He's coming back. I promise."

Ellie said through her massive tears, "Is Daddy gonna call us todaaayyy? I made a picture for him, and I wanna tell him what it looks liiiiike."

"I think he'll call today. I'm almost sure of it. And you can tell him about your picture then, okay?"

Willie's crying subsided just a little, and he said, "Can you take us to the park, then, Mommy?"

"Of course, I'll take you. After we have breakfast, we can get dressed and go. Now, you guys, go on downstairs to watch TV. Everything's gonna be okay. Daddy's gonna be back real soon. All right?"

Together they said a somber "Okaaayyy"; then they got off the bed and walked out with their heads hanging low, still sniffling and wiping their noses.

As soon as they got out of the room, and I made sure I heard them turn on the TV downstairs, I closed the bedroom door, crawled back in bed, shoved my face into my pillow, and cried like I hadn't cried since '99 when Weston left me after he tore my house up. And I was crying even harder than that. I tried to cry every tear I could out of my system, because I knew I couldn't keep having random spells with the kids around. So I just let loose as hard as I could.

For about twenty minutes, I sobbed. Until the house phone rang. It scared me, and I thought it might be Weston, but it wasn't.

When I picked up the phone and barely squeezed out a hello, Yolanda said, "Katrice? Girl . . . oh, my God . . . are you okay? Thomas told me what happened. I'm *so sorry*."

And then I bawled some more in her ear. "Yolanda—I can't—I can't—do—do this shit. I can't do it. What are we—gonna do—without Weston?"

My hysterics scared her. "Oh, my God . . . I'm . . . you know what? I'm on my way over there. Okay? Just hang on. I'll be there in twenty minutes. Where are the kids?"

"Down—downstairs watching—TV. I'm supposed—to make them breakfast and take—take them to the—par-park la-later."

"Okay . . . Katrice . . . breathe, girl. You need to breathe. I'm on my way. Try to get yourself together so the kids won't freak out. I'm leaving now. Hang up the phone."

"O-okay."

And I hung up.

I got off the bed and went into the bathroom so I could put a cold rag on my face and try to cut down on the puffiness in my eyes. I put the cover to the toilet seat down and sat on it; then I just stared at the floor for about a minute. Finally I got back up and fixed my face as best I could, and went downstairs to make the kids' breakfast.

They stayed quiet while watching TV, but I could tell they were still sad and confused about what was going on. They weren't talking, laughing, or even arguing over the TV channel, like they usually do. They just sat there looking at *George of the Jungle* with blank expressions on their faces. They didn't even look at me when I passed them to go into the kitchen. Thank goodness for that, because my eyes were still red and puffy.

I started their oatmeal and eggs, and then I heard Yolanda come in with Lydia. I had unlocked the door for her on the way past.

The kids seemed to brighten up a bit when they saw their sister, and the three of them started talking while Yolanda came and joined me in the kitchen.

When I looked at her, I started crying once again.

She walked up to me and cradled my face, then looked at me seriously. "Hey. No more tears. Come on, Superwoman. You can do this. You *have* to. You gotta hold it down, girl. No tellin' how long this ride is gon' be, and you can't be usin' all your energy cryin', boo. I'ma be here for you as much as I can, and as much as you need me, but you got them babies out there, who don't know what the hell is goin' on. If you don't pretend like it's all good, they're gonna know it's not."

I just nodded while I let the last of my tears drop, then splash to the floor.

She wiped my eyes, then asked me in a low tone, "Now. What'd you tell the kids happened to Weston? 'Cause whatever you told them is what I'm gonna tell Lydia. We gotta have the same story."

"I told them he had to go away really early this morning to take care of some important business that was gonna take a while, and he didn't have time to say good-bye, but that he'd be back soon and he'd call."

"Okeydokey. That's the story, then. Now wipe your eyes. And move outta the way and lemme get in here, girl. You 'bout to burn up the kids' oatmeal."

I let out a small chuckle, thanked her, then let her take over so I could get myself together again. I got some paper towels for my face, sat down at the table; then I tried to figure out how I was gonna get through the day without my husband—and without crying every hour.

Close to nine-thirty that morning, after the kids had eaten and I had gotten a grip on reality, the house phone rang. Yolanda had already told Lydia about Weston and had gone to the store for me; I was doing the kids' dishes. Lydia and the twins were still watching TV. When I picked up the phone in the kitchen, it was the operator telling me there was a collect call from Weston at the Glenn E. Dyer Detention Facility, and asking if I would accept the charges.

"Yes . . . yes . . . put him through."

He sounded ashamed. "Hi, babe."

"Hi."

I had so many mixed emotions that I couldn't really bring myself to give him the cheerful hello he was probably looking for. But I was happy as hell to hear his voice.

There were a few seconds of silence between us at first; then Weston asked, "You okay?"

I kept my voice low. "Don't ask me that right now,

please. It's been a rough morning already. I miss you. The kids miss you. They're confused. Are *you* okay?"

"Not really. I didn't sleep at all, my body hurts, I miss you and the kids . . . and . . . I'm scared. What'choo say to the twins about me?"

After I told him, I let him know Yolanda told Lydia the same thing. He said that was a good idea; then he told me what he wanted me to tell his boss.

"Tell him the truth, babe."

"Are you sure that's a good idea?"

He thought for a second, then said, "Okay, no . . . don't tell him the whole truth. Just tell him I was drunk and I got in a fight at a bar and I ended up in jail. Tell him . . . we tore the club up, it was a bad fight, and everything's up in the air right now. And tell him I'm sorry. I don't wanna lie to him. He a man, he'll understand. We go way back. He knows I'm good people . . . that I don't git in trouble. After I find out what the deal is, then if I have to, I'll call him myself and explain in more detail . . . but I ain't gon' give him everything. That's our business."

"Okay. If you're sure . . ."

"I am. And tell the fam, the real deal. Don't hold back. They know the history. I don't wanna hide nothin' from them. I would call 'em all myself and explain, but I don't have a lotta time on the phone, so I need you to do it. And tell Mama I'ma call her tomorrow."

"Okay."

We both paused.

Then he said, "I'm sorry, babe. I know I fucked up, and I know you mad as hell at me. I don't know what else to say."

So I wouldn't start crying again, I said, "You

should talk to the kids before you have to hang up. They're expecting to hear from you. Lydia's here, too. Hang on."

I called the kids into the kitchen and told them Weston was on the phone.

Ellie got on first. "Hi, Daddy! I made you a picture! It has flowers and trees and the sun and a dog, and I made you smiling again. What time are you coming home?" She waited for his response, frowned a bit, then said, "Okay. Yes. I love you, too. Yes. Okay. Here's Willie. Bye, Daddy. See you when you get home."

Willie jumped on and shouted, "Hi, Daddy! Mommy said she'd take us to the park today 'cause you can't take us. Can we go next Saturday with you?" He waited. Laughed. Nodded and said, "Yeah." Laughed some more. Then said, "Okay. Yes, I'll be good. Okay. Have fun doing your business, Daddy. Okay. I love you, too. Bye, Daddy." Then he handed Lydia the phone.

"Daddy, are you gonna be home at eight so I can call you? Oh. Okay. Oh. Well, I'll just wait until you call me, then. No. Mommy did. Yeah. Okay, I love you, Daddy. See you when you get back."

Then she handed me the phone. I told them, "Okay, you guys go on back in the living room and lemme talk to your daddy."

They all ran off, feeling better since they had spoken to Weston.

I got back on, and he said, "I gotta go, babe. I'm sorry. I'ma call you back tonight."

"Okay . . . Weston . . . I love you."

"Not as much as I love you, babe. I gotta hang up. Wait for my call tonight, okay?"

"What time?"

"I don't know yet."

"Okay, bye."

Yolanda and I took the kids to the park together; afterward, she took them home with her so I could come back and make the rest of my calls about Weston's situation in private and try to get some rest. She said she'd keep them for the night, since I had to work the next day for a few hours. I told her I'd pick them up when I got off. That was perfect, because with all that had been going on, I didn't have time to call my clients and reschedule them. I didn't wanna ask Angela to fill in for me because I knew she was booked for the day.

I called Steve, Weston's boss, first. I informed him as Weston had instructed, and surprisingly enough, although he was very disappointed, he understood. He said he had been in that same situation once before in the past, and his wife had to do the same thing I was doing—make the my-husband's-locked-up phone calls. He told me he knew of a great attorney named Lincoln Simpson—he defended Steve in his case and got him off—and said he would see if he could get Simpson to take on Weston's case. Steve's wife was able to hook that up back in the day because Lincoln was married to her cousin. He also said he'd get in touch with Weston's clients and tell them he was out of town on an emergency, and would work something out with them until further notice. Then he told me to have Weston call him ASAP, and I told him I would.

Next I called Mama and Daddy and spent over an hour talking to them about what had happened.

They were totally shocked, and they felt awful for both of us. They told me to let them know if there was anything I needed, especially with the kids; then they said they would keep Weston in their prayers.

I called P.J., but his phone was off. I didn't bother leaving him a message because he's terrible with listening to them in a timely manner. I figured I'd have to catch him later.

Then I called Chantelle and told her what had happened. After she got past the surprise, she told me how sorry she was, and, of course, to let her know what she could do to help. I asked her to relay the details to Sabrina, Rishidda, and Genine for me, because I was getting weary with all the calls and having to rehash the events. She agreed, and I told her I'd get with all of them during the next week, after I had a chance to figure out my life and adjust my work schedule, since Weston wouldn't be there to do his part with the kids.

I called Tiki and Charles, and also Joan-Renee, but I ended up having to leave them messages. I gave them the two-minute version of the story on their voice mails, then told them to get back to me when they could.

I saved the call to Weston's family for last, because I knew it would be the longest one. I did a three-way call with Lorraine and Sonny and told them everything. Lorraine cried, and Sonny was devastated. Of course, I had to hold it together so I wouldn't cry, too. After we got past all the emotional stuff, we stayed on the phone for another two hours. Sonny told me that Weston had issues with anger growing up and used to fight a lot as a kid. Weston had told me some of that, but Sonny really

laid the details on the line. I was surprised at some
of the things he told me. Like the fact that Weston
cracked a boy over the head with a glass bottle full
of soda when he was nine because the boy knocked
into him and didn't say "excuse me." And about a
time when Weston was eleven and blackened a boy's
eye, all because the boy wouldn't move out of the
seat he wanted to sit in during a class they had together. Then there was the time when Weston was
six and he shoved a boy out of a swing and he fell on
his face, and two of his teeth got knocked out, because Weston was mad that the boy beat him to the
swing during a race. There were other stories, too,
and I was shocked. A few of them Weston had already told me, but he left out some details, which
disturbed me a bit. I guess Mama was right—I *was*
lucky he didn't hit me the night of the wedding. Of
course, then he'd be dead, because if I didn't kill
him, like Mama said, she would have.

Lorraine told me that after Sonny left, things got
even worse, and Weston's anger issues increased.
She was worried about him, because for a long time
he shut down mentally and wasn't himself. He was
always respectful of her and his siblings, but it
didn't take much to set him off, and she was concerned that one day someone would make him
mad and things would get out of hand.

I told her Weston would call the next day, and I
also asked her to please let the rest of the family
know what was going on so I wouldn't have to do it.
Sonny and Lorraine wanted to make a trip out to
California right away to see about Weston, but I
told them to wait until we found out what was going
on. They both agreed, and I told them I'd keep in

close touch with them about any details that came up. Lorraine offered to come stay with me and the twins. I thanked her, but told her I could manage. I knew Mama and Daddy would be around, if need be; plus, I had Yolanda and the rest of my girls, if things got really tough.

After I spent all afternoon talking to everyone about Weston's misdeed, I was worn the hell out, and I went upstairs to take a well-deserved nap. I actually fell right asleep and didn't wake up until about six-thirty that evening. Shortly after seven, I started feeling sick, and about fifteen minutes later, I went and threw my guts *all* the way up. Stress does that to me, and considering the amount I was under, I was surprised it didn't happen sooner. I didn't bother trying to eat afterward, because I was afraid I wouldn't be able to keep anything down.

Around eight-thirty, Weston called back. I was still mad, but hearing his voice made me feel better, and our conversation was less strained than that morning. I told him I made all the calls, and what Steve had said. He was glad to hear about Steve trying to get him a lawyer, because he wanted someone he could trust. He said if the lawyer was good enough for Steve, that was good enough for him. He was most concerned about Steve's response, because he really loved his job and didn't wanna put a damper on his relationships with anyone he worked with. He told me he'd take care of talking to Dr. Owen at a later date. His main concern was keeping his job secured at the gym.

I didn't tell him that Lorraine cried, because I knew that would make him feel bad. I also didn't tell him about all the things Sonny had told me about Weston's childhood. I decided to keep that information to myself. We had enough going on without me bringing up old stuff from the past. I was disturbed about the things I had heard, though, and wondered why Weston held back so many of those details. I started thinking maybe he didn't want me to know, for fear I would look at him differently.

He couldn't talk long; so again, we said our I-love-yous and I-miss-yous, and had to call it a night. He told me he'd call as much as he could and to tell the kids he loved them and would talk to them the next day.

I stayed up for a while, but that didn't last too long because I was thoroughly beat. I finally went ahead and turned in around ten. While I lay awake, I prayed for the strength to get through the madness ahead, for Royce to wake up from his coma ASAP, and for Weston to be back home with us in record time.

Then I ran my hand across the emptiness in the space next to me, where my husband should've been, and cried myself to sleep.

17

WESTON

The only thing rolling through my mind when they slammed them loud-ass bars behind me was *What the fuck did I just do?* I just stood there, looking at the wall in front of me. The dude on the bottom bunk said, "Cool. I finally got me some company up in this piece." I wanted to tell his crackhead-looking ass that I wasn't hardly about to be his company. I was halfway hungover, I was tired, my body was aching like I had just got through playing in a football game gone bad, and it was only about three degrees up in there.

I threw my pile up on the top bunk and tried to figure out how the hell I was gonna get my busted body up there. The eight Hennessy shots I guzzled were almost in the wind, and I was feeling every bit of the fight I had just had with Royce. Especially my face. It was throbbing like it had a heartbeat, and

I was scared to see what it looked like under the bandages. That black punk bitch sliced me so deep, I thought he was about to hit a bone. My right eye was completely shut and stuck closed. Felt like I had *three* eyeballs under my lid instead of one. Every time I breathed, my broke-ass ribs moved like they were floating around in my midsection. I couldn't even get me a full breath because I think Royce's dirty ass collapsed one of my lungs when he hit me with that elbow move in my chest. The left side of my mouth was five times as big as the right, from where I fell against the table when Royce pulled that *Kill Bill* stunt and popped me in my damn kneecap.

Dude must have seen me trying to figure out what I was gonna do, because he asked me, "Ay, man . . . you need me to be on the top bunk? You look like you got'cho ass *fucked up* in somebody fight tonight."

I looked down at his scrawny ass and came back with "Yeah, but I ain't the one layin' in a coma. He is."

He looked at me like he was scared I was about to break one of his twig-ass legs in half; then he said, "Word? You did 'im like *dat?*"

I didn't answer his stupid ass.

He asked me again, "So you need me to be on top?"

"Nah, man. You can stay where you at. I don't need no help."

"A'ight, den."

I went on and made that move and climbed up on the bunk, but it hurt so bad I thought my body was about to break apart. I wasn't about to switch places with his dirty, stankin', might-have-scabies ass. I didn't know *what* kinda germs he was laying up on, and didn't wanna find out.

Once I got up there, the bed was so hard, it felt like a piece of wood. It was twice as cold up top. Hell, I thought heat was supposed to rise. I just wanted to go to sleep, but this chitchatting pipe smoker wanted to have a conversation.

"Ay, dude . . . so what'choo up in here fo'?"

"Didn't I just tell yo' ass I put a nigga in a coma?"

"Yeeeuh, but I'm sayin', though . . . what was y'all scrappin' 'bout? Some money or a bitch or what?"

"Why you all up in my business like you know me 'n' shit?"

"Naw, it ain't all like dat. I'm just tryina see where you at, dawg."

"Where I'm *at*?"

"Yeeeuh . . . you know . . . how you do what'choo do . . . how you git down 'n' shit."

"What'choo need to know all that for?"

"Nah . . . I'm just sayin'—"

"Ay, man, you know what? I'ma need you to shut the fuck up. We ain't 'bout to be friends. I ain't tryina have no conversation wit'cho glass-pipe-suckin' ass. So you just do what'choo do and lemme do me while I'm here. And mind yo' goddamn business."

"Glass-pipe-suckin' ass? Man, how you jus' gon' come up in here and start talkin' all kinda sh—"

"Shut the *fuck* up!"

"Man, you ain't gotta git loud. I was jus' sayin' . . ." He finally shut it down and left me alone.

I didn't wanna eat. Hunger wasn't what was on my mind. All I wanted to do was see my family. I missed my kids, missed my wife, and missed all the comforts of my home. I didn't get to make the twins

their breakfast Saturday morning. I missed them
jumping around on the bed when they got up; I
couldn't see the picture my Boo Boo made for me;
I didn't get to help Willie put together his little
Lego tower, like I promised him I was gonna do that
afternoon—and Katrice is not into that—that was
our project. I didn't get to take them to the park,
like I said I would; and Sunday I was supposed to
take them and Lydia to Children's Fairyland, and
now that wasn't gonna happen. My word is my bond
with my kids. The only time I missed doing anything
with them is that weekend after I found out about
Pop, but I was home at least. They saw me. They
knew I was there for them in other ways. It's different when you don't do stuff with your kids because
you don't feel good; but when you're just not there,
it's messed up for them. Now I didn't know *how*
many more activities I was about to miss. It gave me
a headache just thinking about the looks on my
kids' faces when Katrice had to tell them I was gone,
and didn't know when I'd be back. I knew they were
gonna cry. Then if they cried, I knew Katrice would
cry. *I* would cry if I had to do what she did. How can
you not cry when you're breaking your kids' hearts?
Which, of course, was my damn fault.

Before we go to sleep, me and Katrice usually lay
in bed and run our mouths for about an hour or so.
We talk about what we did during the day—funny
things that happened, things that made us mad,
conversations we had with people, stuff we wanted
to call each other and say in the moment but were
too busy, and even what we ate that day. Just everything that goes on when we're not together during
the workday. That's our time to catch up, since our

mornings are so crazy with getting the twins out the door and rushing here and there; then we get home at different times and then it's back to the kids and dinner and playtime and all that. By the time we finish with them, we're tired as hell. But we gotta have time for us, so that's when we do it. I *need* that. We sleep naked a lot of the time, except on weekends 'cause we know the kids come busting in the room early in the morning, and sometimes she lays on top of me and puts her head on my chest while we talk. She says she likes to feel my chest rise and fall when I breathe, and then when I'm talking, she likes to feel the vibration of my body. That turns me *on*. That's some romantic-type shit that I never really had with a woman before her. I like when she does it, anyway, because I like to feel her warm body— especially her titties covering my chest. They got even *bigger* after she had the twins, and I can't get enough of 'em. The best part about it is sometimes she'll get turned on, and while I'm in the middle of a sentence, she'll just sit up, straddle me, grab hold of Dangerous—which makes me straight *instantly*—and then she'll slip him in and start riding me real slow and sexy. Then we close out the conversation and go at it for about thirty minutes, and after that, we shut everything down and go to sleep. I almost felt sick, thinking about not being able to feel her next to me and on me during the night. She sleeps on her side, and I usually put my thigh over her body because she loves when I do that; and then I scoot real close to her and press my front against her back and put my arm around her. She says that puts her right to sleep—next to me giving her a healthy dose of Dangerous, of course.

Now I was stuck in a freezing-cold, musty, smelled-like-stank-feet jail cell barely bigger than my master bathroom at home.

I had to shit real bad, too. I was dreading the moment I had to do it in front of my cellie, plus get within five inches of the thing they called a toilet in there. But my stomach was gurgling and I had a serious load built up that I had been holding for about five or six hours, so I knew I had to make something happen or I was gonna end up letting loose right there on the bunk. I also didn't want that dirty crack-head freak looking at me. I knew I didn't have the energy to whoop his ass if he did, so I just hoped he would keep his red, smoked-out eyes to himself.

Taking that dump was the hardest thing I had to do. The toilet was way too small for my almost-six-foot-four ass; it was filthy; it was loose; and when I looked for the toilet paper, there were only about four squares left on the goddamn roll. What the hell was I supposed to do with that? Wiping shit takes at least *sixty* squares—well, it does for me—and then I still need those fresh-wipe things that Katrice keeps religiously in the bathroom—for those extra-soft ones that stick to your ass crack—not like the solid ones that drop out clean and you wipe and get on about your business and don't have to worry about skid marks in your draws two hours later. The water at the sink barely worked, so now my ass was crusty, and I couldn't soap up my hands like I needed. Plus, it stank like hell, and I was embarrassed about that because my cellie was right there to get his nose hairs burned out by the aroma.

* * *

I couldn't wait to get to a phone so I could call home. When I finally got my chance, I was scared, because I knew Katrice was still hot with me, but I had to talk to her and the kids. Plus, we needed to talk about what she was gonna say to my people. I felt bad that I had to make her do all that, but it wasn't like I was gonna get much done with the little time they gave us. Also, I wasn't trying to call a bunch of different people collect. When she got on the phone and all she said was hi—and it wasn't even an enthusiastic one—I felt rejected. But the worst part was talking to the kids. I had to hold back my emotions. They all wanted to know what time I was coming home, and it hurt my heart to have to lie. Lydia asked me about our eight o'clock phone call, and I had to tell her I wasn't gonna be home for our calls for a while and I'd have to call her when I could. But my baby girl is sharp, and I was scared she was about to ask me what kind of business I was away doing. She's known for calling me out about stuff. She gets that from me. I'm good for calling folks out in less than a second, and dare 'em to think too long before answering me. That always tells me a lie is about to come out their mouth. But I was glad she took what I said at face value and let it go. Willie asked me about going to the park the next Saturday, and I had to tell him no, then work around the question and start making little jokes so he'd laugh, or else he'd be stuck on that subject indefinitely. Another thing he picked up from me. It's hard for him to move on to something else when a particular thing is lodged in his head. He needs confirmation on every damn thing. That whole scene was enough to make me wanna shoot myself.

Katrice sounded a little less mad by the time I called her back, but I know her. She probably blew my ass up in that journal she writes in. I've never looked in any of her journals—I would never disrespect her like that—but I know when she gets mad at me, them pages be smokin'. Probably burns a hole right through 'em, calling me names and cussing me out with that special pen she uses. I don't even wanna *know* what kinda poison she puts in there about me. But, anyway, I knew it would take her a minute to let that anger go, so I just accepted the fact that she might be a little cold to me our first few conversations. I guess I couldn't blame her. I messed up our whole program. Now she had to figure out how to work it without me. She told me Steve said he had a lawyer for me, who got him out of a legal jam kinda like mine a long time ago. I needed to hear that good news because it wasn't like *my* ass knew anybody.

At one point, it hit me that I was probably gonna be slapped with attempted-murder charges, and if Royce died, it would be straight-up murder, and then I'd be sent to San Quentin for life . . . or close to it. When I thought about it, I knew I'd kill myself before a week went by, because I wouldn't be able to stand not seeing and being with my family. Plus, Mama and Pop would both be heartbroken and destroyed by that. And what would my kids think? What would they do without me? But, really, what would I do without *them*? I don't do too good with those kind of adjustments. When I left Chicago to come out here with Eric, I was homesick every twelve hours. About nine different times, I told him I was about to pack my bags and go home. The only reason I didn't was because I got a good job working at a gym and the money was right. Plus, I had met this girl who was laying the pussy on me *righteously,* and I wasn't really trying to let that go; so I just decided to go ahead and stick it out. It took me about six months to finally get comfortable, and then I was cool. But thinking about a prison sentence keeping me from my family was a whole other issue altogether. I knew one thing: this was about to be my worst nightmare, and I was hoping like hell it didn't last too much longer.

I had never really been into praying and God, and all that, but once I started thinking about my possible reality, I made up for a lifetime of not praying. I started asking the Man in Charge to please work something out for a brotha so I could get back to my wife and kids, where I belonged.

18

KATRICE

October 27, 2007, 6:56 P.M.

This one is probably gonna be extra long since I'm about four days behind in entries. I just haven't had the energy to do it, and, to be honest, a couple of days I actually forgot because there's been so much going on. It's been exactly a week since Weston went to jail, and it's been absolutely wretched. I don't think I've slept more than fifteen hours since that night, especially since I found out that Weston's being charged with attempted murder. That nearly killed me. Steve got Lincoln Simpson to take on the case. I hope this works out. Steve went to visit Weston on Tuesday. Weston told him the real deal about the fight, although he did say he didn't tell Steve that I cheated on him. He just told him Royce was a guy from my past who kept trying to break us up, and he had had enough, and that's how the fight got started. Somewhat true, I guess. Anyway, Steve totally understood. He told Weston about how Lincoln defended him back when he had his moment in time and ended up in jail after his bar brawl, and Lincoln got him off; Steve was sure Lincoln could help Weston out. I'm so glad they have a good relationship. They've known each other for years, even before Steve became his boss. And I like him. And his wife, too.

I had to work my original schedule because I had too many clients depending on me; plus, I woulda felt bad about backing out of my obligations at the last minute. I don't like to cancel appointments unless I'm sick or the kids are sick. But all this crap with Weston just messed everything up; and even though I wanted to call all my clients and try to reschedule them, I realized that wouldn't work because there probably would never be a better time to schedule them—especially with me not knowing from one minute to the next what was gonna happen with Weston. So my Superwoman ass just sucked it up and went to work all last week. Yolanda kills me with that! She's so funny, calling me "Superwoman." I love her.

I haven't been able to bring myself to tell Angela what's going on with us. Even though we do talk more now, and I'm starting to kinda like her a little, I don't want her in my business like that, just yet. I don't know her well enough for that. I did tell her that Weston had to go out of town for a while on business, and that things were a little rough around the house, which was why I'd been so tired. Of course, she told me to let her know if there was anything she could do. I probably won't, though. Thank goodness Mama came and stayed for four days, because I needed help with the kids and getting them from school on the days that were supposed to be Weston's. I'm glad Daddy knows how to fend for himself. She cooked and cleaned and played with the kids, but things were still hard. They miss their daddy, and even though he calls them every day and assures them that his business will end soon, and he'll be home again, they don't understand what that's about, and the next day, they're asking me what time he's coming home. Hopefully, the next couple of weeks will be better because I did call my clients and let them know I had to change my schedule because Weston is "out of town for a while," and that I needed to move some of them around so I could get the kids after school. Fortunately, they were all okay with it. My regulars understand, and they don't bitch about stuff like that.

Part of the reason I couldn't wait till the week was over is because I knew I was gonna go visit Weston today. But it wasn't anything like what I expected. First of all, we only had thirty minutes to visit—how do they figure? You can barely eat lunch in thirty minutes, much less catch up with a loved one. Then the worst part was I couldn't touch him. I know they said there'd be no physical contact, but I didn't realize there'd be a damn window between us, so we couldn't even touch fingers at the very least. I almost broke down in tears. I haven't touched him since he kissed me good-bye right before he left to go pick up Eric and go out Friday night. That nearly killed me. How inhumane is that? You can't touch your own husband who's locked up and you don't know when he's getting out? That's just WRONG. Period.

But, oh, my God . . . his FACE. The bandage that was on his left cheek was off, and I almost screamed in horror when I saw what was under it! Weston told me Royce cut his face open with a piece of glass off the floor when they were fighting. It looked atrocious! That dirty bastard! He ruined my husband's beautiful, perfect face! I know for a fact it's never gonna heal right. There's just no way. He's gonna be scarred for life—unless he has some type of corrective surgery. Oh, God . . . I just realized something . . . now both me and *Weston are physically scarred for life because of a fucked-up interaction with Royce. How ironic that is. I wish I'd never met him in high school. He's turned out to be one of the worst people I've ever known, for various reasons. He told me about the rest of the fight as well; but I couldn't bring myself to ask him what the hell Royce said to him about me sucking his dick. I'm positive that remark took place during their fight, but I didn't wanna get into that again. Weston still looks really bad. His ribs are still messed up; his eye, even though it's open now, is still puffy and discolored; his arms are still all scratched up; his lips are still kinda swollen; and he's limping. It was hard for me to look at him while we talked, because I just kept staring at all his wounds.*

He was glad to hear the kids were doing a little better about him being gone. I squeezed in as many stories as I could about them in the little funky-ass thirty minutes we had; and he smiled the whole time, which made me feel good. He loves his kids to death. That half hour went way too fast, though; I can't wait until I can get back there again.

I finally talked to P.J. and filled him in on everything. I miss my brother. I wish he was here. Florida is just too damn far away for him to be living. I mean, I'm glad he and Lateshia are doing well, but, damn . . . it's times like these when I need my big brother here to guide me and help keep my head together and make me laugh like he always does. It's just not the same on the phone. Of course, he said he completely understood where Weston was coming from, and said he probably would've done the same thing if he were in Weston's shoes. It figures. Men always band together when it comes to that. I'll never understand their way of thinking on that subject.

I was only able to talk to Joan-Renee for about fifteen minutes a few days ago. At least, I got to tell her the necessities. She was so sad for me. Damn, I miss my girl.

I talked to Tiki and Charles on the speakerphone at their house the other night for, like, four hours. They were floored about the Weston-Royce thing. Charles said he hoped Royce's dog ass never woke up; then he realized what that meant for Weston and said he was sorry and that he didn't mean that. He's just still so mad at Royce. I guess I don't blame Charles. And he can hold him a SERIOUS, SERIOUS *grudge! He's relentless when it comes to not forgiving people. I'm glad he loves my black ass! Ha ha ha! God, I miss them. Tiki's shop is doing well. She has a bunch of clients, and she's happy. Charles's new House Burgers is, of course, pulling in hellafied bank. I'm glad he let Rishidda and Robert take over this one out here and not close it down, because I don't know what I'd do without my Big Bang Beefer Cheeseburger at least once a week. As a matter of fact, I need to stop over there after I leave work tomorrow. I'm way overdue.*

Me and the girls also finally got a chance to catch up on stories, which I needed, because I've been so on edge this past week that I needed to relax with my crew for a while. I'm so proud of my girl Chantelle! Man, I needed to hear that good news! I knew she'd make her mark in the art world eventually, and now she's about to have her fifteen minutes of fame . . . which will hopefully be more like fifteen years. I can't wait to see her in action in February. I hope Weston's out of jail by then. And Rishidda! Hot damn! She's finally coming out of her shell after all these years! It's about time; I've been worried about her. I mean, she's doing fine as far as Cash being dead, but she never gives any guy the time of day, and that's just not normal. We've been trying to get her to date for years, and she just keeps avoiding it. I can't wait to see what this dude looks like, because he has to get the seal of approval from the rest of the crew before he can officially be welcomed. Hee hee! And Genine. Her time is gonna come, I know it. At least Warren is supportive and not acting like an asshole about it. Sometimes men just don't do well with stuff like what they're going through, and they don't know how to give their woman the support she needs when she's tweaking on what happened. I like him, though. He's a good guy. And he better marry my girl, dammit! I wanna be a bridesmaid at one of my crew's wedding sometime before 2010! Sabrina and that new dude Ty seem to be doing okay. I haven't really spent enough time around him to know if he's right for her yet; but from what I've experienced of him, he's decent. She's sprung, I know that much. She talks about him all the time. It's nice to see my girls happy in relationships for once. I don't really know about Chantelle, though. She's so into her art that she's not really giving serious thought to getting involved on a long-term level with any guy. But she's definitely getting plenty of dick, I know that. I wish she'd slow down a little, though. She's been with, like, four or five different guys sexually this year, and even though she swears she's careful, still . . . shit happens. I just don't want it to happen to her.

After I left my visit with Weston, I went to meet up with the girls. Daddy said he'd keep the twins for me during the day while I took care of my own stuff.

Mama ran off to Vegas with her senior group, so he was going it alone. He said he needed the company, anyway, so he was glad to have the kids with him.

Chantelle asked us to meet at her house because she said she had something to tell us and she didn't wanna have to tell the story more than once, so we just decided to have a girls' day over there. I invited Yolanda, but she and Thomas were taking Lydia to Thomas's mother's house out in Sacramento and would be gone for the day.

We all gathered in Chantelle's cozy living room on her fluffy carpet, which I love. That girl really came up over the years. Her crib is fly, and, of course, her artwork covers the walls. She's so damn bad! Rishidda brought the four bottles of Alizé Gold Passion, and Sabrina brought the Chinese food from Yang Chow.

After we all got settled in with our food and wine, I said, "Okay, look, you guys . . . we can't be talkin' about anything sad, bad, or upsetting. You know I got enough issues at home, so whatever's said here, we need to be able to cheer about it. Agreed?"

Sabrina said, "Well, then, I guess we won't be asking you how things are going with your husband's situation, huh?"

I smiled. "You are astute, my dear. Five times no. I wanna hear what's goin' on with *you* guys. We haven't talked in weeks. What the hell have I missed? I'ma sit here and drink and stuff my face while you guys gimme some dirt . . . some good dirt. Y'all heffas betta make my day. So who's kickin' it off?"

Chantelle said, "*Welllll* . . . I might as well since I told y'all I had somethin' to dish about."

With a mouthful of scallop chow mein, I said, "Fine, get to it."

"Okayokayokay . . . y'all ready?"

Genine said, "Girl, if you don't come on!"

Chantelle hopped up off the floor and started dancing around like a maniac; then she screamed at the top of her lungs, "I finally got picked up by a gallery to do my first exhibit!"

I nearly spit my food out.

Sabrina shouted, "Aw, *hell* yeah! She did the damn *thang*!"

Once I swallowed the remnants of noodles that were left in my throat, I jumped up and attacked her with a hug, screaming, "My girl, my *girl*! You a bad bitch, I hope you *know* dat! I *knew* it was comin'!"

Genine shouted, "It's about time! Congrats, girl!"

And Rishidda said, "For real! Girl, how many years you been tryina make this happen, now?"

Chantelle said, "Girl, like, ten!"

I sat back down and said, "You ain't lyin', 'cause I remember back in the day when you used to cry about how you wanted to get into a gallery and show the world what'choo could do. You remember that night when I was tellin' you about my first date with Weston, and you gave us the whole scenario about your fabulous artist life wit'cha big house in the Oakland hills and ya fine-ass man?"

"Do I remember? Girl, I can almost recite what I said, word for word!"

"I heard that, girl!" Genine chimed in.

Rishidda said, "Okay, so come on . . . sit'cha bad ass down and spill the deets! Who, what, when, where?"

She plopped down all wild on the floor again and cheesed like a lottery winner as she told us her story.

"Okay, so you remember I told you I had my eye on this one gallery that I had seen on the Internet . . . the one in San Francisco . . . the Mystic Law Art Gallery?"

We all nodded.

"Okay, well, one night about a month ago when I went out with one'uh my many men . . . I think it was J.B. that night . . . he took me to this place in S.F. for dinner, and it was across the street from the gallery. It was still early, so after dinner I told him I just *had* to take my ass over there and see what was up. So we go, it's fly—the art is on hit. So then I went to talk to the curator. His name is James Moore. Oh, you guys, he is so damn nice. We started talkin' and he was tellin' me that he's a Buddhist . . . he does that Nam-myoho-renge-kyo thing—"

Sabrina interjected, "That *what*?"

Rishidda sat straight up and shouted, "Girl, you betta shut up! So does Dianne!"

I asked, "Dianne . . . your therapist?"

"Yes, girl! She told me about that stuff when I was seein' her. I even went to a coupla meetings with her a few years ago. It's interesting."

Sabrina asked, annoyed, "What are y'all talkin' about?"

Genine jumped in, saying, "That thing Tina Turner does . . . you remember . . . in *What's Love Got to Do with It*? The girl from the group came to her house and showed her how to chant, and then after she started doin' it, she got all strong in the mind and started whoopin' Ike's ass up in the limo! That was classic!"

Sabrina said, "Ohhhh, I know what'choo talkin' about. Yeah. That was funny as hell!"

Rishidda said, "I wonder if they know each other. I'ma hafta call her and ask."

We all shrugged, and Chantelle went on.

"I don't know . . . but, anyway, y'all . . . we talked for a long time, and I told him how long I been doin' my thang and that I was tryina find a gallery that would take me on so I could do my first show. So he asked if I had any samples of my work, and, of course, I didn't, since I wasn't in my car—'cause y'all know I keep a portfolio in the ride. But you know a sista is always prepared in some kinda way, and I had a picture of one'uh my favorite pieces in my wallet so I pulled it out and showed it to him, and he liked what he saw. Then he asked me if I wanted to come back that next week and bring some actual pieces so he could get a closer look at my work. So we set up an appointment for that next Wednesday, and I went in there with about seven of my best pieces, plus my portfolio with everything in it—all hundred and fifty pictures—and blew his mind wit' my talents, y'all! He was so impressed that he said he would take a few and see how they sold, and if they did, he'd see about gettin' my ass in there for a show sometime after the New Year! Woo, lemme git me a swig right quick—"

She grabbed an Alizé bottle and took it to the head, and we all burst out laughing. Then she continued. "Okay, so then"—she smacked her lips—"he calls me up about ten days later and says that the three pictures he took were gone, okay? Sold like slaves! And I fell out my chair, y'all!"

Rishidda cracked up. "Girl, you ain't got nare bitta sense! You's about a silly ho!"

Chantelle said, "I might be a silly ho, but I's 'bout ta be a rich ho, ya heard meh?"

Genine said, "I know I did! Okay, so finish, finish . . ."

"So, okay . . . he says they sold, people was all up in his grill about who I was, where could they find more of my work, woop woop, yamp yamp. Then he says he's gon' see about havin' me do a small exhibit in, like, early February of next year that's gonna run until the end of March—I get to be the featured artist! So I almost kiss this dude, okay?"

I asked, "So, wait . . . what's a small show?"

"He said like twenty pieces. I'ma come wit' some new work, though. Fresh out the basement."

Sabrina said, "That's a lot, girl."

"No, compared to those people who have, like, twice that amount on display, it's small. But you think I give a damn? I'm just glad to be puttin' my art in a real live gallery and havin' the public have a chance to view and buy it. You know I made bank sellin' on eBay and all that, which is cool, but this is the real deal, y'all!"

Rishidda told her, "Okay, so get back to the details . . . when? What time?"

"Okay, so he said we're lookin' at early February. He thinks the opening reception might be the ninth, from six to ten P.M. He's gon' call me to confirm that, though. But this is about to happen for real and for true! I'm 'bout ta git everything I ever wanted in my career!"

As I raised my glass of wine, I said, "And on that note, all y'all put'cha glasses in the *urr*, as Chingy would say, and let's git this toast on!"

Sabrina said, "But 'Telle can just raise the whole bottle on this one."

Chantelle said, "I know that's right. I sho' am 'bout to!"

She grabbed a bottle and the rest of us put our glasses up, and I said, "Okay . . . to our girl's big break . . . to her success . . . to her prosperous future in the art world . . . *and* to her kickin' me down some'uh them ends when times get hard."

She smiled and said, "And ya know I will, girl."

They all laughed; then we said, "To our girl." We clicked glasses and downed our drinks.

After we put our glasses down, Rishidda said, "Okay . . . my turn."

We all looked at her in surprise.

"What'choo lookin' at me like that for? Y'all act like y'all the only ones that can have good news. I got a little somethin' tasty fo' ya!"

Chantelle said, "Well . . . come on wit' it, then."

"Well . . . ya girl had her a li'l datey-date last night."

Genine hollered, "*Woooo,* tell it, girl! Gone then!"

Sabrina smiled, threw her left hand in the air, then shouted, "Praise *be* got-dammit! Sheeda 'bout ta git hers! More dick stories added to the pot!"

We all fell out laughing; then I said, "Okay, then, sista-girl. Give it up, give it up . . . who, what, when, where?"

She smiled deviously. "It was Keith Grayson, the counselor at Cash's school."

We all screamed in pitches loud enough to break fifty windows.

As I pushed her over, I said, "*You slick-ass bitch!* You been tippin' and dippin' and ain't said a damn thang! You know you wrong!"

She was all smiles. "Wait a minute, boo. I had to make sure it was right before I came wit' all the vitals."

Chantelle told her, "Well, you need to quit stallin' and say wassup, 'cause now you dun started it up in here!"

"Well, I told you Cash has been actin' up lately, and I been havin' to go up there to the school and talk to his counselor about his work habits and his attitude in class. So this last time, about a week ago when I went up there, Keith was comin' outta his office— it's like three doors down from Mr. Dunbar's office— that's Cash's counselor—"

Sabrina interrupted, "Yeah, yeah . . . forget all them insignifs. Git to the askin'-out part."

"Shut up, girl . . . lemme tell my story. So he's comin' out. He sees me. He stops, lookin' at'cha girl like she got *everything* he needs and wants. He lookin' kinda right his *damn* self. He says hi and asks me how I'm doin'. Tells me I'm lookin' *real* nice, and we get to talkin' a little bit. I wasn't in no rush, and . . . I was feelin' ready, y'all."

Genine said, "And it's about that time, too."

Sabrina said, "Okay? Say dat fuh real!"

Rishidda continued speaking. "So, anyway, he invites me to come into his office and sit down for a few so we can talk, and I went my ass the hell on in!"

I said, "As you should!" Then I took in another mouthful of chow mein.

We all laughed; then she went on. "So I go in, sit on down, and we talk for about an *hour,* y'all. Wait—hol' up—*wit'* the door closed—y'all ain't hearin' me, though!"

Chantelle shouted, "Woooo, yes indeed, yes in*deed*! Teddy Pendergrass dun already tol' yo' ass ta close it in the first place!"

More howling and laughter.

Rishidda said, "Right—riiight. So he tells me he's been tryina get me alone so he can see about me for a *minute.* Said he wants to talk to me, take me out, and get to *know* me. But'choo know before I can let that happen, I gotta find out the 411 on his ass, 'cause Rishidda Denise Hamilton can't let'choo see about *her* till she sees about'*choo* first."

I cosigned with "All right, now! That's how you work it, girl!"

She pointed at me. "Please buh'lieve!"

Genine asked, "Okay . . . so what'choo find out?"

"Okay, he's forty-three. He has two daughters by his ex-wife—they live in Houston with her. He been counselin' for ten years. He got a house in Berkeley. He just bought a 2008 Cadillac Escalade—"

Sabrina screamed, *"Holla!"*

"And he likes to go to jazz concerts and shoot pool and—oh! He likes to *cook*! Said he wants to open a little restaurant one day!"

I pounded my right fist on the floor and shouted, "Holla three times on that! Gone git'cha man, girl!"

"*And* he gives to charity! His mother died of cancer, like, nine years ago, and he said he gives two hundred dollars a month to the American

Cancer Society, no matter what. Said he's never missed a month since his mother died."

Chantelle told her, "Girl, if you don't git'choo summa dat, I'ma take *my* ass up to the school and show him what's good!"

Rishidda said, "Can't let'cha do dat, baby. 'Cause after we talked, I gave him my card and told him he could gimme a call later and we could see about that date. Girl, *whyyyy when I got home,* not five minutes after I walk in the door, his ass calls me talkin' 'bout he don't wanna wait till later. He wanna talk about a date *now*! So we end up talkin' for another *three hours,* okay? And after that, wasn't nothin' else to say about it. We had made plans to go out last night, and lemme *tell* you—that man knows how to treat a woman! First he took me to Kincaid's in Jack London and we got our seafood on. Then after that, we headed on over to Yoshi's to the jazz club, and, ladies . . . ya boy treated me like I was a queen sittin' up on the throne. Just lavished me all night with whatever the hell I needed and wanted. Told me I was beautiful, intelligent, and he was lucky to be out with *me*! Did y'all hear what I said?"

Genine said, "Ain't missed a syllable, girl! But git to the after part. I wanna know . . . did he git a little taste of what'choo got?"

"Wait, now—you aheada thangs. I ain't done yet. After we left Yoshi's—and y'all not gon' believe this, 'cause I *still* don't—we stop at the store and his ass goes in and buys a bottle of wine—don't even ask me what kind, 'cause I was so sprung by that time, I didn't give a damn *what* kinda alcohol he bought.

It coulda been some rubbin' alcohol, for all I gave a hell!"

We screamed at that one.

"So then we drive, right? And I'm like, 'Boy, where you takin' me?' and he just tells me to sit back and relax . . . enjoy the ride. So we talk and laugh, and the next thing I know, we headed up into the hills in Berkeley. About two minutes later, why do we pull up to the Berkeley Rose Garden?"

Sabrina jumped up and ran around the room, waving her hands in the air like she had just caught the Holy Ghost. "Stop, stop, stop—stop! You killin' me, girl! Not the Rose Garden! Say it ain't so!"

"Oh, girl, it was *very* so! We get up there and it's all warm outside, and I had never been up there before, so I didn't know *what* to expect. Well, then he pulls out a blanket from the back of his Escalade, grabs the wine, two little plastic wine cups, *and* my hand, and he takes me to this little spot to sit down. Then he pops open the wine, and we sit and he wraps the blanket around us both, and we talk and drink wine for two hours! Oh, Lawd! It was like outta one'uh them romance novels! I got so damn comfy that I ended up tellin' him all about Cash and how he died, y'all . . . and you know how I feel about rehashin' that part of my life. I couldn't believe I went that far. I prob'ly was halfway drunk, though, 'cause I had a few drinks at Yoshi's, and then we were drinkin' wine, so you know. But, anyway, I'm talkin' and tellin' him all about it, and he was just all up into every little thing I was sayin', okay? So then he tells me how attractive it is that I was so strong for my kids, and that he admired me for pullin' myself through that whole ordeal and still comin' out such a positive woman. I coulda did his ass right there on the spot for that!"

I said, "Girl, you hit pay dirt wit' this dude, I can feel it!"

"I think so, too, girl, 'cause wait—after we leave there, he asks me if I'm ready to go home yet, and you *know* I wasn't. So I tell him no, and then he says he only lives, like, five minutes away and asks me if I wanna come back to his place and talk a little more. Well, hell, I was high, feelin' good, and he was workin' it so damn right that I just went on and I told him yeah. So we go back to his crib—which is tight, by the way—and we sit in fronta his fireplace and talk some more, and next thing I know, it's one-thirty in the morning. You know I never leave my kids home for that long by themselves, so I got kinda nervous— even though Cash's ass is sixteen . . . but you know what? I just wasn't ready to go. So you know what ended up happenin'?"

Sabrina shouted, "You broke him off! Hell yeah! I knew it!"

"No, boo . . . come back, come back. I called Cash and told him I would be later than I expected, and he was like, 'That's cool, Mama. You need to have you some fun. We a'ight. Do what'choo do.' So that's exactly what I did. I laid up on Keith's floor with him, by his fireplace, and we talked till we fell asleep. And that's where our asses stayed until he woke me up at seven-fifteen this mornin', talkin' 'bout 'What'choo want for breakfast?'"

Genine said, "You know what? I can't do this no more. You off the chains wit' it now! *Breakfast?*"

"Honey, that man went up in that kitchen and threw down like ya boy Emeril and made some kinda fancy-ass omelet with cheese and spinach and onions and mushrooms. And then he made some home fries and some fresh-squeezed orange juice, and we sat down at his kitchen table and ate us a hearty-ass meal, okay? Girl, my clothes was wrinkled, my breath was hummin', my hair was lookin' like Don King, but he didn't give a hot damn. After we ate, I told him I needed to get home to my kids, 'cause I had never left them alone overnight, and do you know he got right on up and gladly took my ass home—all respectful?"

I said, "Okay . . . now please tell me . . ."

"Yes, honey. After I thanked him and told him how much I appreciated everything he did for me, and what a good time I had, I laid summa this sweet tongue on his fine ass so good, he damn near passed out!"

Everyone jumped up and hollered, and Rishidda just smiled like she was the happiest woman in the land.

Then I said, "So your *hot* ass just got home not too many damn hours ago!"

"That's right, baby. And I *will* be seein' him again tonight, so part two of the story *will* be served up at the next rap session."

Sabrina bellowed, "Well, hallelujah and *amen* up in this bitch! My girl dun went and caught the biggest, baddest fish out there!"

She said, "I hope so, ladies. I'll let'cha know. Now, who's gon' top my story today?"

Sabrina told us, "Well, all I got to say is I'm gettin'

banged right and treated well. That's all I care about right now. Me and Ty are cool, and until further notice, that's where I'ma be spendin' my free weekends."

And Genine said, "Well, I'm doin' better with the whole baby ordeal, and Warren is takin' good care'uh me. He asked me last week, all outta the blue, if I still loved him. I looked at his ass like he was outta his mind. Then I asked him why, and he said because ever since I lost the baby, I been kinda distant and actin' like I don't want him to touch me. I told him it didn't have nothin' to do with how I feel about him—I'm just still goin' through it. I didn't even know he was trippin' until he asked me that. Then he told me that's why he quit talkin' about gettin' married— 'cause he thought I didn't want to anymore. I told him I thought *he* didn't want to anymore and that's why he quit talkin' about it. So then we talked for a long time and started gettin' our bond back—and then . . . well, you know what happened after that."

Chantelle quipped, "She put it on him till his head spun off, that's what!"

We laughed; then Genine responded, "Girl, just about! We ain't so much as rubbed up against each other in over a month. I started thinkin' our bond was on the way down the tubes. But we needed that, though. It's like that's what's been missin' lately. . . . We ain't had that physical closeness. So once we worked out that kink, we got back to our regular way. Thank God, 'cause I'm damn sho' not tryina start all over wit' somebody new—not at this stage in the game."

Rishidda announced, "Girl, but I *am*! And I'm feelin' good about Keith. But I'ma take it slow, though. When it's time for me to put it down, you know I'll fill ya in."

I told her, "Well, you know what, Miss Hamilton? You deserve *everything* good that man is about to give you. It's been eleven years. It's time for you to get yours and run with it. I'm happy for you, girl. The universe owes your ass somethin' great. I'll never forget how you helped me through that Weston ordeal that day. I meant what I said, too. . . . You *seriously* saved me. No lie."

She smiled at me. "Thanks, Trice. And you know what? You and that husband of yours . . . y'all gon' make it through this little storm. He'll be home soon. Watch. Somethin's gon' happen to where he'll be home sooner than you think. Y'all got too many people prayin' for you—somethin' good *has* to happen. You just gotta believe that, honey."

"I'll try. I'm just glad I got my girls to keep me sane, or else I don't know what I'd be doin' right now."

Genine said, "Well, you know we here for you. Whatever you need. Ya girls always got'cha back. Fo' *liiiife*."

"I know you do. And I love all y'all for it."

Rishidda said, "Right back at'cha, girl."

19

WESTON

Even though I already knew it was a possibility, when it became a reality, things were totally different. You know how people always say they see their lives flashing before their eyes when something life-threatening is happening to them? Well, I always thought they were just spouting off dramatics, but you know what? That's exactly what happened to me at the arraignment when the judge bypassed the battery charges and blasted my bubble of hope to smithereens by telling me that I was officially being charged with attempted murder. His words rang in my head even louder than Royce's dick-sucking comment. I started breathing all heavy, my knees got weak and felt like they were about to buckle, my heartbeat turned choppy, my stomach sank through the floor, and I thought I was about to hurl. My hands shook like I was having convulsions, my forehead started sweating, my eyes started tearing up, and then all I saw was my whole life going down the drain. I saw myself as a kid, smiling and playing with my brothers and sisters. I saw myself hugging and laughing with my parents. I saw myself looking at Katrice the day I met her in the shop, and remembered how I knew I was gonna snag her. I saw the look on her face when I asked her to marry me. I saw Lydia and my twins being born. I saw all their little innocent, smiling faces flashing through my head, over and over, as I played with them. I saw my parents collapsing in devastation behind the news. I saw Yolanda, Thomas, and the rest of my boys looking distraught, and I imagined Katrice's destroyed face and reaction when I had to tell her about it. Then, right after that, I had visions of me being convicted, then getting carted off to San Quentin forever, and then getting a Dear John letter from Katrice, saying she couldn't stay married to a criminal with a life sentence, and that she wanted a divorce so she and the kids could move on with their lives. All that ran through my head in the span of about thirty seconds, but it seemed like an entire movie was playing during the thought process.

But that wasn't all. The judge wouldn't let me out on bail because Royce was still in the vicinity, and since I was in such a violent rage the night of the fight, I guess the judge thought I might do something stupid like try to dust Royce's ass off while he was in the hospital. Like I would really be that dumb. I couldn't believe that. In my worst days in life, I never thought I would be standing up in a courtroom, being told that I was half a breath away from going to prison for life for trying to kill a man. Yet there I was. In living color. Black as the day is long.

Beat down physically and ruined mentally. Possibly on my way to a life that I knew I wouldn't be able to continue to live if I had to be separated from my family forever.

I waited as long as I could to tell Katrice the news that day. Matter of fact, I waited until the last minute at phone time because I didn't wanna have a long conversation with her about it. I knew if I called with only a few minutes to spare, I would have no choice but to get off the phone—and that's the way I needed that call to go down. Just like I thought, she was an emotional wreck, and it hurt my heart so bad to hear her crying like that. I had to actually pretend I needed to hang up faster than I really did. For once, nobody was waiting for the phone, but I lied and said there was a line because I couldn't take listening to her sob. Plus, I didn't wanna break down and cry, too. So I rushed up off the phone and told her I'd call her the next day. I hated to do that to her, but the situation was just too messed up for me to deal with. I spent the rest of the night laying awake, staring at the blank walls like a zombie, wishing I had never even called my boys and said I wanted to go out that night. I woulda never encountered Royce then, and I would be living my life as a free man, like I was supposed to be doing.

On Saturday, Katrice came to visit me, and I thought the worst part about being locked up would be not seeing her, but I was wrong. The thing that hurt the most—next to not seeing my kids—was sitting right in front of Katrice, face-to-face, and not being able to touch her. That visit we had was torture. I almost didn't want her to come see me anymore after that. They had that joke of a window slapped up between us with some goddamn air holes in it so we could hear each other, and that was it. The same window was there when Steve came to see me on Tuesday, but that was different. I didn't wanna touch Steve.

Katrice looked so beautiful, I almost couldn't stand it. She did something to her hair, as usual. She pulled it back in some kinda French bun—not a regular one, 'cause she hates those—and it was clipped real tight—not a hair outta place—and her features were real defined because of that. I could see every part of her perfect face, not like when she wears her hair down. I loved it. When she pulls her hair back, her eyes seem even bigger, her cheekbones stand out, and her lips look even more succulent. And I couldn't touch one single part of her. I don't know why they torment people like that. It's bad enough your ass is locked away from everything you love, but to have your woman sitting three inches away from you and then be forced to have to deal with the fact that you can't get your touch on, that's some bullshit. Then they wonder why folks go crazy in the pen. Bastards.

I didn't want her to see that gash on my face from Royce's slasher-film move, but I had to take the bandage off so the wound could air out. It was all damp and slimy feeling, and I didn't want it to get infected. People were already looking at me like I was some kinda kin to Scarface, so I knew what it would do to her when she saw it. Sure enough, she looked all horrified and distraught, and I thought she was about to bust out crying. I went on and told her what happened right quick so we could get that out the way and move on to another subject. We only had thirty measly minutes, and I damn sure wasn't trying to spend it all talking about Royce. I wanted to hear about my kids. That was hard because I felt left out when she was telling me all the funny stories about what they did and said during the week.

I had a dream the night before that woke me smooth up outta my sleep in a sweaty panic. I dreamed I came home from work and Royce's bitch ass was posted up in the living room in my recliner, watching TV, drinking my beers, and eating my tortilla chips, all comfortable and relaxed like he was paying bills around my shit. I asked him what the fuck he was doing in my house, and it was like he couldn't hear me—like I didn't exist or something. He didn't even look my way. Then Katrice walked right past me and went and kissed him on the mouth, all passionate, tongue and all; then she sat in his lap like she does me, and started caressing his face and rubbing his bald head like she was all in love with his ass. They started talking, but I couldn't hear a word they were saying. I was about to start going off on both of 'em, but then Katrice got up and walked away, and the twins came over and jumped in the chair with him, hollering, "Daddy, Daddy, we love you!" I couldn't take that shit, so I blew my fuckin' top. I walked over and snatched my kids outta the chair, and they started screaming and crying and struggling and acting like I was a kidnapper. That hurt my feelings. Willie kicked me, and then Ellie bit my arm and started howling for Katrice to help her. Katrice came rushing up to me and started slapping and punching me and hollering, "Take your filthy hands off my babies! Get outta here! Leave my family alone! How did you get in here? I'm calling the police!" I didn't understand what the hell was going on, so I just stood there with my mouth

wide open, trying to figure out what she was talking
about. Royce got up and walked all up on me like he
was ready to get it cracking, and all of a sudden I
pulled out a twelve-gauge shotgun and blasted his
brains all over the living room—right in front of the
kids and Katrice. They all started screaming and
crying, and then the twins started yelling, "You killed
our daddy! We hate you! Leave us alone!" Then Katrice fell to her knees and threw herself over Royce's
body and started shrieking about how I killed the love
of her life, and she hated me and would never forgive
me. About five seconds later, four cops came busting
in the door and started beating me with batons until
I fell to the floor unconscious. As soon as my body hit
the floor, that's when I woke up, spooked outta my
mind, and I never went back to sleep after that. I just
laid awake and stared at the ceiling all panicked,
scared that I was never gonna get out of jail and be
back with my family again.

Yolanda came by later that day, too. Her hours at
Whole Foods were all over the place, but she told me
she'd get by to see me as much as she could. She said
Lydia was doing okay with the whole "business trip"
excuse, but a couple of times, she whined because she
didn't understand why I couldn't call her at eight
every night. One time she asked if Yolanda could
drop her off with me so she could spend the night.
Lydia promised she wouldn't get in the way and I
could still do my business, but that she wanted to see
me. She's used to seeing me at least once during the
workweek, because I pick her up from school on
Tuesdays—and we still talk at eight just so we can say

good night—and then she sees me again at some point on the weekend. Yolanda said she told her it was a grown-up business trip and kids couldn't be there. Lydia didn't like that, and she had an attitude for the rest of the night. That bothered me because I didn't want her to start thinking I was gonna be throw-ing our father-daughter plans off on the regular.

I also started tripping off Pop again, with him having HIV and all. It was still running through my head, and I kept thinking about what if I never got out of jail, and my pops died and I didn't get to spend time with him. I don't cry that often, but when I thought about everything I had to deal with, my frus-tration and anger brought me to tears for a few min-utes. I was glad Basehead was still 'sleep, because it was bad enough I had to drop my loads in front of him; I didn't need him to see my ass crying like a bitch.

All my prayers were going toward whatever Steve's lawyer could do for me to help get me outta the jam I had got myself in. When Steve came to see me, I told him what really happened at the club and explained who Royce was, with the exception of the fact that Ka-trice had cheated on me. He told me not to worry, and that Lincoln could work it out because he was known for getting people out of tight situations. He worked a major twist and kept Steve out of prison. He was up on some serious charges, too—he was facing involuntary manslaughter. It's a good thing we had the relationship we did before I got in trouble, and he knew I didn't get involved in illegal deals, because I needed someone on my side that could vouch for me. I had some problems when I was a kid—I beat down quite a few dudes in my day—but as an adult, I learned how to tame my temper so I wouldn't be knocking people around every week. I can get outta control every now and then. I know that about myself, so I knew in order to stay outta the prison system, I would need to work on that. I trust Steve, too. We talk a lot, and he tells me things he probably shouldn't even be telling me.

I met him way back in the day when I first started working at 24-Hour Fitness. He was the one who interviewed me. At the time, he was only an assistant manager, but he told me he was working his way up to the top, and he finally got there. I knew after the first ten minutes, me and him were gonna hit it off. He was the coolest white dude I had ever met. I knew I was qualified for the job, but I already knew he was gonna hire me just based on our connection. We used to hang out a lot in the beginning; then after his wife had a few kids, that changed. But we still went out and got our drink on every now and then, and they even had me over for dinner a few times before I met Katrice. They couldn't make it to our wedding, but when we got back from Chicago, they threw us a big dinner party, and Steve hooked us up with a free three-night stay at the Bellagio Hotel in Vegas. Somebody he knew worked there and always gave him and his wife freebies. It sure is good to know people with clout, I can tell you that.

Now that I had what seemed like a good lawyer, I prayed he could do for me what he did for Steve. I prayed on it like my ass was sitting up on death row waiting to be executed and was trying to get a stay.

20

KATRICE

November 8, 2007, 10:36 P.M.

Today was a bad day. Very bad. That's all I got to say about it. I'm too tired to say anything else. But what I will say is that I can't wait till this is over with, because what happened here tonight can't keep happening. It's too much to deal with. Thank God I have a solid support system, or I would surely slit my wrists . . . or at least maim myself in some way.

The stress of Weston's absence was taking its toll on me for sure, but it was even harder on the kids. Things got out of control when I completely flipped my lid on Willie, and the next thing I knew, the whole household was in an uproar.

I was in the kitchen with Willie, cutting his chicken

breast into little bits so he could eat his dinner. Ellie had already finished hers and gone into the living room to watch television. It had gotten to the point where I had to start separating them at dinnertime because they spent more time talking, playing, and giggling than they did eating. So I started having Ellie eat twenty to thirty minutes before Willie, which they didn't like, but I didn't care. Too many nights had gone by where the food on their plates got cold, and then they complained about not wanting it anymore. Goodness knows we don't have money to throw away on perfectly good food, so I had to devise a plan to move away from that problem. Weston said I was cutting into their bonding time; I told him they have plenty of time to bond before and after dinner, and cutting into that thirty minutes wasn't gonna hurt them one bit.

Anyway, Willie was already restless and tired, and I was frustrated about the whole Weston thing, as usual, so both of us were on edge. I set his plate in front of him with the meat cut up, nice and small, and then turned to leave the kitchen. All of a sudden, I heard Willie moan, "*Nnnoooo, Mommy.* It's not right."

I turned and looked at him, confused. "What's not right?"

"The meat. You didn't cut it right."

"What do you mean I didn't cut it right? You like it small. It's small. So what's the problem?"

"You didn't cut it like Daddy. Daddy cuts the meat in shapes. Like squares and stuff. These don't look like that."

I had forgotten all about that. Weston has this thing where he sometimes cuts the kids' meat into fun shapes and then sets them up on the plate in shape order. I had done it a couple of times when Weston didn't get home until after the kids ate, but I didn't do it quite as good as he did. At the moment, I wasn't in the mood to try to do his work any type of justice.

"Okay, well, there's not gonna be any shapes tonight. Just eat it like that. It's fine."

He whined, "*Noooo.* You hafta cut it like Daddy does, Mommy."

I hate it when he whines. It works my nerves to the core.

"It doesn't really matter what shape the meat is in. As long as it's small, it's fine. Besides, it's not on your plate for you to have fun with. You're supposed to be eating it, Willie. And quit that whining. You know I don't play that."

He kicked his feet on the legs of his chair, tantrum-like, and whined even louder, "It does too matter! I don't like it cut regular! I want you to cut it like Daddy does, or I'm not eating it!"

"Whoa . . . *excuse me,* mister. Who you talkin' to up in here like that?"

Do you know my child actually had the audacity to say, and with much authority, "You, Mommy! Cut it like Daddy does!"

"Boy, have you lost your *mind*? You don't talk to me like that, *ever*! You hear me? Don't'choo *ever* fix your lips to speak to me that way again!"

And then, acting just like his father, he hopped his happy ass out of his chair, turned toward the kitchen door, and had the nerve to start stomping away from me. But I shut his little ass down real fast.

"Willie! Stop, turn around, and look at me! *Right . . . now!*"

He stopped cold in his tracks, but he didn't turn around. Such a Weston move.

"Little boy, you got *two seconds* to turn yourself around or it is *on!*"

Finally he turned slowly, and when he faced me, all I saw was demonic rage in his young eyes. He looked *exactly* like Weston, so much so that it made me wanna burst into tears. I missed him like a madwoman, but at the moment, I couldn't give in to those emotions. My son was in the throes of disrespect, and I most definitely couldn't have that.

"Now you *get* back over here and eat your dinner— the way it's presented to you! I cut the meat the way I cut the *damn* meat! Period! When your daddy comes home, you can have him cut your meat to your heart's content, but right now, this is the way it is!"

He just stood there, rocking back and forth on his heels the way he always does when he's trying to figure out how to get himself out of trouble. The demonic rage in his eyes changed to one of challenge— the same look I get from Weston when he doesn't wanna be wrong but knows I'm right. It infuriated me that my son was taking things to that level, and I simply lost my composure.

"William Weston Porter, I am *not* playin' with you! You're actin' *real* stank right now, and I'm not havin' it! Move your ass right this second and get it back to this table, or I will whoop it in ways you'll *never* forget!"

The shock of my stabbing tone scared him to tears and jolted him into motion. He ran back to the table, howling at the top of his lungs; then he scrambled into the chair and screamed out in anguish, *"I want Daddyyyyy!"*

I slammed my hand down on the table so hard that it shook like we were having an earthquake; then some of the peas on his plate popped up like popcorn, jumped onto the table, and rolled onto the floor.

I screeched in his little petrified face, "Well, you know what? I want Daddy, too! But Daddy is *not here*! He's not here! It's just the three of us, kiddo—so you *better* find a way to deal with it!" Then I growled, *"Now eat!"*

He continued to scream like I was beating him senseless as his face turned red and all his little neck veins nearly popped open. I was too pissed to attend to him anymore. I turned to leave him drowning in his tears, and Ellie was standing in the kitchen doorway, holding her favorite doll by its braid, practically dragging it on the floor, with tears streaming down her face.

Before I could ask her what was wrong, she sobbed, "Mommy, why you yellin'? Why you makin' Willie cryyyyyy? Stop yellin' at Willieeeee!"

I can't describe the aching I felt in my heart when I saw my baby so distressed by all the commotion. I dashed and grabbed her up, then held her as close to me as I could.

"I'm sorry. Mommy's sorry. Don't cry, sweetie. Mommy's just upset. Everything's gonna be okay. It's all right."

"No, it's *not*! Daddy's gone, Willie's crying really loud, and you're yelling and hitting the table! It's *not* okaaayyyy!"

Her doll went soaring to the floor and bounced on its plastic head; then she wrapped both her arms around my shoulders and buried her wet face in my neck as she continued to cry her little heart out.

Willie was still bawling and screaming for his daddy.

I knew then that it was time to call for help.

Willie never did eat. After I left him in the kitchen crying, I calmed Ellie down, took her upstairs, put her in her jammies and into bed; all the hoopla wore her out. When I came back downstairs about fifteen minutes later, I noticed it was much too quiet in the kitchen, so I stuck my head in the doorway to see what my meat-traumatized son was doing. He was sound asleep with his head on top of his crossed arms on the table, snoring like Weston. I couldn't bear to wake him up right then; I wanted to take advantage of the quiet in the house. So instead, I let him sleep a little longer while I went to make my call.

"Thomas . . . is Yolanda there?"

"Ay, girl—yeah, she's here. What's wrong wit'choo? Why you soundin' all frustrated?"

"'Cause I am. My damn household is falling apart, and I'm about to start breaking furniture in a minute."

"You and the kids okay? Sound like you need a breather."

"I do. And . . . no, we're not okay—mentally, I mean. I was calling to see if Yolanda could take the kids tomorrow."

"I don't see why not. Hang on, lemme get her."

"Okay, thanks."

A minute later, Yolanda got on the phone.

"Hey, Miss Superwoman. Yo' cape fallin' off?"

"Girl, what cape? That thing *flew* off in the wind the first week Weston was gone. I can't take much more of this."

"What's goin' on?"

"Willie and I got in a . . . a fight."

"A *what*? I *know* you didn't just say you had a fight with a five-year-old."

"Yes, the hell I did. Screaming and shouting and stomping—the whole nine. It was awful."

"Well, where is he? And what happened?"

"He's asleep at the kitchen table, with his head next to his dinner plate full of cold food."

As I filled her in on what happened, she was highly amused by all of my dramatics; but in the end, she got stern on me.

"Katrice, you need to stop this. Seriously. I don't know why you're just now reaching out for help."

In the background, I could hear Lydia saying, "Mommy, lemme talk to Katrice. Is Daddy home yet? Lemme say hi."

Yolanda told her, "No, you can't talk to her right now. We're in the middle of an important conversation."

"Lemme talk to the twins, then. Is Daddy home?"

"Lydia—no, no, and *no*. Now go back upstairs. Stay outta grown folks' business. You can talk to them later. *Out*."

Then I heard Thomas yell, "Lydia! Come clean up these crumbs you left in here! I *told* you about that crap! You not gon' have us wit' ants all through the house like last time!"

Lydia's voice faded away as she said, while heading

in his direction, "*Okaaayyy.* I was just tryina talk to Katrice. I'm comin'."

Yolanda said, "Sorry, girl. Anyway, look— what'choo need me to do? 'Cause this is ridiculous. You shoulda called me long before now. I told you to let me know if things got to be too rough, and now it's past that point. You're screamin' at your son like the Exorcist, damn near breakin' tables, and you're throwin' his peas across the kitchen— not cute, boo."

I burst out laughing at that one. "Girl, you're stupid. Thanks, though. I needed that laugh."

"I know. That's what I'm here for. So what else can I do?"

"Can you just take the kids for the evening to-morrow?"

"That's it? Just for tomorrow?"

"Yeah. I got somethin' I need to do, and I gotta get my head together before I do it."

"Why don't you at least let me take 'em until Sunday night? It's Thursday, girl, have the weekend to yourself. You need it. And besides, Whole Foods finally gave me a few days off. I don't hafta be back at work till Monday."

"You wanna keep 'em for three days? That's too long. I don't want 'em to feel like they're being abandoned. They already think Weston's never coming home."

"Honey, lemme tell you somethin'. If you don't take a break, you're *gonna* abandon them . . . on a freakin' street corner. Your ass is gonna dump their screamin', cryin' behinds off somewhere in the cuts of East Fourteenth Street and skid away like a psycho bitch. So bring me the kids. Go find your Super-

woman cape and sew it back on . . . and get yourself
together. Lydia can see her siblings, and you can . . .
I dunno . . . go watch some porn or somethin'."

"Yeah, right. Not likely. It's no fun to watch without
Weston. There's no . . . you know . . . action afterward."

"Girl, you do *not* need Weston there with you to
engage in afterward action. You better light your
own damn fire."

"Please. I haven't had to light my own fire in so
many years, I don't even think the pilot would work."

"Hmph, you get a big enough dildo and I bet the
flames'll pop out every which-a-way."

We cracked up; then I said, "Thanks, girl. I gotta
go. I need to get Mr. Attitude up from the table and
into bed. I'll bring the kids by after I get them from
school."

"Okeydokey. I'll have the door unlocked for ya."

"Okay, thanks."

"Toodles."

After I hung up, I went back in the kitchen and
stared at Willie for a minute. A feeling of sadness
rushed over me. I wondered how many more nights
like the one we just had were waiting for us in our
future. Then I wished Royce would hurry and wake
his comatose ass up so I could finally find out my
husband's looming fate.

After I dropped the kids off with Yolanda, I did
what I had been thinking about all day, and still
wasn't sure I wanted to do it. I went to see Royce in
the hospital. I had been thinking about doing it

for days on end, and after the whole Willie thing, I decided it was time.

I knew he was still in a coma, but I felt like I needed to see the other party involved in what went on the night Weston ended up in jail. It wasn't a pity visit. I had a specific purpose for going there. I had been doing some reading and research on coma victims and whether or not they could actually hear people talking to them. I had seen many a movie and TV show where victims' friends and loved ones were constantly hovering over them, talking as if they could hear every word being said. So I decided to look a little further into it and see what I could come up with.

It turns out there have been many studies that showed that because coma victims are considered to only be in a very deep sleep, their brains are still functioning—just on the lowest level possible. Hell, their ears still work; their hearts are still pumping; they're alive. Royce may have been in the deepest sleep there was, but since he was still among the land of the living, I thought it was time he heard a few of my words. I did read in several articles on the Internet that you have to be careful what you say to coma victims. Apparently, they're in a very sensitive state, and any negative talk may send them even deeper into darkness. So even though I was pissed at him, I made sure I didn't say anything that might make things worse.

Before I went in his room, I asked if there were any visitors in with him and was told no. Thank goodness, because I figured people from his family would surely be hanging around the hospital. I didn't know any of them, what they looked like, or where they lived, and

I wasn't trying to find out, either. I didn't even know if his dad still lived in Maryland, because Royce never finished telling me what the deal was with them. I wasn't trying to be faced with any of his people asking me questions about who I was or how I knew Royce. Most of all, I didn't want anyone asking me if I knew what had happened.

When I stepped in, I was kind of freaked out. The room felt so eerie and somber. I walked gently to Royce's bedside and just stood there looking at him for several minutes, shocked at his appearance. All the tubes and gadgets that were hooked to him were scary-looking, to say the least; and he looked so gaunt.

After I got through studying him, I figured I better hurry the hell up and get down to business before someone came busting in on me and I had to answer questions. First I just reached out and touched his frail-looking, limp hand. I was almost afraid his eyes were gonna pop open on me when I did, but he didn't move a muscle. I ran my index finger over the top of his hand; then after I was sure he wasn't gonna move, I slipped my whole hand underneath his and held it. Again, this had nothing to do with me caring about him in a romantic way. I was trying to jar him. I wanted him to feel some kind of connection. I hoped he'd feel the warmth of my hand. I hoped somehow he'd know it was me holding on to him. After about thirty seconds, I squeezed gently; I covered his hand with my left hand, while still holding and squeezing with my right. Then I prayed softly, out loud, "God, I know this is all my fault. And I'm sorry. I should've never, ever done what I did. But please wake this man up as soon as possible. Please. He doesn't deserve to die. And I need my husband back at home. Please. I don't know how many times I'm gonna hafta say sorry, but as many times as I need to, I will. I just really need You to bring Royce back, and please find a way for my husband to come home to his family *very, very soon*. Please."

I let my head hang low in silent prayer for a minute or so, and then I stared at Royce's face. Not that I expected it, but there was still no sign of anything coming from him. Then I moved closer. I got right in his ear, like I had seen so many people do with coma victims, and said in a soothing tone, "Royce. This is Katrice. I know you can hear me. You *have* to wake up. You can't stay in this coma. And you *cannot, cannot, cannot* die on me. I need you to wake up. Please hear me. Everything I love is at stake. You *have got* to come back *right now.* I'm sorry about all of this. I really am. None of this was supposed to happen. *Please . . . wake . . . up.* I need you to be okay."

Nothing. Absolutely nothing. Just the beeping of the machines among the silence in the room. Looking at him lying there near death, I realized I meant what I said. He didn't deserve to die. And I did care whether he was okay or not. But that was as far as my feelings for him went. Yes, to be honest, my main concern was him not dying so Weston could avoid being convicted of murder. But I also wanted him to be okay so he could move on with his life, just like I wanted to move on with mine, with my husband and family.

I sat for a few minutes more, still holding his hand, hoping he felt me there, and thinking about the past—coming to terms with everything that had happened because of that one night when I wasn't strong enough to stay true to the man I really, truly loved. Then, after another round of silent prayers for his speedy recovery and Weston's even speedier release from jail, I let go of Royce's hand, and let go of the past. Then I got up and left.

When I got to work on Sunday, I was so upset that I could hardly focus. Weston's legal proceedings were well under way. He told me that Lincoln had some evidence that he felt would work to Weston's advantage, and that Lincoln would fill him in when the time came. Things were about to really get going, and I was scared outta my mind. But the worst part was the judge wouldn't set bail, so there would be no getting Weston out that way.

I was glad I only had a few people coming in, because I didn't think I could handle much more than that. I hadn't been eating much because I was so scared and stressed out, and I was exhausted. And it showed.

While I was setting up, Angela walked over to me, put her hand on my shoulder, and asked, "Katrice? Child, I don't mean ta be all in yo' business . . . but are you okay? I been watchin' you lately, and you jus' seem like you really goin' through it, honey. You and them sweet babies all right at home?"

And that was all she wrote. I broke down in tears right then and there. Scared poor Angela half to death. She grabbed me and hugged me, then sat me down, since I was too hysterical to sit myself down.

After she let me cry for a minute, she finally said, "Well, okay now. Look like it's *my* turn ta help *you*

through a stormy day. What in the *world* is goin'
on, child?"

I know I said I wasn't gonna tell Angela my business, but there was no way I was gonna be able to
maintain with all that I was holding in. So I just said
the hell with it and told her everything. I told her
who Royce was and why he was looking for me,
what our history was, and all the happenings that
had taken place up until that moment. I had to get
to the point fast because the shop was gonna open
in thirty minutes, but I managed to get everything
out that needed releasing.

When I was done, she said, "*Katrice!* Why the hell
didn't'choo say somethin' ta me? You been runnin'
'round here lettin' all this mess tear you apart, and
now you up here havin' a nervous breakdown."

"Well . . . I mean . . . we don't really know each
other that well. I'm a very private person, except with
my closest friends and my family. They're the only
people I really let in. I don't just talk about my issues
with people I don't have a history with. I'm sorry—
no offense—but I just didn't feel close enough
to you."

"Well, I understand. I don't blame you, honey. I
just wish I had known because I woulda done somethin' ta help you out. You been comin' in ta work
every day like ain't nothin' wrong, when you shoulda
been takin' some time off. I coulda helped out wit'
some appointments. You know I live for doin' hair.
You shoulda at least asked me ta help in that way,
child."

"I wanted to several times, but I just couldn't. I
mean, Tiki and I used to do that kind of stuff all the

time, but you're new here. I didn't wanna start trying
to do that with you so early on."

She sighed, then patted me on the knee. "Oh,
child. You need ta learn when ta ask for help. You
can't do everythang by yo'self. Especially wit'
what'choo got on yo' plate. And speakin'uh stuff
on yo' plate . . . what'choo been eatin' lately?"

"What?"

"Child, when's the last time you had a meal? I
mean a *real* meal. You been eatin' a lotta junk lately.
I been watchin' you. McDonald's here, Burger King
there—you don't usually do that. Make me wonder
what them babies'uh yours been eatin'."

"I've been too stressed out and tired to cook meals
lately, so I just make the kids sandwiches and soup
and stuff . . . and sometimes I make them frozen
dinners—then I call it a day. They ate some leftover
chicken and vegetables the other night. Well, Ellie
did. I told you what happened with Willie. For me, I
just eat whatever I eat and say forget it. I don't have
the energy to think about much else."

She paused, looked at me real hard, then said,
"Katrice, I'ma tell you what I want'choo ta do, and
I know you gon' wanna say no, but I really think it'll
be a good idea, if you just give it a chance. Okay?"

"Okay. What?"

"I want you and them babies to pack some stuff
up . . . and come stay with me for a little while. You
need help, honey. You ain't takin' care'uh yo'self,
and you cain't take care'uh them kids right unless
you do that first."

"Oh . . . no, Angela. No—thank you for the offer,
really—but we couldn't do that. It's okay. I'll be
fine. That's—"

She put her hand up to stop me from talking. "Uh-uh, child. Now listen . . . I got plenty'uh room. Honey, I got a cleaner-than-clean four-bedroom home all to myself."

"Why in the world do you have that many rooms?"

"The extra three . . . they fo' my grandbabies . . . just in case my daughter come 'round and start speakin' ta me again and let me see the kids. I just know she will one day, and when she do, I wanna have me a place for the kids ta sleep and play and run around free in. I even got all they rooms decorated. You and the babies can stay in them rooms, child. I got my own bathroom in my bedroom, and y'all can use the guest bathroom down the hall. It's plenty'uh food stocked up, and, honey, I can cook my ass off, okay now? I raised four healthy, good-eatin' kids myself. I can cook anything and everything. Y'all need ta be eatin' somethin' more than some ol' sandwiches and soup and fast food. And . . . ta tell the truth . . . I could really use the company. I'm lonely in that house a lotta times. It'll be nice ta have some kids runnin' 'round makin' some noise and bringin' thangs ta life. It's time fuh you ta let people help you git through yo' hard times. Come on, stay wit' me for a minute. I won't bother you if you wanna be lef' alone. And if you wanna talk, that's fine, too. It's plenty'uh space. You can do whatever you need to do . . . jus' . . . lemme help you. And while I'm helpin' you, you'll be helpin' me . . . a lot."

I was speechless. And once again, I was glad Mama set the record straight for me, because in that moment, I totally understood why people always say watch how you treat others, because you might need them someday.

"Are you sure? I mean, my kids will run you ragged."

"Honey, that's what I want. I miss them days'uh runnin' after my grandbabies. They was the light'uh my life. And I just adore them precious kids'uh yours. They so well mannered and smart. I would love ta spend some time gittin' ta know them better. And while I'm doin' that, you can take better care'uh *yo'-self*. Just come stay for a week. If you ain't feelin' it, then we can say we tried, okay?"

"Thank you so much. I mean, really . . . this is so nice of you."

"Child, I'm gittin' somethin' out the deal, too. I got my selfish reasons for wantin' y'all there. So why not just help each other for a while?"

"You know what? Okay. We'll—we'll do that. It might even be fun."

"I know it will. And, hopefully, me and you can git ta know each other better. So come on by when y'all git ready. Y'all can come tonight if you want. Jus' lemme know what'choo wanna do. And far as you and these clients, you need ta use me, honey— 'cause you *know* Miss Angela Brown here can *do* her some hair, okay? If you need me ta fill in, jus' say the word."

"Okay. I'll try to make sure I keep that in mind. It may not be easy for me, but I'll try to utilize you . . . if that's what you want."

"That's what I want, honey."

21

KATRICE

November 22, 2007, 9:30 P.M.

This was the hardest day out of all the days that Weston's been gone. It's Thanksgiving, and my husband wasn't here to enjoy the holiday with his family. I went to see him today while the kids stayed with Angela, here at the house, and I almost wish I hadn't. He was so agitated about everything. He's on edge about his legal issues, he misses me and the kids, and he's restless and angry. The kids whined all day long about how they're tired of Weston's business, and they want him to hurry up and come home. I just keep praying Lincoln will be able to work some serious twists for Weston and get him back to us so I won't have to tell my kids that their daddy isn't coming home at all. Then I'll have to tell them the truth. I'm praying hard that day never comes. It would destroy them forever. And me, too. All I have to say is if ever there was a time when I needed God to come through for me, it's right now.

I invited Angela to come with us to my parents' for Thanksgiving dinner, since she doesn't really have anyone. Her sister, Virginia, left town with her boyfriend, and since her daughter still isn't speaking to her, she would've been all alone. I couldn't let that happen. Especially since we've been staying here with her, which I've said in every entry since we got here, has been really good for us. And fun. It's been more than a week, and it looks like we'll stay another week or so. Good thing we live close by, so I can just pop on home and pick stuff up when I need it. And check the mail. The kids really like her, and I have to admit . . . so do I. And she wasn't lying when she said she could cook her ass off! Damn, that woman could put Emeril outta business! I been grubbin' like an Ethiopian since we got here! And she just does it like it's no big deal. I mean, I can cook, too, but damn! I'll have to see if she'll let me in on some of her recipes, because the kids can't get enough of her meals.

Also, me and Angela have talked a lot over the past week, and I'm learning so much about her and her life. She's really smart, too. Funny how the way someone talks can throw you off track with their intelligence. I always figured she was just minimally educated because her grammar is so poor sometimes. But at dinner tonight, she started telling us about how she went to Howard University and majored in business, but she dropped out early because she had her second child. She already had Kelly, and was trying to balance motherhood and school; but when she got pregnant again, she knew she wouldn't be able to handle it all, so she made a choice. . . . She chose her kids. Can't say I blame her. I would've done the same thing. Damn. I really gotta get better at giving people more credit.

I'm so glad I got a chance to see P.J. today. God, I love my brother. After this Weston mess is over, I need to make sure we take a trip out to visit him and Lateshia. I guess I better get used to doing that, since it's clear they're not coming back here. He's happy, though. And I'm glad. Man, if it weren't for him and Daddy tonight, I don't know how I would've made it through dinner. I feel really sorry for women who didn't have fathers and/or brothers growing up. They're irreplaceable.

I was sad all day, but I had to keep that from showing so the kids wouldn't start asking me questions. They're very intuitive, and one little frown or grimace on my face and they're on me: Am I mad? Why am I sad? Are they in trouble? Who did what and why? So I did my best to put on a nice little front for them, and with Angela's help, that went over well.

Willie asked, "Mommy, how much longer is Daddy's business gonna be? He's supposed to be here for the Bird Day. He's always here when we eat the bird."

Right on top of his sentiments, Ellie said, "Yeah, and he always makes the special fruit punch for us to drink. Can't you call him and tell him to come home, just for Bird Day?"

Angela stepped in for me, because I think she knew I was close to the edge.

"Hey, now, y'all. You know what? Yo' daddy's takin' care'uh some real important stuff, and sometimes grown folks gotta do that kinda thang on holidays, like this one. But don't'choo worry, he's gon' be back real soon. And he not gon' make it a habit'uh missin' holidays. He just had ta do it this one time.

But he's gon' be callin' soon, and when he does, y'all just let him know you love him and tell him you waitin' patiently for him ta come home. Okay, now?"

Willie said, "Okay, but can we save him some bird? Maybe he can eat it when he comes back. Daddy likes to eat left-behind food."

I laughed. "'Leftover food,' Willie. That's what it's called. Left behind means someone doesn't want it, or they forgot it."

"Okay, but can we save him some?"

"Sure. We can put it in the freezer and when he gets back, he can pop it in the microwave and enjoy it then. How's that?"

"Okay. It's a plan, man!"

Angela and I cracked up. My kids say the funniest stuff sometimes.

Then Ellie just had to ask, "Mommy, is Daddy gonna be home for when we open presents under the Christmas tree? Is his business gonna be done by then? Because I'm gonna make him a really big, pretty picture and it's gonna be the best out of aaallllll the pictures I ever made. When he opens it up, he's gonna be soooo happy because he's gonna like it the best."

My heart dropped a little, but I said, "Well, Ellie Kat, I hope so. He's not sure just yet, but as soon as he is, he'll let us know. You go ahead and start getting the picture ready for him. When he does get here, you'll be all set to surprise him. Okay?"

That seemed to be enough for her.

"Okay. But can you buy me some more crayons? Mine are getting small."

"Yep. We'll get whatever you need so you can draw your daddy the best picture ever. Now, you guys, go back upstairs and finish getting ready. We need to be at Grammy's soon."

They both said, "Okay" together and bolted off.

I turned to Angela and said, "Thank you. This is getting really hard. Holidays and special occasions are the worst. They almost freaked out on me on Halloween when Weston wasn't here to take them trick-or-treating. He usually does that with them, and then I check the candy when they get home. I forgot about it this year because there was so much going on with Weston being gone at that time, and at the last minute, the kids came running up to me all frantic and asked me if Weston was gonna be coming home to take them to get candy on Treat Day— that's what they call it—and I had to get in gear and step in for him. We ran around all evening looking for costumes and all that stuff, and I was on the verge of tears the whole damn time. This has *got* to end soon. I can't take having to lie to my kids' faces too much longer. Angela, if he doesn't get out, I don't know *what* I'm gonna do."

"Okay, well, first of all, you not supposta be even thinkin' like that. You supposta be makin' plans fo' yo' husband ta come walkin' through that door like he comin' home from work or somethin'. You cain't be havin' no negative thoughts. Ain't no room fo' that mess. It's gittin' down to the wire, and yo' husband needs all the positive energy he can git from all'uh y'all. So don't be comin' 'round me sayin' stuff like, 'If he don't git out,' 'cause then, I'ma hafta put'choo over my knee, Miss Katrice."

"I know. You're right. It's just harder than I thought. And I'm scared to death. Can I be scared, at least?"

"Of course, honey. But that's about it. Be scared, but keep them positive thoughts in fronta yo' mind. Come on now, let's go in here and git these pies outta the oven so they can be cooled off when we leave."

When we got to my parents', I saw the rental parked outside and knew it was P.J.'s. I couldn't wait to get in the house and attack him with hugs.

Me, Angela, and the kids filed in with the food we brought. Angela headed straight for the kitchen, since she had most of the stuff. As soon as I saw P.J., I screamed at the top of my lungs. I put down my bags and ran into his arms and nearly knocked him over. I hadn't seen him since last Thanksgiving, and I missed him like hell.

After I flew into his arms and we almost went falling to the floor, he laughed and said, "Wassup, Kit Kat? I missed yo' silly butt! Hol' on . . . don't knock a brotha over! You 'bout to break my back!"

"I missed you, tooooo! You have *no* idea how much! How long are you guys staying?"

"Till Sunday. We gotta git back. Teshia gotta work on Monday."

I finally let him go and moved on to hugging Lateshia.

I said, "Hey, Mrs. Vincent! How's married life been treatin' you? It's been over a year now. Do you wanna strangle him yet?"

She looked at him, smiled, then looked at me, and said, "Well . . . he *a'ight*. I prob'ly coulda done better. But since he asked, I just went along with it."

He kissed her cheek, then said, "Whatever, woman. You know you love all this right here! You cain't *live* without a brotha!" Then he turned to look at the kids. "Now, where my niece and nephew at?"

They ran over to P.J., shouting in the same tone, at the same time, "Hi, Uncle P.J.!"

"Y'all gimme big hugs now. I ain't seen you in a year. Man, look at'choo! So big! Damn, Kit Kat, what'choo been feedin' 'em?"

"That's not me, that's Weston. Whenever he eats, they eat, even if they just ate. It's ridiculous."

After I said that, I got a pang in my heart. In the midst of the happy moment, I remembered that my husband was sitting in a jail cell, missing all the fun. P.J. saw my facial expression change and told the kids, "Okay, y'all go help Grammy and Grampy set up. I'll talk to y'all in a little bit, a'ight?"

They ran off, and then Angela came back out. After I introduced her to P.J. and Lateshia, she and Lateshia headed back to the kitchen to help out with the food.

P.J. draped his arm over my shoulder, kissed my face, and asked, "You a'ight, Kit Kat? I know you feelin' this shit right about now."

I held back my tears. "God, P.J., it's killin' me. And there's *nothing* I can do to help him. It takes every bit of energy I have to keep myself together in front of the kids."

"I'm sorry, baby sis. This is fucked up. But you gotta keep ya head up, girl. You gon' be a'ight. He'll be home soon."

Daddy came from the kitchen and joined us.

"Well, what we got here? My kids actin' like they love each other today?"

I said, "Hey, Daddy," then kissed and hugged him.

P.J. told him, "Baby sis just goin' through it right

now. I'm tryina let her know it's all good. Her man'll be home soon."

I got ready to cry, and Daddy said, "Okay, Chick-adee, come on. Let's take a little trip to the back porch. You too, P.J."

We all went out back and sat at the table. Then I buried my face in my hands and cried like a two-year-old.

After about a minute, Daddy finally said, "Treecie, you gon' hafta pull it together. I know this is hard, but you can't keep breakin' down like this. You know them babies pick up on all that stuff. You go back in there wit' puffy eyes, and they gon' be askin' who made you cry."

"Daddy . . . I'm just . . . everything's all messed up. And it's all my fault."

P.J. asked, "Why you say that? You didn't do noth-in' wrong."

"Yes, I did! I should've *never* gone with Royce that night. None of this would be happening if I had just told him no and stayed my ass at the reception, where I belonged. Now my husband might be going to prison because of some mess that *I started*. God, I'm so mad at myself! What the *hell* have I done to my life?"

P.J. said, "Come on, Kit Kat. I mean, I know you messed up, but what's jumpin' off right now . . . that ain't on you."

Daddy added, "He's right, Chickadee. Yes, you were most definitely wrong, and you paid for it back then. You went through hell because of what you did, and I think you learned your lesson. But this current situation is not your doing. I'm sorry, but *Weston* is responsible for what's happening right now. He's a grown man who knows what he should and shouldn't be doing. If he started that fight, he was wrong. No matter what the reason Royce is in town or how many times he came to see you, or even what happened back in the day, Weston had no business attacking him. Especially knowing he has a wife and three kids to provide for. If he wanted to confront Royce, he could've done it verbally. No one *made* him jump on that man. He made a conscious decision to do that, Treecie. If you ask me, he let his insecurities take over, and *that's* what made him do what he did. He felt threatened by Royce, even though he had no reason to be, and that drove him over the edge. And you can't take responsibility for his actions. So now it's *his* turn to pay for what *he's* done. Now, personally, I don't think he's going to prison. I just don't."

"How do you know that, Daddy? This is *so bad*. I really do think he was trying to kill Royce."

"I'm not saying I know for sure. I'm saying I just don't feel like it's gonna go that far. And you need to start thinking that way yourself."

"I know. Angela already scolded me earlier about that."

P.J. said, "Yeah, I mean, Weston's a good dude. He don't get in trouble. He ain't never been arrested before, right?"

"True."

"Okay, so judges take all that into consideration. These lawyers today, they know how to git a brotha outta a jam, especially if they was keepin' it together before they got in trouble. And it's prob'ly a lotta stuff you not even thinkin' about, that could work to his advantage."

"Like what?"

"I don't know, but I bet'choo it's stuff that lawyer can use to get him off. You know how many times I dun seen brothas git off for doin' *way* worse crimes than Weston? Too many to count. All it takes is a dude who knows how to work the system, and he *can* keep a brotha outta prison. I mean, you see O.J. walked, and you know how close they was to havin' his ass on death row. But Johnnie Cochran was on top'uh his game. I'm tellin' you, that's all it takes. Just let him do his job, and you keep yo' head on straight. It's gon' all work out."

"Thanks, y'all. P.J., I need you here. I miss you like crazy. Why'd you guys hafta move so damn far away?"

He grabbed my hand and kissed it. "Aw, girl, you don't need me here. You doin' fine on yo' own. I'm only a call away, though. You know that. Besides, you got this ol' man right here to keep yo' silly ass on track."

Daddy raised his eyebrows and looked at P.J. playfully. "Oh, really? I don't know who you think you callin' 'old,' wit'cha not-that-far-from-bein'-fifty ass." He popped P.J. upside the head.

"Ay, ol' man. Don't be uppin' me. I still got six years ta go."

"And they'll be here before you know it. Now look. I'm hungry. I'm goin' in the house to dip my fingers in some pots before we eat. Treecie, wipe your face and come on here. And bring ya old, wrinkled brother with you."

He got up and left, and P.J. and I sat outside and talked for a few more minutes.

Afterward, he said, "Come on, Mama Kat. I'm

hungry, too. You gon' be okay? Just git through dinner and you home free."

I wrapped my arm around his waist, plastered a kiss on his cheek, and said, "Yeah. I'll be all right. Thanks for the pep talk. You know I love you to death, big brother."

"Of course, you do, girl. But I prob'ly love yo' ass more. You always gon' be my little Kit Kat."

We walked in the house, arm in arm, and for the first time in weeks, I felt like things were gonna be okay.

22

WESTON

It was getting harder and harder for me to keep my composure. Every day I was locked up felt like the walls of that damp-ass jail cell were gonna close in and squeeze the life outta me. It didn't help in the least that it was Thanksgiving and I was missing all the family fun, plus the good eats. The jail food tasted like something outta the bottom of a garbage can. Half the time, I didn't eat because the shit looked so unappetizing. I probably lost fifteen unhealthy pounds in the first three weeks just behind skipping meals.

I was off my workout schedule, too. I was used to getting up before the household in the mornings and going into the basement to do my workout for an hour before going to work. I never missed a workout, even when I was sick. It was like brushing my teeth or washing my ass—it had to be done or else I didn't feel right. I had special equipment that I was accustomed to using. Now I was all off-track and I didn't like how my body was feeling. I also needed to start rehabilitating my busted knee, because it was getting stiff from all the cold air hitting it and from me not being able to exercise it like I needed to. Plus, the bed was too damn small for me, and I spent most of the nights half sleeping because I had to concentrate on not falling off the damn thing and crashing to the floor, breaking more bones than I had already broke in the fight.

Basehead was still my downstairs-bunk neighbor, and he was making me wanna do to him what I did to Royce. Always wanting to talk and get in my business. Then when I would go off on his stank-breath ass, he acted like *I* was the one with the problem. One night he almost drove me out my mind. He was down there beating his meat during the wee hours of the morning, and he thought I didn't hear him moaning and groaning, and then growling like an injured bear when he came. I wanted to jump off the bunk and snap his pencil-thin neck. It's one thing to see that on TV, but when you really are stuck in a jail cell with a cracked-out, meat-beating, yellow-toothed, white-lipped fiend, who's always trying to get in your business, it's a whole different story.

My body was still bruised; my ribs were still sore; my face started looking worse and worse by the day as the skin closed up and started to darken; and I coulda sworn I was losing some of the sight in my right eye. Royce was a strong dude. I'm surprised he didn't knock my eye out the back of my goddamn head. I never fought a man that could hang with me on the throw-down tip until him. I don't know what the hell kinda training he had, but I definitely met my grappling match with him.

Katrice came to see me before her and Angela and the kids left for Thanksgiving dinner at her parents', and I think I hurt her feelings, because I was in a bad mood and didn't really feel like talking. She barely made it in time, too. She said she had a hard time getting away from the kids because they were whiney all morning about me not being there. When she got ready to leave, they started crying and saying how they wanted to go with her wherever she was going. Then Ellie threw a tantrum—which she never does—that's Willie's thing—and Katrice didn't know what to do with her. Angela had to step in and play second grandmother, since Ellie wasn't paying the least bit of attention to what Katrice was telling her to do. I like Angela. I'm glad Eleanor told Katrice to stop treating her like a chunk of dirt on the bottom of her damn shoe, because she's good people. I knew that when I met her. Sometimes Katrice doesn't give people a chance. She told me Eleanor called her snooty, and it's true. She was all hurt by it, and I had to tell her it wasn't as bad as she was making it out to be. It ain't like she's a stuck-up bitch; she just doesn't like to let new people in. She's used to her little clique. Plus, she was hurt that Tiki left her. I told her to quit tripping and let that woman move on with her life and start fresh and be happy. But she didn't wanna hear all that. She told me I didn't understand, then got mad and went and pouted. I just laughed at her. Then she told me I was being insensitive. I just laughed at her some more. She kills me with that. Like I'm supposed to fall at her feet every time she's hurt because I told her the truth. That's my baby, though. She can be snooty all she wants. I love her exactly the way she is.

My boys came to see me, too. They had all been up to the jail to visit before then, but it was nice to see all of 'em on the holiday. Made a brotha feel cared about. It was also good for me to get to talk a little shit with them for a few, since me and Katrice only talked about serious stuff when she was there. Even when she was telling me funny stuff about the kids, it was still a serious topic, because I knew she was trying to tell me as many stories as possible before our time was up. But when me and my boys hook up, we talk about lighthearted topics. They crack jokes and have me rolling. We talk about men stuff. It's just different. I need that kinda interaction once in a while. A man needs to be able to just chill with his boys and talk about nothing in particular. Nothing stressful. They know what I need when it comes to lightening the load on my mind. Next to Katrice putting it down in the bedroom, that is. That's always the number one need for me when I got stress taking over my brain. But since that wasn't happening, having my dawgs come through was a nice change.

I talked to the fam for a little while. I called when I knew they'd all be there at Mama's so I could have a chance to say something to everybody. They all sounded like they were having the time of their lives. That's where me and Katrice and the kids shoulda been. Matter of fact, we were planning on going out there to surprise them the day after Thanksgiving. But, of course, I ruined that, too. Good thing we hadn't bought our tickets yet, or that woulda been a bunch of money down the damn tubes. Cornell had got him an older woman named Bridgette—a thirty-five-year-old with two sons, Anthony and Daronn. I was kinda worried about him messing with a woman who already had kids, but he was sprung off that pussy, so I knew I wasn't gonna be able to steer him away from her. She was all he talked about when I got on the phone with his ass. He said they made a good couple. I told him I'd hafta see about that. Kevin was still with Alfreda, and he said he might be ready to pop that question soon. I told him to take his time and make sure she's the one. He swore she was, though. I met her a coupla years ago when me and Katrice took the kids for a visit. She's a cute little thing. She only came up to Kevin's hip because he's so damn tall, and she's only five-one or five-two. Hell, the twins are taller than me, and I'm almost six-four. Whatever. As long as they're happy with the women they got. And my baby sister! Man, Tamika was doing the damn thang, for real! She had just got a job at Temple University as a student counselor and advisor. I can't believe my Meekymu is all grown up and professional. LaMonica and Earl told me they were thinking about packing up Dante, Christian, and Minea, and moving to Florida. I told them Katrice's brother and his wife lived there, and they should call Katrice and have her hook them up so they could find out more about it. And Leslie and Joe had just closed the deal on a new house. Pop sounded okay. He was still depressed, though; and Mama was right there to help him out. I was glad they were still on good terms. It woulda been real bad if their relationship was still on the rocks and he was going through all that HIV mess alone. He probably wouldn't be able to stay clean. I hate to say that, but I know my pops. He's not good with stress, either. I got that from him, so I know about it. I was just hoping it wouldn't be too long before I'd be able to see them all again.

I liked Lincoln a lot. He knew the legal system like the back of his hand, and he was always on top of his game every time we talked. Not only that, but his ass was serious about getting me the hell outta jail. That's the kinda dude I needed on my side. Someone I could feel confident about. He made me feel like I had a chance at freedom. Steve had told me Lincoln was the best, and that when he was on the case, people hated to go up against him because he was so good at his job. Once I got to really talk to him, I saw what Steve was talking about. That dude didn't miss a note. I knew he had some evidence that he was looking into that might help my case, but he also told me he couldn't get into the details yet, but that things were coming together.

One thing was for real, and that was I needed my black ass outta that place before Christmas. If I had to miss one more holiday and hafta listen to my kids cry on the phone because I wasn't there, or be forced to make collect calls to Chicago and listen to everyone being all joyous while I was wasting away in hell, I didn't know what I was gonna do—to myself—or to anyone around me.

23

ROYCE

I thought I heard my mother calling for a nurse. She was saying, "Hurry . . . he's waking up. His eyes are moving!"

I couldn't figure out if I was dreaming or what. My body felt weighted, and my head was hurting. A few seconds later, I heard this white lady talking to me. She had a pleasant voice. Then I felt her touching me. I couldn't quite get enough breath.

Then my eyes opened real slow, and all I saw was her smiling face hovering over me. And a hospital room. And my parents sitting off to the right of me. I didn't understand what was going on.

The nurse's voice was soothing. "Well . . . hello there. Welcome back, Mr. Jordan. It's about time, honey. You gave us quite a scare, there. How ya feelin'?"

I still didn't get it.

I looked at my parents and wondered what they were doing sitting together. I hadn't seen them in the same room with each other since I graduated from high school.

My mouth was dry, and my focus was a little blurry. I tried to move my lips to talk, but nothing came out at first. Then I started struggling to say something. I was getting frustrated.

The nurse said, "Waaaiiit a minute, Mr. Jordan. Hang on. I know you have lots to say, but just take your time, honey. We're not going anywhere. We been waitin' a long time to see those eyes of yours. Just relax. Take it slow."

Ma started crying, and Dad sighed in relief, then looked up at the ceiling and mouthed, "Thank you." He then looked at me and smiled.

I just wanted somebody to tell me what the hell was going on, why I was in a hospital bed, and why I couldn't get the words out of my mouth that I wanted to say.

The nurse started talking again. "Okay, now . . . you're safe, and you're gonna be all right. Just try to stay relaxed."

I felt tired, so I closed my eyes again. Everybody panicked.

Ma said, "Baby . . . baby? Nurse, what's happening to him? He closed his eyes again."

I heard her say, "Okay . . . okay . . . Mr. Jordan? Honey, you still with us?"

It took me a second, but I finally opened my eyes again, since it seemed like it was gonna be a problem if I didn't. Ma started crying again, and Dad put his arm around her. And I was still trying to figure out what they were doing together.

I cleared my throat. I looked around some more. Ma grabbed my hand gently.

I looked at her and wanted to smile, but I couldn't make my mouth do the motion.

The nurse started taking my vitals and talking to my parents. "He'll be okay in a little while. He just needs some time to adjust. May take him a few minutes before he can talk."

Dad asked, "But he will talk, right?"

"I'm sure he will. Just give him a little time." Then she smiled at me and said, "I'll be right back, okay, honey?" and she left the room.

I dozed off again.

I don't know how much time passed, but when I opened my eyes, Ma, Dad, the nurse, and a doctor were all staring at me.

The doctor said, "Hi, there, Mr. Jordan. I'm Dr. Peterson. Can you tell me how you feel? Can you verbalize that for me?"

I finally was able to squeeze out a slow, strained "I'm . . . tired."

"I know you are. We won't be long here. Just got a few things to take care of and then you can get some more rest. Now, can you tell me your first name?"

I cleared my throat again, then forced out, "Roy . . . Royce."

"Very good. All right, I'm gonna ask you some more questions, and I want you to try and answer them the best you can, okay? If you can't, don't worry about it."

"Okay."

"Do you know who these people are?" He pointed to Ma and Dad.

"Parents."

"That's right. Mr. Jordan, do you think you can tell me their names?"

I looked at Ma and said, "Barbara . . . Hathaway." Then I looked at Dad and said, "Royce. Jordan. Junior."

Everything I said was real slow.

The doctor said, "Very good." Then he paused before he asked, "Do you know what year it is?"

I had to think for a few seconds before I answered, "Two thousand . . . seven?"

"Right. Now . . . do you know how old you are?"

"Thirty-ni—um . . . forty?"

"Good. Do you, uh . . . know where you are? What state you're in?"

"Ummm . . . I'm in . . . California. Oakland, right?"

"Yes. That's right. Now, can you tell me . . . the last thing you remember doing?"

That was an easy question. Or so I thought. "Talkin' . . . Tony."

The doctor asked, "You were talking to Tony?"

I nodded.

"Who's Tony?"

"Friend."

"And . . . Mr. Jordan . . . do you remember . . . when that was?"

I looked around the room for a second and thought back; then I said, "Coupla days ago. I think."

Everybody started looking at each other funny.

Then the doctor hesitated before he asked me, "Okay, now . . . can you tell me . . . what date that was? Do you think you can remember that?"

"Um . . . Oc-October—ninth. Tenth. Somethin'. I don't know. The other day."

I noticed the doctor was writing down everything I

said. Then I saw Ma about to start crying again, and Dad looking worried. I was wondering what the hell I could've possibly said wrong.

More questions from the doctor. "O . . . kay . . . October ninth or tenth. Hmm . . . so, do you remember what you and Tony were talking about? Do you remember where you two were?"

"No. Yeah. I think . . . going to eat."

"You and Tony were . . . talking about going to eat, or you were somewhere eating?"

I started getting confused and annoyed, and the doctor noticed.

"Okay. That's enough for now. Let's take a little break."

But I needed to know what was going on, for real, so I started asking some questions myself. "Why? What happened? How come I'm in the hospital?"

Nobody said anything. They just stared at me.

I asked them, "What's the date today?"

Dad looked sad when he said, "It's, um . . . No-November . . . twenty-fifth."

My mouth flew open; then after a few seconds, I said, "*It is?* I don't . . . understand. . . ."

Then Ma said, "You had another seizure, baby."

I looked at Ma in total dismay, then, scared to death, I asked, "I did? Again? When? I haven't had a seizure in . . . years. What I do . . . black out at the wheel like I did last time?"

The doctor said, "I think we need to take a break."

But I didn't want to, because I was terrified about the info they were laying on me.

"No. Wait . . . what happened to me? I had a seizure . . . where?"

Dad said, "At a bar. Well, more like a club."

"Where and when?"

"You had a, uh . . . fight on October nineteenth. At Kimball's."

"With *who*? I don't even remember going to Kimball's. Last thing I was doing was talking to Tony. Way before October nineteenth."

Dad scooted his chair closer to me. "Trè, do you know a man named Weston Porter?"

For a second, I had to think about why he was calling me Trè. Then I remembered he calls me that because I'm Royce the third. The fact that I didn't catch on to that upset me. But not as much as him asking me about Katrice's husband. I didn't know *where* that came from.

"Nah. I don't know him. I mean, I know who he is . . . kinda. My friend's husband. But I've never met him. Why?"

I did remember Katrice, clear as day. And I remembered that I was upset that she was married to Weston. And I was mad I had to say that out loud.

"Do you remember seeing him at Kimball's?"

"Dad . . . I don't remember *being* at Kimball's. Besides, I don't even know what that dude looks like, so how would I remember seeing him?"

"Well . . . you had an awful fight with him that night. The two of you went flying through a window, and that's when you had the seizure. And then . . . you fell into a coma."

I couldn't believe what my dad was saying. And I was aggravated because I didn't remember a damn thing he was telling me that had happened.

"*What? Why?* I mean, I'm . . . I don't . . . know—"

The doctor said, "Mr. Jordan . . . I *really* think you need to take a break for a few minutes. This is a lot to absorb. Just relax." Then he looked at Ma and Dad and said, "Would you two . . . come with me, please?"

Then everybody left the room, and I just laid there, confused and pissed-off. I've had epilepsy since I was eight, and every time I have a seizure, I lose a little memory. But never as much as this time. I might lose a coupla hours, *maybe* six at the most. One time I did lose a whole day, and that scared the shit outta me. That was the time I seizured, then blacked out at the wheel of one of my dad's cars from the lot while I was test-driving it, and I ran into a garbage Dumpster. Dad was with me, and, fortunately, we weren't seriously hurt, but Dad said I hit my forehead on the steering wheel real hard. I wasn't allowed to drive for six months after that. But from what they were telling me, I had lost about ten days, had been in a coma for five weeks, and somewhere in there, I had a fight with Katrice's punk-ass husband and didn't remember it. That made me mad as hell.

I tried to think back and recall, but the only two things I had stuck in my head were talking to Tony while standing outside his house, and the last encounter I had with Katrice. Even that was fuzzy. All I remembered was her telling me no about something and her looking at me like she didn't give a damn about me. I couldn't remember what I asked her, or if I made her mad, or even what day it was when I was talking to her. All I really remembered was the fact that she turned and walked away from me like she didn't wanna have anything to do with me, which hurt my feelings. But no matter how hard I tried, I couldn't bring back the conversation or remember why I was in her shop that day. I also remembered that one of the reasons I came to Oakland was to try to steal her heart from Weston. From what I could tell, I obviously failed at that.

I thought if I closed my eyes and tried to relax, I would be able to remember some events and start putting the pieces together. The only thing that happened was I went to sleep.

The next time I woke up, there were two cops standing near my bed, talking to the nurse and my parents. They scared the hell outta me because I was trying to figure out what kinda trouble I could've gotten into while I was asleep.

They wanted to interview me about the fight. They had a million and two questions that I couldn't answer because I didn't remember a damn thing except what I told the doctor earlier. What pissed me off was they kept acting like I was trying to hold some details back or something, like I knew what happened and just didn't wanna tell 'em. Ma and Dad kept trying to explain to them that I have epilepsy, and that when I seizure, I lose memory; but they acted like they didn't believe them, either.

I did find out that the bartender said he served me three Long Island Iced Teas; nobody could seem to tell them what exactly happened between me and Weston before we started fighting, but that we were throwing down like we were in a boxing ring, knocking people over and breaking tables left and right. Weston was on top of me when we went out the window; he was kicking me in the head before the cops took him down; and he was in jail because of it. I found all that out by them asking me if I remembered any of that. Of course, I didn't. Not one minute of it. I was still back on the ninth or tenth of October when I was asking Tony where the rib place was that he was telling me about so I could go get my grub on. That much I did finally recall after everyone left the room the first time, right before I fell back asleep.

After about fifteen minutes of harassment, the cops finally got frustrated and left. Actually, it was more like I got mad because they wouldn't stop trying to make me remember about that night, and Dr. Peterson saw the conversation was frustrating me, so *he* put 'em out. I was glad, because my head was hurting and I was tired as hell. All I wanted to do was go back to sleep and hopefully start remembering what happened in my life between talking to Tony and ending up in the hospital.

I still couldn't figure out what happened with Katrice, but the more I thought about it, the less I wanted to know, because with everything I had just found out, I figured I'd better leave her ass alone. Especially since her husband was in jail because of something that went down with me. I could just see me trying to talk to her after everything was over with, and her spitting in my face. If I could've just recalled the details of our last conversation, I might've been able to gain some perspective on what was going on. But all I had was some snow in my head, which is what happens every time I seizure. Whatever I lose is gone for good. If I remember any of it, it's in bits and pieces, and it's out of order and doesn't make any sense.

To tell the truth, after the cops left and I realized how bad everything was, all I wanted to do was take my ass back to Maryland so I could get better and try to put my life back together. I knew there was never gonna be a chance for me to get Katrice where I wanted her, so I started making plans to cut my losses and go back to the East and let her go for good. My mind was too gone for me to try to back-track and figure out where I went wrong with her that day. All I had in my head was that look she gave me that basically said, "Get outta my *damn* face and don't *ever* come back." So even though I didn't want to, that's what I planned to do, since it seemed like my mission was shot to hell. If I could ever get out the hospital bed.

24

KATRICE

November 25, 2007, 5:10 P.M.

*OH, MY GOD!! Royce is finally awake!! Thank the
LORD!! I had almost given up hope after I went to see him
on the ninth and nothing happened. I mean, I really
thought we were screwed and that he was either gonna die
or never come out of that damn coma! But I talked to
Weston a coupla hours ago, and he told me he just got word
that Royce woke up today! This is exactly what we need to
lighten the load on Weston's case. THANK YOU, GOD,
NO MURDER CHARGES! I'm SO relieved! I was about
to start losing my damn hair over this mess. God, I'm
begging You, PLEASE GET MY HUSBAND OUT
BEFORE CHRISTMAS!*

*I've spent the last two hours on the phone with everyone
I could think of, filling them in on the news. Tiki actually
clicked in just as I was about to hang up from talking to*

Mama, so it was perfect because we hadn't had a chance to talk for a minute. She was just calling to check in on me and make sure I was doing okay. She said she was worried and had been wanting to call me, but with all her clients and stuff, plus the time difference, it just wasn't happening. But also, Charles has had the flu for the past two weeks and hasn't been able to go to work and she's been nursing him. I told her all about Weston's news, and she was so excited. I also told her I got the beautiful card she sent me last week, letting me know how sorry she was about our troubles and reassuring me that she's always here for me. I knew that, anyway, but it was nice to read it in a card. I miss her so much! I told her about us staying with Angela and how we'd probably be here until the end of the month, and how I had adjusted my attitude toward her, courtesy of Mama. She was glad. She knew I was struggling with that. I told her as soon as the Weston catastrophe was over with and we could get ourselves back on track, I'd be out there for a visit.

I also finally caught up with Joan-Renee today and told her the news. Damn, we've been playing phone tag for weeks! She's really tired, though. Having two small children is no joke, even if you do have a husband. I thought when Weston and I had the twins, things would be easy, because there are two of us, but I was WAY wrong! Maybe it would've been with only one, but two at the same time is a whole other story. She promised to scan me some recent pics of Scarlett and Archer. She's so bad at that stuff. I always have to get on her about keeping me up to date with my little godchildren. I wish Joan-Renee were here, too. We're like two peas in a pod. I still laugh about how when we first became friends in the fifth grade, people didn't understand our bond, and they used to tease us and call us the salt-and-pepper girls. Stupid asses. Like we were the only pair of white-and-black friends in school. Hell, there were about three other pairs just like us. But I guess they didn't hang as tough as me and Joan-Renee. My girl. I remember that time her stepdad tried to bust up our friendship. He didn't get us, either. And you know what else? I miss her fudge! Damn, it was good! I'm gonna have to call her back and tell her to make me some and send it to me. I lost the recipe, too. Gotta have her send it to me with the goods.

No sooner than I got in the door from work, Angela's house phone rang. I almost didn't pick it up, because I wasn't expecting a call from Weston until later that evening. But since I was standing close by, I went ahead and answered.

It was the institution with a collect call from Weston. First I was surprised; then I got kind of scared because I thought something was wrong.

Before I could even say hi, he burst out, "Babe . . . babe . . . babe . . . Royce woke up this morning!"

I screamed, "Oh, my God! He did?"

I never told Weston I went to visit Royce that day. As a matter of fact, I didn't tell anyone. I figured I should keep that to myself. It was just something I felt I needed to do, and I didn't feel like having people judge or criticize the action.

"Yeah. I was scared as hell he was gon' die and I'd be stuck wit' murder on my head. But we outta the woods now. I can breathe a little."

"God . . . I'm so relieved! I've been sick about this every minute of the day."

"Shit, not *you*. I told you I ain't been sleepin' good 'cause every day that goes by is another day his ass could die on me . . . on *us*."

"Okay . . . so what happens now? Wha'd Lincoln say? Can Royce talk?"

"I don't know all the details. He said all I need to know right now is Royce's awake and Lincoln's lookin' into some new details for the case. He can't really discuss it right now, but I trust him. I told you he had somethin' else he was investigatin' before this, so now I guess it's some other details added to it. He just said be patient, let him do his thang, and by the time we go to court, he'll fill me in."

"Well, when's that? The court date?"

"I'm not sure yet. But as soon as I find out, you know I'll call you."

I heard someone say to Weston, "Ay, man . . . come on . . . other folks tryina use the goddamn phone."

"Ay—babe, I gotta git off. They on me right now about this phone. Do me a favor and call Mama for me and tell her. I'ma try to call you later. I love you."

"Okay—love you, too."

After I hung up, I just stood in the middle of the living room in shock. It was the moment we'd been hoping and praying for since the night of the fight. While I was definitely glad Royce was finally awake, I was also scared stiff about what he might say once he got to talking. Since Weston started the fight, there was no telling what the hell would come out of Royce's mouth. I didn't know how he felt, what he was thinking, or if he would do or say something crazy to jack Weston's situation up even more. All I could hope for was that Royce would do the right thing—whatever that was—and not cause any more trouble for us. I was also worried that once he was out of the hospital, he was still gonna be hanging around town, trying to take care of whatever the hell

brought him to Oakland in the first place. I figured
that never got resolved, since he was still here on October 19, and was all up in the club. To be honest, I
just wanted him to take his ass back to Maryland and
never come back here again—regardless of the fact
this was his hometown.

I jumped right back on the phone and called Lorraine. She saw my name on the caller ID and started
talking without saying hello. "Katrice . . . what's
wrong? Everything okay? What's happening with
Weston?"

"Everything's better than okay. . . . Royce woke
up this morning! Weston just called and told me!"

"Oh, my God! Oh! Thank the good, good Lord!
That's been at the top of my prayers since I found
out about that coma! Thank you, Jesus!"

She got real quiet on me, and I got scared. "Lorraine? Are you okay?"

She had started to cry. "Yeah . . . I'm okay, baby. I
was just takin' in the good news and saying a silent
thank-you to my Savior. I was so scared my baby was
in for the worst. But we're on our way . . . we're on
our way. There's *nothing* more powerful than prayer,
I tell you."

"You're right about that."

She pulled herself together, then asked, "So what
now? Is he talking?"

"You know what? I don't know. Weston doesn't
have all the details. He's gonna let me know as
soon as he finds out what's going on. It's really scary
that we don't have all the info, but Steve assured
us that we're in good hands with Lincoln. The main
thing is we're not looking at the possibility of murder

anymore. I thought I was gonna go insane if he didn't wake up . . . or if he died."

"Well, I hope this attorney is on the job, because things could still be messy. No telling what Royce will say, or may have already said."

"I know . . . I was just thinking that, too. I'm hoping he just tells the story like it is and doesn't make any extra stuff up. Really, I wish he would say Weston didn't start the fight. But we know that's not gonna happen. If anything, he'll be mad as hell because he ended up in the hospital because of it. I just don't trust him right about now."

"And you shouldn't. Not one bit. But you know what? We've gotten this far with our prayers—we need to keep 'em up, so the next thing is Weston getting out and not going to prison. I really hope he gets some help once he's out. I love my son with all my heart, but he's really gotta work on his temper. You have no idea how many times Sonny and I had to talk to him about going off on people when Weston was growing up. I really don't know where he got that from. Both Sonny and I are such mild-mannered people. And there was never any reason for Weston to be so angry—well, prior to Sonny leaving, but he was fourteen then. This temper of his has been out of control since he was a little boy—you remember what we were telling you last month."

"Yeah, and I'm still disturbed about some of those stories. I mean, like I said, Weston told me about a few of those instances, but that other stuff? I don't know why he never mentioned any of that to me before. Maybe he thought I'd think he was a monster or something and not wanna be with him."

"I wouldn't be surprised if that was the reason. Sometimes my son is very selective about the information he gives out. It all depends on who he's giving it to and how it's gonna make him look."

"Yeah, but, Lorraine . . . this is *me*. He should know I'm not going anywhere, and that he can tell me whatever. It's just part of his past—it's not who he is right now. I mean, we've known each other almost ten years, and not once has he tried to beat up on anyone or cuss anybody out. Okay, well, there was that one time when we took the kids to the movies last year, and the guy at the register tried to say Weston didn't pay for one of the kids, and he did, and they got into it. Weston threatened to put his fist through the window and knock the guy's ass smooth out if he didn't stop accusing Weston of trying to gyp the theater. The guy was so scared he just said never mind and let us go through. I was shocked, but I was mostly embarrassed because people were staring and whispering, and the kids were looking at Weston like they weren't even sure if they wanted to *go* to the movie after that. I didn't even say anything to him about it when we got in and sat down because I was scared he was gonna yell at me . . . and you know I wasn't gonna have that. So I just stayed quiet and let him calm down."

"See, that's what I'm talking about. He needs to get to the bottom of why he does things like that. I can't do anything with him. He hears me when I scold him about it, but he's not listening. It's like he just flips at the drop of a dime sometimes." Then she paused. "Katrice . . . tell me the truth . . . has he . . . ever—"

"Hell no! He's *never* raised an unjust finger to the kids, and he's *damn* sure never raised his hand to me. The weird thing is, it's like he has control of himself when it comes to us. Even the night of the wedding when I thought he was gonna clobber me, he didn't. And I'm telling you . . . I honestly thought I was gonna hafta put your son in the hospital that night. Because if he had hit me, you don't even know how *on*, it would've been. And that's the God's-honest truth. Sorry to say . . . "

"Don't be sorry. If he *had* hit you, no matter what you did that night, whatever he got back, he woulda had it coming. And that's my son, and I'm sayin' that. I'm tellin' you . . . I don't play that. The night Sonny almost hit me, I felt the same way. And I'm just a small piece'uh thang, but I tell you what— if that fist'uh his had even *grazed* me, I probably woulda killed him. With his own shotgun. End of story. It's bad enough men beat their girlfriends and wives and whatnot—but to lay violent hands on the women who gave them children? Time and time again? Even when they didn't want to sometimes but did it for *their* ass? After risking multiple health problems and even childbirth death every single time? Hello, girlfriend? They betta *all* ask somebody."

"You ain't lyin'. But you don't hafta worry about that over here. We're good. And I'm not scared of his Big-Bad-Wolf self, either. Sometimes I think he's more scared of *me*."

Lorraine laughed. "Okay? And he should be!"

Then I paused and got real serious. "But you know what? This is making me think about something that happened a couple weeks ago between me and Willie, and it really scared me."

"What happened?"

I told her about the night Willie and I got into it over his meat-cutting issue and how awful it was. I hadn't really talked about it with anyone except Yolanda, but it stayed on my mind because it was a side of Willie I had never seen, and it shocked me to the point where I wondered how the hell we even got there. Willie has his moments, for sure, but that one was completely new to me, and I never wanted to go through that kind of thing with him again. All the talk about Weston and his temper brought me back to that day, and I started getting scared that Willie was headed in the same direction.

Lorraine said, "You know, Katrice . . . people don't realize this, but kids are just . . . like adults in children's bodies. They have personalities and minds of their own . . . and sometimes we don't understand that. We treat them like they don't know what they're talking about, but really they know exactly what they're saying—they just don't have the vocabulary to articulate certain things. And when they act up—or in Willie's case, act *out*—we think it's just 'cause they feel like being bad. But a lotta times, they have something going on in their minds that they can't tell us about because they just don't have the words. I've seen it *all*, honey. I raised six kids, and lemme tell you, it was like living with six little grown-ups who couldn't always speak their minds, but they always found a way to act out those frustrations."

"But he's five, Lorraine. What could he possibly have on his mind besides kid stuff? I mean, I got the feeling if he were much older and could've done it, he would've cussed me out. And that's no joke. The thought of that scared me. You should've seen the way he looked at me. It was like I was the ultimate enemy or something."

"Well, first of all, Weston got that meat thing from Sonny, 'cause he used to do that for the kids a lot."

"I know . . . he told me about that."

"But just because those kids are only five doesn't mean they don't have real feelings about stuff. That boy missed his daddy. He just wanted to feel close to him. Having the meat cut like Weston does it was the way he wanted to feel that closeness. But because he *is* five, it's not like he could tell you that, since his vocabulary is still so limited. All he could think of was you needed to do what he needed you to do so he could feel better. That meat thing is routine, right?"

"Pretty much. He doesn't do it all the time, but he does do it quite a bit."

"Okay, well, if there's one thing kids get attached to, it's routine. You break that pattern, you gon' have problems. They don't understand why all of a sudden stuff they're used to stops happening. Hell, adults don't even like change, so how you think kids feel?"

"That's true. . . . I didn't think about that. I feel bad now. I feel like I should've known that."

"How could you? This was the first time his routine was ever really broken. And since Weston wasn't there to keep it up, he wanted *you* to do it. In his mind, if you cut the meat like Weston, it would've made him feel connected to his daddy, even though he wasn't there to do it himself. That's all he really wanted. Just a little connection to his daddy."

"God, Lorraine. How am I supposed to know all this stuff?"

"You're not . . . right away. You just pick things up as you go along. This is your first time out. And you happened to get two for the price of one, so you got thrown in the advanced seat right from jump. It takes time to learn what your kids need. I had six chances, and I still had problems along the way. They were all totally different kids with different needs. But don't worry too much about it. You were both upset and frustrated, and it was a learning experience. Now you know. Kids need that routine. And if one parent isn't there to do it, they gon' want the other one to step in. Especially in a situation like yours where Weston was gone and Willie was really feelin' his absence."

"No wonder he was so mad at me. I just thought he was acting like a brat because he was tired. But he really was pissed. I guess it makes sense. . . . I didn't even *try* to cut the meat like he likes it . . . like Weston does. I just told him it wasn't goin' down. My poor baby." I shook my head.

"Ah . . . he'll get over it. He probably got over it the next day. Kids bounce back fast, too."

I chuckled. "That's true, too, because the next morning he acted like nothing out of the ordinary happened the night before, and I was expecting him to act up all day because of it. He just moved on like it was all good."

"See. He's fine. He just had a moment . . . like all people do." Then she laughed. "I bet'choo one thing, though. Next time he asks you to cut the meat like Weston, you won't hesitate!"

I cracked up. "Okay? You got that right! We not goin' through that mess ever again!"

"I know you won't!"

"Well, thanks for the Child-Rearing 101 lesson. I'm glad I brought it up. I was really thinking we were gonna have major problems in the future because of that."

"Oh, you gon' *have* problems in the future. You'll have so many, you won't be able to keep the damn things in order. But you'll be fine."

I breathed a sigh of relief. "Thanks. I feel a lot better. But, look, I gotta go. I need to call the others and let 'em know what's up. As soon as I hear anything else, I'll call you. Okay? Oh, and can you tell Sonny for me? Tryina save on minutes. Between the collect calls here at Angela's that I hafta pay for, the calls at our house, the calls at the shop, and my cell phone minutes, I'm damn near broke."

"You need some money, baby?"

"No—I didn't mean it like that—I shouldn't have said that. I just meant it's adding up, and I need to watch myself, that's all. We're okay on the money tip. But thanks."

"Okay, well, you let me know if you're not. I got me a nice stash put away, and you know whatever you need is yours."

"Thanks. I love you, Lo."

"I love you, too, honey. I'll call Sonny right now."

"Okay. Tell him I said hi and I love him, too."

"I will. Talk to you later."

After Lorraine, I made the calling rounds and gave everyone else the good news. Of course, they were all relieved and said they would keep praying for Weston's release from jail. When Angela came in with the kids—she picked them up from my parents' for me—I had to wait a few minutes before I could tell her what was going on because the kids wanted to chitchat. Naturally, I couldn't deny them that, especially since Weston wasn't around. Once I had entertained them for about twenty minutes, I left them in the TV room and went to talk to Angela while she was making dinner.

I kept my voice low. "Angela . . . Weston called not too long ago. . . . Royce woke up this morning!"

Her face lit up; then she put down the colander full of greens she had just washed, threw her hands in the air, and started dancing around in a circle. Finally she stopped and said, "Child, that's wonderful! God is *so* good, I tell you! I knew some righteous thangs was gon' start happenin' 'round here befo' too long!" She grabbed me and hugged me real tight.

"You did, I know that. And thank you for helping me stay positive. I needed every bit of your encouragement."

After she released me, she said, "Oh, child . . . we all need help stayin' strong sometimes. So what now?"

"Well, we don't have all the information yet. Weston said Lincoln told him all he needed to know for the moment was that Royce woke up, and that Lincoln was looking into some other evidence that might help the case. I wish I knew what the hell he was talking about. It's making me nervous."

"Honey, it's gon' all come out in the wash soon enough. Don't't'choo worry 'bout it. I believe that man knows what he's doin' and he's takin' good care'uh yo' husband. I feel it, child. . . . Y'all almost through this hurricane, and it's gon be a overload'uh sunshine once it's over."

"I hope so, Angela. I really do."

25

WESTON

I didn't wanna get overexcited about Royce being awake and what that might mean for me, but my ass was relieved as hell. I knew I still had to deal with the attempted-murder charges, but the fact that murder was out of the way took ten loads off my mind. Never in my life had I prayed for a dude I didn't like to be okay—until this happened.

Lincoln had me kinda scared when he kept telling me to sit tight while he looked into the stuff he wouldn't tell me about; so one day, I asked him what was up with that. Not that I didn't trust him, but I just wanted to know why all the secrets. He said it wasn't that he was trying to keep it secret, but he needed to make absolutely sure of what he was telling me before he gave it all to me. He told me about this one time back in the early days of his career when he was representing a client and he came across some big news about a victim. He rushed back and told his client about what he had found. Then a day or two later, he found out the information he got wasn't all the way accurate, and he had to change his story with his client. The dude started acting like Linc didn't know his job anymore and started second-guessing him every time he came at the client with new info after that. From then on, Lincoln promised himself he wouldn't reveal evidence to clients until he was 100 percent sure it was on point first and he had the whole story. I told him I understood, and to go on and do his thang and let me know when it was time.

The time came on the evening of December 13 when I met with Lincoln and he said the words I had been praying for with everything I had: PLEA BARGAIN! I was so happy and relieved, I jumped my ass up and actually hugged that man. Hard. And long. Like I ain't never hugged anybody before— not even Katrice. To tell the truth, I even dropped some tears behind it. All I could think was that this man had just got me my life back, when it was looking like I might hafta pack it in and call it a day. He made it possible for me to go home and spend the holidays with my family. I could finally see my kids and make up for all the things I couldn't do with, and for, them while I was locked up. I could have my wife back in my arms again and not take our daily routine for granted anymore, like I had been doing for a while up until the fight. I had got so comfortable, I forgot that in a flash I could lose it all with one wrong move on my part—or somebody else's.

When you're comfortable, you don't think about what life would be like without everything you love until you're forced to be without it all—whether you screwed yourself all by your lonesome or you had some help. I didn't have any words to express how grateful I was to have Steve in my corner, and to have a dude like Lincoln on my side, working like a slave to get me outta trouble. He didn't even know me. I had never had anybody go to bat for me like that before who wasn't part of my family or a close friend. It was like he really felt I deserved a second chance, and he did everything he could to make it happen. The whole thing just made me realize how important it is to have people who believe in you, even when you fuck up royally. Sometimes it's so bad that you can't help your own damn self outta the mess you got in, and only someone who thinks you're worth the effort can step in and help you. Steve and Lincoln were those people, and I was damn thankful.

Because the cops actually witnessed me stomping and kicking Royce in the head repeatedly, which is what really caught me the case in the first place, I was told the agreement was that I would have to plead guilty to reduced charges of aggravated battery. After that, I was looking at a two-year suspended prison sentence with five years' probation and a list of conditions that included no drinking, no contact with the victim—like that would really be a problem—2,500 hours of community service, anger management, psychological counseling, and restitution. That meant I would be paying for all of Royce's hospital bills, plus any additional therapy he might need later, and also paying for the damages to the club—but Royce would be paying for some of it, too, since he did help tear the place up with me. That part hurt me a little bit, though, because I knew I would need to use the money I had been saving to open my gym to pay for all that. But if it meant staying on the opposite side of those steel bars, I knew I was gonna do whatever I had to, even if it meant going broke. As long as I had a job, which Steve promised me I would when I got out, I could start over and rebuild. It would take a while, but that was just something I was gonna have to deal with. I figured a dream put on hold was a hell of a lot better than a dream I couldn't fulfill because I was in prison.

I knew that even though the potential murder charges were off my head after Royce woke up, there was still the attempted-murder issue, and I could still be up Shit Creek if something didn't happen to make that go away. When Lincoln came to me and presented the evidence that made it happen, I realized I owed both him and Steve my life.

I knew I was looking pretty good when we had met before and discussed the main factors: It was my first conviction, I was a model citizen in good standing with the community, and I was *past* drunk, which meant I wasn't in my right mind. In the end, they couldn't find any real witnesses to state exactly what had happened between me and Royce—only the bartender, a couple of bystanders, and some of the security guards gave statements and said they saw us and everything that happened after we started fighting, but they didn't know how the fight got started. So there was no real proof that I had started it—*and* I was under severe emotional distress because of the news about Pop, which is the reason I went out drinking in the first place. I didn't even think about that one. But then Lincoln came at me with the thing that *really* saved me. First he told me Royce has epilepsy and has a long history of seizures. That shocked the hell outta me—I just couldn't picture somebody like him with that kinda problem. It just goes to show that even if somebody looks and acts perfectly healthy, anything could be wrong with them. Anyway, Lincoln started telling me that because of Royce's history with seizures, he's not supposed to be drinking—and he had about three drinks before me and him got down; and with the fact that he cracked his head on the curb *before* I started kicking him, it would be hard to prove that I actually caused the seizure he had out on the sidewalk. The cops tried to say everything was my fault because they saw me kicking him—even that I caused the coma—but now with the whole epilepsy thing, they couldn't really pin that on me. Not saying I didn't have something to do with it, but they couldn't prove how much, if anything at all. Then Lincoln told me the best part, and I swear I thought he was trying to be funny at first when he said it. He told me when Royce woke up, he couldn't remember a *single* thing that happened that night. Not only that, but his memory was stuck about ten days before the night of the fight. I really didn't believe him at first. I asked him if he was sure. He said he was. He said Royce couldn't tell the cops a single thing about October 19. He kept talking about what he did a week prior to that day. I always saw stuff like that on TV, where coma victims wake up and all of a sudden have amnesia, and I used to think it was all fake—I guess just because I never met anybody personally or heard of anybody who had experienced amnesia before—but apparently coma victims forget major events all the time. Sometimes they remember later, and a lotta times, they never do. And then with Royce having that seizure, it messed him up even more. Since he couldn't say what happened, that shot his whole deal down. With all that going on, they knew taking the case to trial would be a big mistake. The prosecutor, though, damn sure didn't want my ass to walk, so they came to an agreement.

After my meeting with Lincoln, I called Katrice to tell her the good news, and she almost passed out. She was screaming and hollering and hyperventilating and crying in my ear like she had won the billion-dollar lottery or something. But I guess she had. Her husband was coming home, and now she didn't have to tell her kids the truth about their father, and that he was never coming back. I know she thought about it every second of every day— what she was gonna do if she had to break that kinda news to them. I was beyond ecstatic that my kids wouldn't have to go through that trauma, because I was sure it would've damaged them for life. I definitely wouldn't have been able to handle that.

The next day, December 14, when I got my walking papers, was the happiest moment of my life— right up there with marrying Katrice and watching all my kids being born. I just couldn't believe all the luck and protection that was thrown my way. I kept thinking about how crazy it sounded that Royce couldn't remember anything from that night. I was actually scared his memory was all of a sudden gonna come rushing back to him and then I'd be back in the hot seat and my release would be interrupted. But after I thought about the fact that he had been out of the coma for three weeks and still couldn't come up with the truth, I figured I was safe, and I finally stopped tripping off it.

From then on, my mind was only focused on getting home to my family, enjoying my freedom and the holidays in peace, and never, ever doing anything to put our setup on the line again. Thanks to good friends and a load of prayers, I was finally about to make that happen.

26

ROYCE

I had been out of my coma for twenty days, and I still couldn't remember a damn thing I needed to remember about my life after October 9 or 10. It was driving me crazy, too. Every time I would go to sleep, I would have these off-the-wall dreams about fighting a heavily distorted-faced Weston at the club—a club I didn't even remember being in—and the two of us thrashing around, knocking all the blood out of each other. But when I would wake up, none of it rang a bell. None of it seemed familiar. One night I even dreamed we were fighting and I cut his face with a piece of glass off the floor in the club. Of course, I couldn't make out any of his features. But it was him. Or should I say, it was *supposed* to be him. I cut him deep, too. I even felt the anger when I did it. That dream was the most real to me because it was like I was really there in the moment. But when I woke up, my memory was still blank. It was just a dream. Another night I dreamed he was kicking me in my ribs. That night he looked exactly like the dude from that movie *The Elephant Man*. But because dreams are so damn twisted, what happened was he all of a sudden turned into me, and then I was kicking myself. I felt the pain in that dream, and it woke me up.

Every single day, all I thought about was the fact that I was almost killed in a fight with my archenemy and had absolutely no recollection of any of it—not to mention the ten days before it happened. Then I was mad as hell because I found out they were letting Weston's ass outta jail, and he was going home to Katrice. My whole mission with her was shot, and to tell the truth, the more I thought about it, the more I wished I had never tried to see about her. The only good thing I was getting out of the ordeal was he had been ordered to pay for all my hospital bills and physical therapy. I was glad to hear that, since I wasn't trying to spend up my money paying for an incident I didn't even remember— even though I had health insurance and most of it would've been covered. We had to split the cost of busting up the club, though; and I was pissed about that, since I didn't remember what I was responsible for breaking.

Since I had so much time to myself while laying up in the hospital waiting for my body to heal well enough so I could be released, all I did was sleep and think. I realized after everything that had gone down between us—from high school until that moment— I really never had a chance with Katrice. I was delusional about that. She only went with me that night so she could have part of what she always wanted to have with me. Deep down, I knew that. I just didn't wanna admit it to myself. I mean, she liked me as a person and she was attracted to me—that much was true. She got past my reasoning for rejecting her in high school. We had a good time talking before she fucked me so good, I almost went blind—and then I was ten-times sprung. But she wasn't trying to be with me. That was obvious. She left me in the middle of the night and went running home, scared about what was gonna happen with Weston.

I knew something went down between them after that night because that's when Charles called and threatened to shank me if I didn't leave her alone. But obviously they worked everything out because when I talked to Rick, who was at the wedding that night and who went to high school with us, he said he ran into Katrice one day in 2002 and she was pregnant and had this rock on her finger. He said she looked like a supermodel and was beaming and cheesing from ear to ear. They started talking, and she told him she got married and her husband's name was Weston Porter, and they were expecting twins soon. I knew that was the same guy, because she said his name right before she left the hotel that night. So when I heard that, I realized how serious she was about that dude. I was hurt. Really, I was mad at myself because I didn't check for her when I should have—in high school—and now she was with some other man and having *two* of his babies.

After our night together, I tried to keep it pushing and get on with my life, but she just stayed all up in my head every damn day, especially after I had that conversation with Rick. I had plenty of female distractions, and I was getting so much first-class pussy, it should've been illegal. But none of the women I was spending time with were really impressing me—the way I needed to be impressed in order to wanna be with a woman. I tried to be with some of 'em. They were smart, attractive women with good heads on their shoulders. But they weren't Katrice. She had that extra-special something that I was looking for. She always did, even in high school. I was just too immature to go for what I wanted back then. So after so many years of letting the situation eat at me, I decided to take my chances and see what I could do about it, even though I knew the odds were slim. I told Dad I was gonna go home for a minute and see about Ma, since her diabetes had been acting up— which was true—and that I was gonna check in with a few friends and visit with them. And while I was there, I planned on spending as much time as I could trying to see if I could backtrack on the mistake I made when I shut Katrice down in high school. Turned out I was a lifetime too late, and now the only thing left for me to do was accept it, leave the past behind, get healed up, and go back to Maryland and try to find a replacement for her.

Although I was born and raised in Oakland, and it would always be where I was from, it wasn't my home anymore. It was only a place I could visit every now and then, but never try to return to for good.

27

KATRICE

December 14, 2007, 12:51 A.M.

WESTON'S COMING HOME TODAY, WESTON'S COMING HOME TODAY, WESTON'S COMING HOME TODAY!!!!!!!!!! THANK YOU, GOD, FOR AN-SWERING ALL MY PRAYERS!!!!! I'm SO FUCKING EXCITED that I know I won't be able to sleep tonight, so I'll probably just stay up. I would've written this entry sooner, but I've been on the phone with everybody all damn night telling them that WESTON'S COMING HOME TODAY!!!!! He called last night and told me they came to a plea bargain and they're letting him out on probation!!! He's gonna be on a tight leash for five years, but who gives a damn? He'll be here with us and that's what counts! And I cannot BELIEVE the turn of events! That whole thing about Royce having epilepsy, a history of seizures, and not being able to remember, just blew my mind! I never knew he was sick. He never mentioned that to me in high school or that night at the hotel. I'd like to say I feel bad for him, but I don't. Not one bit. If he can't remember what happened, *TOO GODDAMN BAD FOR HIS ASS! I* know that was kinda wrong, and I shouldn't be making light of his illness and memory loss, but, hey, that's how I feel. If I can't tell the truth here in my journal, I can't tell it anywhere. But, really, I need not encounter Royce Phillip Jordan III for the rest of my life. I've had more than enough of him, and don't care if I ever see him again. The next time he comes to town, I hope he knows to skip the visit to my shop, because he will definitely get kicked OUT if he doesn't! But after everything that's gone on, I highly doubt he would ever set foot in my presence again. For a hot second, I thought about going to the hospital to tell him that, but after that second, I changed my mind. There's no need. That would only stir up more trouble. I have nothing else to say to him. The only thing that matters now is getting my hubby back where he belongs and getting our life back on track. Christmas is in eleven days and all I wanna focus on is us having the best one ever. We REALLY, REALLY are indebted to Steve and Lincoln for this. But you know what? That's perfectly okay with me.

God, I'm SO relieved! Now I don't have to worry about telling the kids the truth about Weston! That thought has been wearing me down, day after day! I know Angela and everybody else have been trying to encourage me to be positive, and I appreciate all of them, but they weren't in the situation. It wasn't their husband or mate that was locked up, and they didn't have two little innocent children to worry about. I know everybody loves my kids with all their hearts, but at the end of the day, they're just that: mine. And I'm the one who worries about them the most. Well, me and Weston. And since he wasn't here, I had to worry

*about them for both of us. I did the best I could under
the circumstances, but that was by far the hardest shit I've
ever done! It took more energy for me to "keep my head up"
than anything else. I mean, I had to lie to my kids every
day; smile in their faces when I felt like crying; try to entertain them overtime just to keep their minds occupied so
they wouldn't think too much about Weston being gone
and start asking questions I didn't wanna answer; watch
my facial expressions every time they were in the room
with me because they're so damn intuitive that anything
out of the ordinary tips them off and then they're on me
about what's wrong; fill in for him in ways I didn't even
know how sometimes—like building Lego towers and
play-wrestling, when I hate that crap, and CUTTING
MEAT INTO SHAPES! And people wondered why I had
a problem staying positive. But you know what? I think
I did a damn good job running the show while my husband was gone. I know one thing: he better not ever, ever
in his LIFE do this to me again! I'm just glad it's about
to be all over with. I can't WAIT to see, touch, feel, and
FUCK THE LIVING DAYLIGHTS OUTTA WESTON
for as many hours as I can manage to keep Girlfriend
wet!!!! And when she dries out, I'll pour the whole bottle
of lube straight-up in her and get right back to whipping
my girl on Dangerous till he crashes and burns! Oh,
wait . . . do we even* have *any more lube? That's gonna
wreck things if we don't. I'm not cutting my dick session
short for NOTHIN'! Damn . . . lemme go check. . . .*

*Okay, we're good. But, anyway, I gotta try to get at least
five winks of sleep. It's gonna be a long day today, and I
need to be able to keep my damn eyes open. I hope my
clients understand about having to reschedule—either
that or have Angela do them—she said she'd be happy to
fill in. I'm gonna hafta get on the phone around seven*

*in the morning and start calling people. And it's a good
thing the kids will be at school, because I really wanna surprise them and have Weston be here when they get home.
They're gonna flip! I can't wait to see the looks on their
faces when they come in the door and see Weston standing
there! This is gonna be perfect! Okay, dammit . . . this is
ridiculous! I gotta go to bed!*

After I had put the kids to bed, I went upstairs
to relax for a while. I was growing increasingly
weary about Weston's situation because it was getting closer and closer to Christmas, which meant
more questions from the kids about when Weston
would be coming home. They were getting irritated
and antsy because he wasn't around to take them to
the mall to see Santa, like he had done the past
three years in a row; and truthfully, I wasn't thinking about that. There are just certain things that
Weston does that I don't get all that involved in.
He's more the take-the-kids-out-and-run-the-streets
type. I mean, I do my share of taking the kids here
and there, and we have a lot of fun, but Weston is
such a kid at heart, and he's just better at that stuff
than I am. He's much more enthusiastic. Now what
I *do* get into is the shopping for gifts and wrapping
them and tree trimming and baking and decorat-
ing. But because of all the stress I was under, that
had gone by the wayside. So when Ellie started
asking me about Weston being home to open presents under the tree—which, by the way, we *still*
didn't have because I was so busy trying to do both
our jobs around the house that I didn't have the
luxury of thinking too hard about tree shopping—

I knew something needed to happen fast or it was gonna be the Christmas from hell.

I had just changed into my night gear and was about to watch some TV in bed when the phone rang, close to nine-thirty. When I picked it up and heard the collect-call operator, I got scared because I had talked to Weston earlier when he called the shop, and he sounded like he was on the verge of losing his mind. The whole holiday issue had been tearing him apart as well, and it took everything I had to try and cheer him up and put some words of encouragement in his head.

As soon as he clicked through, he said in a strange tone, "Babe, what room you in?"

"What? What's wrong? Are you okay?"

"Just . . . where are you in the house?"

"I'm . . . in the bed . . . why? What's—"

"Okay, so you on the cordless phone."

"Yeah . . . yeah. . . ."

"Where the kids at?"

"Weston, you're scaring me."

"Where are they?"

"I put 'em to bed about thirty minutes ago."

"Okay. I need you to do something for me. It's real important, and you gotta do it fast."

"Oh, God. Please don't scare me like this. What's wrong?"

"Just calm down and listen. Take the cordless and go down into the basement right quick."

"Huh? Why?"

"Babe, you need to move fast 'cause I'ma hafta git off the phone soon. It's people waitin'."

"Okay, okay . . . hang on."

I jumped out of bed and ran down the stairs like a jackrabbit into the basement and flipped on the light.

Out of breath, I said, "Okay, I'm here. *What's wrong?*"

"Close the door."

I closed it. "It's closed."

Then he said, in the calmest voice I had ever heard from him, "Okay, I just need to know . . . if you gon' be able to get here around two o'clock to pick me up tomorrow."

I stopped breathing, pulled the phone away from my ear, stared at it for a second, then put it back on my ear. "*Whaaat?* You're confusing . . . wait . . . what did you say?"

"I said, are you gon' be able to get here to pick me up tomorrow around two? 'Cause my ass is comin' home, babe! I'm gittin' *outta* this mu'fucka tomorrow! I got probation! It's over! This shit is *over*! *Come . . . git . . . me!*"

Then it was obvious to me why he wanted me to go into the basement, because he knew I was gonna act the damn fool that I did when he said that, and he didn't want me scaring the kids to death.

I shrieked and squealed so loud, and so long, that if anyone had heard me, they would've thought I was being attacked like one of those stupid-ass girls in the *Friday the 13th* movies. Then I started bawling so damn hard I couldn't catch my breath, and for a minute, I thought I was gonna faint. My head started throbbing and my heart was pounding so hard, it felt like King Kong was kicking his foot up against my chest. I stomped my feet on the floor like a crazy woman and pounded my fist against the wall; then I collapsed onto the stairs in joyous tears.

Weston finally said, "Babe . . . babe . . . listen to me, okay? I gotta move fast here. Phone time is almost up."

Between tears, half breaths, and snorts, I said, "Ye-yeah—yeah—I'm he-here—okay—I'm—tell me what—hap-pened!"

I listened and cried as he quickly filled me in on everything that went down in the meeting with Lincoln. Since I knew he had to hurry and get off the phone, I kept quiet and tried not to ask too many questions so I could get the whole story. When he got to the part about Royce's epilepsy and lack of memory, I went berserk and started crying even harder. I couldn't believe how the situation was turning out, and all I could think was if it weren't for Steve being in Weston's life, and them having such a good relationship, this might not be happening. God only knows what kind of lawyer the state would've appointed Weston, and what kind of attitude he would've had about the case.

After Weston slammed me with all the details, he said, "Okay, I'm outta time. It's about three dudes waitin' and they lookin' like they 'bout to catch attitude, so I'll see you tomorrow, babe! I'm comin' *home*!"

"Okay—I'm gonna call your mother *right now*. I know it's late, but she'll wanna hear this! I love you—I'll be there tomorrow . . . early!"

"A'ight . . . love you, too, babe. See you tomorrow."

"Bye!"

For about fifteen minutes, I just stayed sprawled out on the stairs, crying and thanking God for coming through for me . . . for all of us. I knew I needed to hurry up and call Lorraine, especially since it was nearly midnight Chicago time, but I felt like I needed to sit there and take in everything Weston had just told me, and really *feel* the happiness and relief that was surging through me on the deepest level I could. I thought about how in less than twenty-four hours, my kids would be reunited with their daddy, and they could finally get back to enjoying their lives again, and that gave me the most pleasure of all. There was no doubt that I was excited for myself, but my babies were totally in the dark about what was going on with Weston, and they missed him so much it was almost a sin. More than anything, I wanted Weston and me to be able to slip this horrendous ordeal past them without having to reveal the real deal and scarring them for life. That was truly my worst fear—having my babies damaged mentally because of the mess the two of us caused. I say the two of us because, technically, it all started with me and my unwise decision. But it was finally over, and I planned on thanking God, Steve, and Lincoln for the rest of my life.

Shortly after ten o'clock, I got back on the phone and called Lorraine. I stayed in the basement because I was sure the kids were still asleep. They sleep harder than I've ever seen any kid sleep in my life. Once they're out, that's it until morning, so I knew I would be okay to stay where I was for a while.

I knew it would scare her that I was calling so late, so I didn't even give her a chance to wonder if something bad was wrong. As soon as she picked up the phone and started saying, "Katri—" I cut her off with "Lorraine, Weston just called and he got probation! He's getting out tomorrow! I'm going to pick him up at two o'clock! He's coming home! He's coming *hooooome*!"

Let me tell you, if I thought I acted a fool when I heard the news, I was wrong. Lorraine dropped the phone and went running around the room, screeching and yelling and sobbing like someone had put her in a straitjacket and locked her in a padded room. "Yes, yes, yessss! Thank You, Jesus! Thank You, Lord Almighty! I *knew* . . . oh, Lord, I *knew* You wouldn't let me down! There is *no* God like my God, none in this *world*! My baby's comin' *hooome*! Thank You, Jeeeesuuus, for givin' my son a second chance! Thank you for savin' and protectin' him and bringin' him home to his *family*! Oh, oh, oh . . . my baby! The weight on my heart is finally lifted! Oh, I can *sleep* now! Thank You for returnin' my baby where he *belongs*!"

And while she ranted and raved, I thanked God again, right along with her, as I reverted back to tears, once again thinking about how lucky this family was.

I waited very patiently for her to get back on the phone so I could fill her in. That took a few more minutes. And I completely understood. Finally she picked up the receiver and said, between sniffling, "Katrice? Baby? You still there?"

"Of course."

"I lost my head for a minute. I'm okay. I'm okay."

"If you hadn't, I woulda been worried about you! I did the same damn thing! And I'm not goin' anywhere until I tell you this story, Lo!"

I gave her every detail Weston gave me, and she cried the whole time I was talking, especially when I got to the good news about Royce.

She said, "Oh, Katrice . . . God is so good! He makes the most mysterious things happen! That right there is truly, truly a miracle if I ever heard of one! *No* memory?"

"None."

"Not a *single* detail?"

"Zip. Just some stuff from about ten days before the night of the fight, and, apparently, even that's not clear. Can you believe that?"

"Well, you know what? I did know this woman about thirty years ago, named Betty, who used to teach at the school with me. She had seizures sometimes and she used to tell us that when she did, her memory was all messed up, too. She would wake up and not be able to remember what she was doing before she fell out. Her husband and children had to tell her what was going on. Sometimes she even forgot what day it was. One time she told me after a seizure she couldn't remember what her youngest son's name was—he had to tell her—and he cried for days over that. She remembered later, but in the moment, she just couldn't recall it. It was really sad. But as far as Royce, I think part of it might have been because he was in a coma, too."

"You could be right. And I don't mean to sound insensitive, but I'm glad he can't remember. If he did, that would've changed everything. I have a feeling Weston wouldn't be getting out if he had."

"But it's all taken care of now, honey! Oh! I'ma hafta call Sonny and wake him up to tell him! This is *exactly* what he needs right now. He's really been suffering over all this. Plus, he's been upset about all the medicine he has to start taking. . . . It's just been a rough time for him lately. He didn't even have a chance to let the HIV news really sink in before Weston got in trouble. That knocked him down hard."

"He's not using, though . . . is he?"

"No. He's clean. He's just hurting, and it's been hard for him to stay afloat. I'm doing the best I can to support him, though. We're getting through it."

"I'm glad, because without you, he might not be able to weather all these damn storms. Okay, go . . . go . . . call him. I'm so damn happy I know I'm not gonna get any sleep tonight! I gotta make a zillion calls right now, so you go on. . . . We'll talk to you tomorrow when we get settled in. I'm gonna surprise the kids with this one! Oh—did you need me to call some more people? Any of the kids?"

"No, baby, I got it. I'm gonna call them after I call Sonny. You go on and take care of your calls."

"Okay! Love you lots!"

"Okay, baby. Love you, too!"

"Bye!"

Before I got back on the phone again, I ran upstairs to check on the kids, just in case one or both of them woke up, even though I was pretty sure that wouldn't be happening. Sure enough, they were calling a hundred hogs and totally oblivious to the happy chaos in the house. I ran straight back to the basement, and even though it was late, I called everyone on the list: all the girls, Mama and Daddy, Yolanda and Thomas, P.J. and Lateshia, Tiki and Charles, Eric and Tamara, and Angela, whose reaction was spiritually emotional as well. She also told me she'd fill in for me if my clients didn't mind her taking over for the day and waiting a little longer. I thanked her profusely and told her I'd call them in the morning. The only person I didn't actually talk to was Joan-Renee, and that was because I really didn't wanna wake her household up at that hour; so I left her a message on her cell because it was after midnight in Texas as well. I knew I could call my brother's house, and Tiki and Charles, because they're all late-nighters; plus, I promised them I'd keep them closely informed, no matter what time of day or night it was.

Never had so much screaming and hollering gone on in one night in my house. Thank God for the basement, or I would've surely wakened the kids and had to explain why I was making all that damn noise. Everyone was emotional, and I must have cried at least twice during each conversation I had. Because I wanted to surprise the kids, I asked Yolanda if she could pick them up at school for me and bring them to the house, along with Lydia, so that when they got there, Weston could surprise them by being home, waiting for them. She said that was fine, and I told her to pack a bag for Lydia so she could stay with us for the weekend and spend time with Weston.

Once I finished the calls and my voice box was worn out from all the strain I put on it, I went back upstairs and started straightening up the house at damn near midnight. I had so much excess energy I didn't know what else to do. So for about forty-five minutes, I cleaned while I wore the biggest, cheesiest smile on my face. My man was coming home, and I absolutely could not wait!

That morning while I was getting the kids ready for school, it was the hardest thing to keep Weston's homecoming a secret from them. Several times I almost told them about it, but then I decided against it. I didn't wanna jinx anything. I figured it was better to wait until I actually got him home before I said anything. Lord knows, it would've been disastrous if I had told them he was coming and then something went wrong. I would've never lived that moment down. Since I was so chipper and peppy, they kept laughing at me and asking me why I was so happy. They know I'm not really a morning person and smiles are hard to get from me that early. I simply told them I got a good night's sleep and felt really good. They accepted that explanation and moved on. Before we left, I told them Yolanda was gonna get them from school because I had to go run an errand after work. Fortunately, we had done that several times in the past, so they weren't suspicious about that move, either. When I told them Lydia was gonna spend the weekend, they were excited as hell. They love their sister to death, and can't wait to be around her.

I spent most of the rest of the morning getting the house completely ready for Weston. The cleaning I did the night before was only minimal, so I went ahead and really got into it. Around twelve-thirty, I went and got dressed; then I ran out of the house and skidded out of the garage in Weston's car so I could go get him. I took his car so he could drive on the way home. I figured he'd feel the freedom a little more if he could get out of jail and get in his own car and drive off.

I ended up having to wait about an hour longer than I expected because processing was so slow; but when I saw my husband come outside those jail walls, I jumped out of the car and raced into his arms like the Bionic Woman. I attacked him so hard I nearly sent us both crashing to the ground. We hugged, kissed, and cried for about ten minutes. No joke. We literally didn't let each other go for about that long. He had never hugged me tighter, either.

Finally he released me, grabbed my face, looked me in the eye, and said, through his sparse tears, "I'm *sorry*, babe. Never again. *Never*. You hear me? I will *never* leave you again, not if I got anything to do with it. I almost went crazy in there wit'out'choo."

"You better not, Weston James Porter, 'cause we can't ever be without *you* like this again, either. Now"—I held his keys up and smiled big—"please . . . take . . . us . . . home. Your kids are waiting."

"They know I'm comin'?"

"Uh-uh. It's gonna be a surprise. Yolanda's getting them from school and bringing them to the house with Lydia. She's gonna stay for the weekend so you can spend time with her."

"Well, come on. I can't wait to see my clan."

After we got in the car, right before we drove off, Weston looked in the mirror and stopped abruptly. "*Babe* . . . my *face*. What we gon' tell the kids? This ain't lookin' good."

I paused. I hadn't thought about that part. But it was a good question. There was no way we were gonna be able to get away from inquiries about how his face got so damaged, so I told him, "Okay . . . well, first we need to stop at the pharmacy and get you some of that Neosporin Scar Solution. It's supposed to be *really* good, even on bad scars like yours. Then . . . we're just gonna hafta tell 'em . . . you had a nasty fall while you were gone. There's no other

way around it, baby. We're gonna hafta nurse that
scar for a long, long time. So just say you fell and
that's that. They won't know the difference."

"You know Boo Boo's gon' ask how I fell. You
know she is."

"Damn . . . you're right."

"Yeah, she gets that from *you,* always wantin' details about everything." He laughed.

I cracked up. "She does . . . I can't even lie! But,
seriously . . . tell 'em you fell while you were working
out at the gym or something. They'll go for that."

"And where've I been all this time, babe? You know
we gotta git this story straight before I hit the door,
'cause if it ain't, we not gon' hear the end of it."

"No, no . . . I forgot to tell you Willie asked me
that a coupla weeks ago, and I told him your business trip was in Chicago. He fell for it and left the
subject alone."

"A'ight, then. That'll work. Long as we don't git
up in the house and start forgettin' what we supposta
say. You know them kids'uh yours'll be on our asses
if it don't sound right." He smiled and winked at me.

"Ohhhh . . . kay. *My kids.* Right. Let's go home
to *my kids* then, please."

"Cool. I'll just take the one with long curly hair
and the eyes that match mine. You can *have* them
other two."

We busted up laughing; then Weston sped off.

By the time we got home, Weston barely had
enough time to take a shower and change clothes
before Yolanda showed up. That extra hour we had
to wait for him to get out threw us off schedule.

Plus, we stopped to get the stuff for Weston's face, too. Although we were pressed for time, we made sure to squeeze in a *seriously, seriously* intense, passionate "quickie" before they got there. It had been far too long, and that was a piece of business that simply could *not* be put on hold any longer. There was no way in *hell* we could wait until after the kids went to bed to release all that tension, so we made *very* good use of the short time we had.

When the front door opened, Weston and I were already sitting in the living room on the couch, cuddled up like nothing special was going on. We couldn't wait to see the looks on the kids' faces when they saw him.

Lydia was talking, and the twins were laughing at first. Then when they got to the living room, still talking and not paying attention, Weston jumped up and shouted, "Ay, where y'all been?"

I wish you could've seen how those kids' faces lit up, how big their eyes got, and the Ronald McDonald smiles that fell across their mouths when they looked up and saw Weston standing there, grinning at them.

Together they all dropped their things right where they stood and screamed at the top of their little lungs, *"Daddyyyyyyyy!"* Then all three of them ran and jumped on Weston like mini football players out on a field. He fell to the floor with them on top of him and they showered him with a ton of hugs and kisses, and he ate up every second of it.

Yolanda and I watched and laughed while Weston relished in reuniting with his babies. After a minute, we went into the kitchen, since it was obvious they'd be on the floor for a while.

Yolanda said, "Well, Miss Superwoman, you did

it. You hung in there and held the fam together. I'm proud of you. I know it was hard."

"Girl, hard isn't even the word for what that was. We're not doin' that *no . . . more,* okay?"

"I heard that. I'm just glad he's back and everything worked out. He got real lucky with this one."

"You ain't neva lied, girl. I was scared as hell."

"Well, now y'all can get on with your lives and enjoy the holidays together. Look, I'ma head on out. Y'all got a lotta catchin' up to do, so I'll just see you when I get Lydia on Sunday. Tell Weston I'll get a hug later. I'ma go out the back door here, girl."

"Okay, and, hey . . . girl, thanks for *everything.* I mean it. You really made things a lot easier, all those times you stepped in for me and helped out."

"Girl, that's what we baby mamas do. I thought 'choo knew that."

We laughed, and then she walked out.

When I got back in the living room, the kids still had Weston pinned to the floor like wrestlers, and they were throwing questions and comments at him, left and right, while lying on top of him. Ellie was in the middle of saying, while touching Weston's scar gently, ". . . But Daddy, how are we gonna get your *ouchie* to go away?"

"Mommy bought me some medicine for it. I'll be okay pretty soon."

Lydia ordered, "Daddy, next time you go away for business, you can't leave us here! You took too long getting back!"

"I'm not goin' on no more of those business trips, baby girl. That was a onetime thing."

"Okay. You better not. 'Cause that is *sooooo* not gonna work for me, okay?"

Weston and I fell out laughing; then Weston said, "Okay. I promise. I won't leave you again."

Then Willie shouted spastically, "Daddy, can you take us to the park now? Mommy said we could go as *soon* as you got back! So can we go now?"

He laughed. "It's too cold out there, li'l man. And it's about to get dark soon. We can go tomorrow."

"Are you *sure* you're gonna be here tomorrow? Last time you left and didn't say bye."

"I'ma be here for sure, man. We goin' to the park tomorrow. I promise. But you know what?" He sat up. "I'm *hongry*! Y'all wanna go git somethin' ta eat?"

They all yelled, *"Yeahhhhhh!"*

"Okay, where we goin'?"

Willie shouted, "Can we go to Barney's for ham-buggers?"

"Yeah, burgers sound good. Y'all want burgers?" He looked at Lydia and Ellie.

Ellie said, "Yeah! And I want onion rings!"

Lydia jumped in with "Can we get shakes, too?"

Weston said, "We can get whatever y'all want."

Willie yelled, "Daddy, Daddy, Daddy . . . guess what? We saved you some left-behind food . . . I mean, I mean . . . um . . . *leftover* food from Bird Day! It's in the freezer!"

"You did? *Thank you*, li'l man. I'ma eat that to-morrow. But right now, we gon' *all* go out to eat. So come on, y'all, go upstairs and put'cho stuff away. Lydia, take yo' bag up there."

They chimed, "Okaaaay," and ran off.

While we waited for them to return, Weston and I stood in the middle of the living room and hugged and made out like new lovers. I felt Dangerous poking me and said, "Down, boy . . . I'll take care of you later." Then I smiled.

He put his hand between my legs and started rubbing Girlfriend. "And I got somethin' for *yo'* friend, too. You can *buh'lieve* that."

"Oh, I know the *hell you do,* honey. And I'm good and ready for it."

We went back to slobbering on each other until we heard the kids scampering down the stairs. Then the five of us piled in Weston's car and went to eat.

When we got home, Weston fell right back into his routine and watched the cartoon channel with the kids, ate tortilla chips, and drank Pepsi—since there'd be no consuming alcohol for him while on probation—and laughed and played with them during the commercial breaks. Even I stayed with them and partook in the celebration. Mostly, though, I just sat there and smiled at the scene before me. My husband was back home with me and his kids, and I was more thankful at that moment than I had ever been about anything in my life.

After we put the kids to bed and Weston made all his family-and-friend phone calls, we spent the rest of the night making up for the two months of sex we missed out on. We worked each other over again and again, only stopping for bathroom and water breaks; then it was right back to it. I had no problem at all with Girlfriend staying wet; Weston made *damn* sure of that, so the bottle of lube stayed in the drawer.

After several hours of lovemaking, talking, and laughing, we took our rightful positions next to each other in bed, nice and naked like we always are after we know the kids are asleep, and Weston held on to me supertight the entire night, just the way I like.

The holidays were fabulous. Steve told Weston to take the rest of the month off so he could spend quality time with us, and said he'd see him back at work on January 2, 2008. Steve had already taken care of contacting Weston's clients and letting them know when Weston would be back at work, so that was perfect.

Once Weston got settled in, we finally got into the Christmas spirit and ran all over town shopping for the kids, buying a tree, and, of course, taking them to see Santa. Because we knew our money would be tight with all of Weston's restitution responsibilities, we decided not to buy each other anything for Christmas, and, instead, just focused on the twins and Lydia. Just shopping for them was enough to put us in the poorhouse alone, but we didn't mind.

There were a few welcome-home parties thrown for Weston between the time he got home and the end of the month. First his boys threw one for him on December 21, and I told them if I found out that *anybody* brought liquor to the scene, I was gonna kick in the door and set it off up in Gerald and Brinda's new crib, which is where the party was. They assured me they had no intentions of getting Weston sent up the river, and they had a safe, alcohol-free bash that I could feel confident about.

On December 23, I invited Steve and his wife, Caroline, and Lincoln and his wife, Cleo, over for dinner, complete with Christmas ham, macaroni and cheese, the traditional green-bean casserole, and my special sweet-potato pie that Weston loves. We had a great time, and Weston and I finally got to express our gratitude to all of them for everything they did.

On Christmas morning, Ellie presented Weston with a gigantic, colorful picture she drew for him that had me, Weston, Willie, herself, Lydia, Thomas and Yolanda, Mama and Daddy, Lorraine and Sonny, and a large dog all standing in a park on a sunny day, with birds flying in the sky and flowers blooming out of the grass. We were all holding hands and smiling. Of course, none of us looked like we were supposed to look, so she wrote our names over the tops of our heads, just like we used to do when we drew pictures for our parents when we were kids. Weston loved it, and told her he was gonna frame it and hang it in our bedroom, which made his Boo Boo very, very happy.

After Yolanda brought Lydia over so she could open her presents from Weston and me, and also drop off her gifts for the twins, Weston spent the day playing with his kids *and* all their toys and games, and acting just as childish as the three of them, while I videotaped, laughed, and shook my head in amusement.

We had a *massive* dinner party at Angela's on New Year's Eve and invited everybody for that—Mama and Daddy and my entire crew, as well as all of Weston's friends—since her house was so big. Angela fried up a ton of snapper and catfish, and she made corn bread from scratch that was so moist, buttery, and perfectly seasoned, she had everybody clamoring for the recipe. She made two pots of greens that were so delicious we even fought tooth and nail to get the last remnants of the damn juice when all the greens were gone. She also made a pot of black-eyed peas and three peach pies. Gerald showed up with a delectable melt-in-your-mouth prime rib that almost made me cry, it was so damn good. He refused to divulge his seasoning method to me, so I told Weston to get on the job and find out so I could make it for his birthday in March. And Weston concocted his famous fruit punch, since he didn't get to make it for Thanksgiving. We ate, danced, acted like fools, and loved every minute of it. Thank goodness Angela had extra bedrooms, because the kids went up to bed and we kept right on partying *way* past the ringing-in of the New Year, and into the wee hours of the morning.

I took a much-needed vacation the first week in January and caught up on my rest, since the last half of December was so damn hectic. By the second week in January, Weston was back on track at work with all his clients, we were back on our schedule with the kids and ourselves, and he was all set up with his probation officer and ready to face the music. It was definitely gonna be a long, challenging road, but as long as we were traveling it together, we knew we couldn't lose.

We were told that Royce had been released from the hospital and had gone back to Maryland right after Christmas. I took *great* comfort in knowing he was finally out of our lives and moving on with his; and once and for all, I bid him, all my feelings for him—and our sordid, twisted past—a resounding and permanent *good riddance.*

28

KATRICE

February 2, 2008, 11:00 P.M.

Today was a very special day, and I saw it coming from a hundred miles away. Sonny and Lorraine finally got back together—in marriage. When Lorraine called in early January and made the announcement to Weston, he was really scared at first, with Sonny having HIV and all. He was petrified that Sonny would infect Lorraine and then he'd have two sick parents on his mind. But once she explained to him that the two of them were very HIV-educated and had all the information they needed to keep Lorraine safe, and that she and Sonny never stopped loving each other and felt they needed to be together—as a couple—to start over—he was happy for them. They said life is too short to pass up being with the one you really love; and if Magic and Cookie Johnson could make it, so could they. Besides, they had been *spending so much time together the last couple of years, it just made sense for them to officially reunite.*

Sonny took Lorraine out to dinner at the Lotus Flower Italian Restaurant right after New Year's—the same location where he proposed to her the first time—except back then it was a soul-food place—and proposed to her again. But here's the best part: Sonny said he always knew he'd marry her again, when the time was right. When they divorced, Lorraine was so hurt at the time that she took her ring off and gave it back to Sonny. Well, he kept it; but not only that, he looked at it at least once a day and said a little affirmation to himself that one day, he'd put it back on her finger for good. He had it resized and then had a brand-new diamond put in, but a bigger one this time. He said since it was a new start, she should have a new diamond. Now I know where Weston gets his romantic side from. ☺ When I asked Sonny how he knew Lorraine would say yes, especially given his condition, he just said, "I know that woman better than she knows herself. She's been waitin' for me to come home for twenty years." I just laughed. But then when I asked him why they divorced in the first place, he told me it was because Lorraine was afraid he'd leave her again, and she couldn't take that chance because it destroyed her the first time, so she let him go. But really, she didn't.

Lorraine told me once, in confidence, that she dated quite a few men over the years, and while she liked them all and she had a lot of fun, none of them measured up to Sonny. But, of course, she wouldn't dream of telling him she wanted him back—she said she made a decision and that was that. At the time, I didn't wanna press her for information about their divorce, but I was always curious. I was glad to see them work things out, even though it took twenty years.

Since Weston's on probation, we didn't wanna push the envelope by asking if he could take a trip to Chicago for the wedding, so Sonny, Lorraine, and the rest of the family came to us, instead. They had beautiful nuptials at the California Ballroom in Oakland, and the two of them looked like teenagers in love. Lorraine's minister friend, Rebecca Allen, married them. They had been friends for over fifteen years, and Lorraine said she never considered anyone else for the job.

All the Porter siblings and their mates managed to make it for the wedding, which was perfect because Weston wanted to see everyone but didn't know when he'd get to go back home for a visit; and he had an absolute ball catching up with them. He and Sonny got to spend some quality time together, and I was glad because I know Weston was worried about his dad. But I think seeing him so happy with Lorraine put Weston at ease, and I feel like now he'll be able to really accept Sonny's condition and be okay about it.

But wait—I just have to talk about my girls for a minute. I finally, finally got to meet Keith Grayson, Rishidda's new man. I invited every-damn-body to the wedding and told them to bring a date if they wanted, and, sure enough, she brought him. He wasn't at the New Year's Eve party because he was with his daughters. But, DAMN, my girl did good! I watched them real close, and I can tell by the way Keith looks at her that he's not letting her go for NOTHIN'! He's perfect for her, because he's well-rounded and spiritual, and Rishidda needs that kind of man in her life. I know she and Cash had something none of us could ever understand—him having been a drug dealer and all that, and them having three kids together—but I have to admit, it's good to see her with someone who's got his act together and is feeling her the right way and not living a life that's gonna put her in any potential danger. Rishidda

could've been killed that day Cash got shot down—and so
could her kids, for that matter. This Keith dude is definitely
the breath of fresh air she's been looking for all these years,
even if she won't admit that she's been looking for one. I'm
so happy for her. And she looks absolutely ecstatic!

Some nice-looking man that worked at the Ballroom
was all up in Angela's face today, and it was cracking me
the hell up! He cornered her twice and had her hemmed up
in conversation while his ass was supposed to be working!
And she was all smiles and laughter, too! I hope whatever that was turns into something she can sink her teeth
into, because she deserves a nice man in her life. I know
she's lonely without her daughter and grandkids, so it
would be good for her to have some male companionship.
She's a really good person, and I'm glad I finally got past
my attitude long enough to see that about her. I know one
thing: he definitely wouldn't go hungry if he ended up
being her man! Hahaha!

Genine and Warren are all the way back on track,
thank God! They're talking about marriage again, and
I'm hoping by this time next year, she'll be Genine Young-
Stewart. I like Warren, and I'm glad she finally stopped
avoiding him just because he was a pest-control employee
back in the day. She cracked me up with that "I'm not
dating some dude who kills roaches for a living" mess! I
couldn't believe her! I'm sure glad he was persistent and
waited the damn five months it took her to finally go out
with him, because they're like . . . what's that line in For-
rest Gump? Oh yeah, "like peas and carrots." She's so
damn crazy. But I'm glad she's found her man.

I think today I finally decided I like Sabrina's man, Ty.
I wasn't so sure about him at first because I never really got
a chance to talk to him; but after we chatted for a bit at the
reception, I see now that he really is into my girl. He's just

kinda quiet, that's all. And I guess that's okay. As long as he's treating her right, we won't have no problems. I'd hate to have to jam some dude up 'cause he messed over one of my crew. 'Cause we don't play that. For real.

And the infamous Chantelle, with her fast ass. She showed up with who she called, "the Chosen One," which, for her, means the one she's doing right now. But quiet as it's kept, I think she actually likes this guy. His name is . . . damn . . . what the hell did he say his name was? Dammit . . . oh yeah, Devon. Yeah, that's it. She likes his fine ass, I can tell you that. She's not gonna admit that right now, though; but I know her so well, it's ridiculous. She held his hand twice, and 'Telle doesn't hold hands unless she's sprung. She tried to tell me she wasn't really holding his hand, he was holding hers. Heffa. I'ma call her ass out about it tomorrow. I made sure I talked to him, too; and he told me straight-up that he's trying to see about my girl full force. I told him to be patient and give her some space. She doesn't like to be crowded. He said he'd keep that in mind. Yeah, that's about to be her new man. I feel it. Her art exhibit starts next Saturday night, and we're all excited as hell about it. I can't wait to see my girl in action, rockin' it like the bad-ass bitch that she is. I'm so proud of her.

Well, 2008 is definitely starting off right. My husband is home, where he belongs, and, apparently, Sonny is about to be, too.

They say you can't go home, but "they" obviously haven't met the Porter men.

Departures and Arrivals

You know they say you can't go home,
but sometimes that's not true.
It all depends on what you plan
on trying to return to do.

There are times you need to leave home
so you can get your life on track.
And once you do, then it's okay
to make your way back.

Some people leave home for the wrong reasons
'cause they're running from their fate.
Too bad they don't understand that fate
will follow them from state to state.

Others are forced to leave
when they've made wrong moves or big mistakes.
And the people they leave behind
are riddled with pain and heartaches.

Then there are those who leave
because their time in one place is done.
Those people leave with confidence
and can walk—not run.

But whatever the reason you go,
learn as much as you can while you're away.
'Cause there's nothing worse than coming back
the same person you left as that day.

Leaving home is about growth and change.
It's about building a better you.
Sometimes the tools needed for construction
are in a location completely new.

At times the growth is difficult,
 you may feel you've ventured to the wrong place.
And you find yourself in situations,
 you thought you'd never face.

Your first impulse is to pack your bags
and go right back whence you came.
But if you did, you'd be a coward—
what a pity and a shame.

The only way to rise above
all the hardships, pain, and strife
is to plant your feet firmly where you stand
and fight with your entire life.

They say you can't go home,
but for some that remains to be seen.
For those who left a manicured lawn
may return to find the grass still green.